# TWIST OF LIME

## A Lynn Evans Mystery

## Claudia McKay

New Victoria Publishers
Norwich, Vermont

Published by New Victoria Publishers Inc., a feminist, literary and cultural organization, PO Box 27, Norwich, VT 05055-0027.

Printed and Bound in Canada

1   2   3   4        2000   1999   1998   1997

**Library of Congress Cataloging-in-Publication Data**

McKay , Claudia.

   Twist of lime  :  a Lynn Evans mystery / by Claudia McKay.

      p.   cm.

    ISBN 0934678-88-X

    I. Title.

PS3563. C3734T88     1997

813' . 54--dc21                                           97-19531

                                     CIP

# Chapter 1

Turning clear, turquoise water into white spray, and breaking the quiet of the hot tropical morning, a big outboard dinghy headed toward a white-gold beach surrounded by mangrove and coconut palms. Beyond the beach, bird and insect calls mixed with the steady scraping from inside a large, neatly-dug square hole. An archaeological crew was uncovering what several thousand years ago had been a Mayan house.

At one end of the excavation, undisturbed by the sound of the boat, Lynn Evans contentedly removed gray ash and red clay from around the bones of a burial. She loved the mystery of this work, the excitement at the discovery of each new piece of pottery, volcanic glass or bone. As the oversized dingy pulled up on to the small wooden pier, Lynn daydreamed about the lives people led long ago on this steamy tropical coast, imagining the big Mayan trading canoes that brought goods from as far away as Columbia in the south to the temples of Mexico in the north. As she dusted the last bits of dirt away from bones with a small paint brush, she thought about the person whose bones lay before her. Those of a woman, a woman who perhaps had sat in a corner of this house weaving some bright-colored cloth, bustled about cooking a meal, or just enjoyed a quiet moment listening to the birds—a small Mayan woman like those she had seen in the market, with dark intense eyes and strong quick hands.

Invited by her friend Sarah Donovan, the chief researcher and boss of this archaeological dig, Lynn had come down to this sandy, palm-covered coast inside Belize's barrier reef for a few weeks to get away from her work as a reporter for the *Hartfield Chronicle*. But instead of sitting on the beach and snorkeling in the warm tropical water among bright colored fish as she had planned, she had joined

1

the other workers in the trenches.

On the mound of dirt next to the excavation, a slim handsome young woman, Ann Wilson, suddenly stopped shaking her large screen. Something about the abruptness made Lynn glance up. Instead of picking the last few bits of pottery and flint out of the screen to put into a labeled plastic bag, Ann had straightened up and was studying the beach with a pained expression as if something was worrying her. Suddenly she started, as if she saw someone or something unwelcome.

Ann's grubby, torn t-shirt and jean shorts only emphasized her perfect olive skin, small-boned frame and innocent dark eyes. It was the sort of look that always intrigued Lynn probably because it contrasted so drastically with her own sand colored hair, gray blue eyes, and pasty pink-white skin.

Ann was new at this too, having arrived a few days before Lynn. Lynn was not sure why Ann was here. Sarah was perpetually short handed and relied on volunteers as well as the students. But Ann was less interested in the research and more difficult to work with than the others. Lynn had observed that Ann could be genuinely friendly, though distant, but she often seemed annoyed, preoccupied and was easily provoked. Still she was a good worker and often took the harder jobs as if she had something to prove. She had been at the screen all morning.

Lynn wondered if maybe she should give Ann a break, take her turn with the screen, shaking out the finer dirt and looking for the small pieces of bone, pottery, charcoal and volcanic glass. But before she could make the offer, Ann stuffed her thick dark hair back into her borrowed canvas hat nervously, and without even glancing at Lynn, said defensively, "What are you staring at?"

Lynn tried to ignored the annoyance in the remark. "I was wondering if you needed a break."

Still watching the shore Ann said sharply, "I can work as well as you. I don't *need* anything." She began picking out bits of pottery from the screen and stuffing them into the bag set aside for them.

Lynn's idyllic mood was shattered. Ann had not been the most cheerful, person to work with, but she was not generally this rude.

Behind Lynn, at the other end of the excavation, one of Sarah's graduate students, Kathy Sinclair, was making a careful drawing of another burial they had uncovered. In spite of a broad hat and the sunscreen Kathy soaked herself in each morning, her skin was pink and peeling. She wiped her face with the red bandanna and pushed her wispy blond hair away from her face. But her genuine good humor seemed to survive all. She said, in her cheerful peacemaking way without looking up, "Lynn loves the screen, Ann. You'd just be doing her a favor. She hasn't had her daily quota of strained muscles yet."

Ann didn't even look up from the screen.

Still annoyed in spite of Kathy's attempted humor, Lynn said to Ann, "At least you *could* occasionally pretend not to be rude."

Another worker who was painstakingly removing the hardened clay floor in the middle of the trench with an ice pick and trowel, whispered, "She doesn't mean to be rude. It's just her way of speaking." Theodora (Teddy) Sarnoff was a rather gangly, undergraduate student of Sarah's. As usual she was wearing her favorite outfit of Lesbian Avenger t-shirt, baseball hat backwards over a partially shaved head and cut-off jeans that Lynn thought must cling to her slim hips by shear will-power.

Ann laughed—a forced sound. "I certainly didn't mean to be rude. You don't need to apologize for me, Teddy; I can do that perfectly well for myself."

Teddy sighed. "I wasn't apologizing, just explaining."

Ann was watching the beach again. Suddenly she dropped the heavy wooden frame of the screen onto the pile of dirt and walked away.

Lynn stood up. She was puzzled as much as she was annoyed. Ann seemed to be exaggerating her rudeness, being theatrical on purpose as if to cover up some other emotion. Was it fear she had seen in Ann's dark eyes in those quick glances toward the shore line?...What had she seen to frighten her? Lynn looked out to sea herself. A large white catamaran had dropped anchor off shore and an oversized double outboard dingy was pulled up on the beach with several people getting out. More tourists to stare at them while they worked? Did Ann know them? Was that why she left so suddenly? She could see Sarah on her way down to meet them.

Teddy, laying down her pick, said sullenly, "Now see what you've done. Can't all of you leave her alone?" Lynn felt bad for Teddy. It wasn't like her to speak up. Most of the time she was a quiet, hard

3

worker, generally cheerful except where Ann was concerned. It was obvious to everyone that Teddy had a crush on Ann who just as obviously found her annoying.

Teddy climbed out to take over the screen and Lynn went back to her scraping.

Sarah came up from the dock bringing the visitors. *Dr.* Sarah Donovan, Lynn reminded herself, once again amused that her rather scatterbrained high school friend had turned into a dedicated and brilliant scholar of Mayan antiquities. As Sarah got closer they heard her usual lecture about the history of the people who had occupied the area a thousand years before the Spanish arrived. "We believe this site was one of the stops for the traders that traveled up and down this coast. Here, as well as at other similar sites on this coast, we find both pottery and flint chips from many different parts of Central America."

With her smooth dark hair in a neat braid, her crisp white shirt and khaki shorts, Sarah looked nothing like the crusty archeologist one might expect to be spending months each year digging in the jungles of Central America. There were only three shirts, two pairs of shorts and one pair of khaki pants that ever appeared on the clothesline beside the house. But every morning at seven sharp Sarah appeared at breakfast looking as trim as if she had just walked off a fashion magazine cover, even though, like the rest of them, she bathed and washed her clothes in the ocean and spent eight or more hours a day working in the dirt.

A shadow fell over Lynn and she looked up. The pink face of a middle-aged man was peering down at her from under a crisp white cowboy hat. "Whatch'a got down there?"

Sarah introduced him. "Lynn, this is Ed Kelly, one of the university's alumni sponsors for our work here."

"It's a burial. They buried people under the floor of their houses," Lynn explained politely.

Ed squinted and looked closer. "Don't see any jade or flint tools or big pots. I thought they buried people with their valuables."

"Not everybody was a noble or a priest," said Sarah. "We are interested in the lives of ordinary people as well."

The man laughed and stood up. "So if there's nothing there—no you know, treasure, why bother diggin'?"

4

Sarah's voice was impatient now—tired. "Everything we find gives us information. What's valuable is the whole picture—the context of remains, what other objects are associated. The position someone was buried in for instance, or the style of a house wall is as important as the type of stone an ornament is manufactured from..."

Ed was obviously bored and Sarah was clearly getting exasperated. To rescue Sarah Lynn picked up the bucket of dirt she had just removed and climbed out to set it near the screen. Lynn said to Ed, "Let me show you some of what we've been digging up."

Sarah's lips silently said, "Thanks, Lynn," and smiled at her.

Lynn led Ed over to a sandy clearing in the jungle covered by a canvas canopy where they washed, sorted, labeled and stored artifacts. Along one side were the makeshift shelves where the season's work sat in plastic bags and boxes, carefully labeled.

Lynn started to repeat what she remembered of the lecture about the dig that Sarah had given her when she first arrived. "The nobles and priests were the ones that were buried with elaborate ornamentation. But they earned the honor. They were responsible for the welfare of the whole community. During a drought like the one that farmers are suffering here this year, they would have made sacrifices...of themselves." She picked up a sharp blade of obsidian. "They would have cut themselves, drawn their own blood in order to bring rain."

Hardly listening, Ed walked around looking in the boxes and bags where trowels, shovels, surveying equipment was kept. Then he went to the shelf with the camps references and records and started looking through Sarah's field notes.

Annoyed, Lynn stopped lecturing and asked, "Are you here in Belize for long?"

He didn't even look up. "Got a real estate deal or two going. This postage stamp of a country squeezed between Mexico, Guatemala, and Honduras turns out to be a good place to invest. Tourist trade growing. Great ruins, great jungle, some real great opportunities." He laughed. "If the Guatemalans don't invade. Those Brits didn't know what they had. Should have hung onto it; kept it British Honduras."

He glanced over at her. "You can buy just about anything in this blessed country." He looked around to see if anyone else was near-

5

by; then said in a conspiratorial tone, "I wanna show you something."
He stepped closer and pulled a cord from under his shirt. Hanging
from it was a green stone disk. He took it off and handed it to her. A
human figure was carved in the surface—a recognizably female figure
with grooves that indicated clothing and a headdress. Was it jade?

"Bought it from one of the native guys. Cost me a pretty penny,
but it was worth it. You can feel the power in the thing." He was
almost whispering now. As he took it out of her hand he stroked it;
there was a look in his eyes—sensual, greedy. "You ever seen anything like that around here?"

Lynn shook her head. "Did he tell you where he got it?"

"Told me he'd show me. I'm planning to go in there, soon as I
can get outfitted. Someplace up in the Maya mountains." He contemplated her calculatingly. "I could arrange for you go along if you
want. It'll be fun."

"It's illegal to take out artifacts, or even to dig without a government permit. It took Dr. Donovan two years to get a permit to do an
archaeological project even with all her credentials."

He snorted. "And look what she's wasting it on." He waved his
hand at the shelves without looking again at their contents. Then he
looked out toward the beach. "This land's not good for much but
maybe a hotel. Got good beaches, high enough building site. Who
owns it anyway?"

"Its a local ranch owned by Jacob and Emma Phillips and they
aren't at all interested in selling." Lynn liked them. Jacob was part
Mayan, part black. Emma was from Belize City and part of the Black
English-speaking community there. Besides paying something for the
being allowed to dig, Sarah had hired Emma to help them cook and
for the use of her kitchen. Jacob sold them fish he caught when he
felt like taking out his small sailboat.

The greedy look was back on Ed's face. "There's plenty others itch-
ing to sell. And who's to know what you do on your own property."

The man was down here looking to buy his own private archaeological site. Lynn knew what Sarah would say when she found out.
But maybe it was all bluff. Lynn tried to be patient, for Sarah's sake.
Sarah thought it was important to have good relations with the public, especially university alumni and even tourists. "The information
being collected here is invaluable. That…" She pointed at the carving

6

now back around his neck, "...doesn't tell you anything. There is no way to know for sure where it came from or even if it's authentic without documentation about the context in which it was found. Without that information it is useless."

"It's the real thing all right. I can feel it. First night I wore it I dreamed..." He looked around and leaned closer. "...I dreamed about a temple filled with gold light and in the middle of the temple was a bunch of crystals—beautiful, all colors and carved. It's a sign. I know I'll be the one to find them. You know about the carved crystals?" Lynn shook her head. "Supposed to be still buried out there. In the light they reflect all the colors of the rainbow, some carved like human skeletons. Very powerful. I saw one once—in Canada, a skull. Even with a little piece, people who are tuned in can read the future. Somebody who had the whole thing..." He shook his head in wonderment. "Why, just think what that guy could do."

Lynn sighed. It was people like this who made Sarah's job so hard. If Ann knew him—no wonder she disappeared.

Ed put his amulet back under his shirt. "You're one of those skeptic types aren't you? I can always tell. It's my intuitive side. If I ever found one of those crystals I know I could read it. I feel those kinds of things."

"So you're trying to buy property so you can have your own private source of Mayan magical crystal?" Lynn couldn't keep the contempt out of her voice. She wanted this guy to go away.

He laughed and nodded, his eyes narrowing. "You bet I will and with the cooperation of the Belize government."

"You have a particular piece of land in mind?"

"You have any suggestions?"

Lynn shook her head.

Ed smiled. "I offered to let Dr. Donovan dig it up if she'd tell me what hunk of land to buy. I'm a generous guy. You should encourage her to take up my offer. With her on board dealing with the officials the whole thing would be a cinch. She could take all the information, the Mayan garbage—as long as I get a crack at the good stuff. I'll even pay for labor."

"But you get to keep your crystal skulls when they show up."

Ed snickered looking at her out of a corners of his eyes. "We both know, Hon, that the government doesn't let anybody keep that stuff."

7

Lynn was relieved to see a woman in a matching pink and white outfit and straw hat coming up the path from the boat dock. He turned to follow her gaze and then stepped away from Lynn guiltily.

"Let's go Ed," the woman called out shrilly. "We'll miss happy hour at the hotel and I promised Mrs. Jennings—" She stopped speaking when she saw Lynn.

Ed winked at Lynn. "You're welcome to come along on my trek up to the mountains."

Lynn said, "Thanks, but I'm needed here."

"Think about it. What an opportunity. Not these peon huts you're digging up. Huge temples, whole cities under the jungle, just waiting to be uncovered. Remember what I told you...talk to Dr. Donovan. Change your mind about going up to the mountain. Dr. Donovan can get me on the radio if you decide to go along."

The pink lady stood just outside the tent looking in as if she thought the contents were contagious. "She isn't interested in your hair-brained, get-rich-quick schemes Ed. Let's go."

Ed laughed. "Doris...Hon, I *am* rich."

Doris snorted. "Then why don't you relax and enjoy it?"

He looked at Lynn rather triumphantly. "I am." Then Ed turned obediently and went with his wife back down the trail toward their outboard. Off in the distance was their wide white catamaran, more lounge than sailboat. Their local black crew waited patiently, one in the dingy and one on board the sailboat. Lynn watched Ed, Mr. Macho-New Colonialist and his wife stroll down the path.

On her way back to the dig, Lynn noticed Ann coming from the direction of the kitchen. She still seemed nervous, frightened. "They gone yet?"

"They're going out to their boat now. You know them or something?"

"Jesus, no. What makes you say that?"

"You ran off so quickly when they showed up—as if you were seriously trying to avoid them."

"Why would I know that SOB?"

"How do you happen to know he is an SOB?"

Ann opened her mouth as if she were about to say, but then she closed it and took a deep breath.

Lynn said, "You know if there is something wrong, something

your worried about—it might help if you talked to somebody. Are you in trouble?"

For a moment Ann stood very still, the brown eyes contemplated her slightly out of focus. Lynn was reminded of her actress friend Sonya preparing herself for a line she had to deliver. Then Ann said angrily, "None of you're friggin' business. You're bad as the other jokers here. Always interfering, telling me what to do. I can take care of myself."

Lynn stared at Ann as she marched back down the path to the tents. The anger had seemed feigned as if she were trying to cover up her real feelings. Why was it she always felt as if the woman was hiding something?

# Chapter 2

After lunch Lynn was sitting on a wooden bench on the rickety, termite-infested porch of the tiny wooden house that was Sarah's office, residence, and laboratory. At the bottom of the weathered gray stairs Sarah was talking to a man who had just driven up to the tiny dock in a wide fiberglass outboard. Lynn noted that everything about him was faded—scraggly blond hair, jeans, salt encrusted t-shirt. Only his skin, sun-baked red and flaky, contrasted.

The man was saying, "One of the little islands, up the river. Nobody lives there—mostly mangrove with a few palms in the middle above high tide." Was that a friendly smile or lechery giving itself away on his sun-cracked lips? "I tell you what; I'll take you over there," he continued, "show you what I found."

Sarah said as she took a plastic grocery bag from him, "Go on up to the ranch house and get some lunch, Marv... Tell Emma I sent you—while I look at this."

He smiled, pushed back his baseball cap. "Thanks boss," and wandered off.

Sarah came up on the porch, pulled a cookie sheet from the stack under the table and dumped out the contents of the bag. She sat down across from Lynn at a wooden table. Then she silently spread out the muddy contents of the plastic bag—a few potsherds, chips of obsidian flint, and bone.

As far as Lynn could see it was the same sort of stuff that covered the surface of this site they were currently digging. "Anything interesting?"

Sarah shook her head. "Not really. Typical for the region." She picked up a couple of pieces and began making a separate pile. "But these...if they were really found in this region...interesting."

10

Lynn could see she was trying to contain her excitement.

Sarah looked up at Lynn. "When Marv comes back, best not to let him know that I am interested. God only knows who we will find shoveling up the place." She shook her head. "Marv usually means well as long as he isn't under the influence, but I'm not sure what he might do for a case of beer. He is basically lazy—so he, at least, won't have done too much damage digging."

Marv came strolling back munching on a sandwich, walked up on the porch and sat down next to Lynn. Sarah introduced them and he smiled, shaking his head. "Crazy, wasting your vacation digging up dead Indian bones."

After he finished the last bit of his sandwich, he readjusted his baseball cap and, squinting in the tropical sun, studied Sarah too closely with red-rimmed watery blue eyes. "So what's it worth to ya?"

Sarah continued putting his collection back in the bag. "The usual, a case of beer."

He smiled calculatingly. "I don't think so."

She handed him the bag.

He waved his hand. "You keep it. No charge. It's no use to me." He pulled out a bag of tobacco and began rolling a cigarette—cool, efficient—waiting.

Sarah went inside and pulled a chart out of one of the cubbies above her desk. Back on the porch she spread the chart out waiting for him to point out the location.

He shuffled his feet and squinted down at the chart.

Sarah sat down on the wooden bench next to Lynn. "Look, I got a lot of work this afternoon. My crew will be coming back from lunch break…"

He lit his cigarette. "There are others 'ud be real interested."

Clearly he knew how much Sarah hated treasure-hunting amateur adventurers. No, Marv wouldn't be likely to use such tactics on her unless he thought he had found something important, something he could market elsewhere. Sarah would have to buy him off if she agreed what he found was significant.

She was saying, "It's on the mainland, not on an island at all, isn't it?"

He hunkered down, his back against the rough sun-bleached wall and shook his head slowly. His smile was calculating. "You read me

11

like a book."

"Two cases, but you have to show me where it is on the map."

He shook his head. "I'll be happy to show you, but I have to take you there."

Sarah sighed. "How much?" Lynn knew how tight her budget was. Would she have to borrow money again?

There was a greedy look in his eyes as he said, "Fifty bucks and two cases...and twenty five percent of any—"

Sarah got up and stood over him with her arms folded. "Get out."

He grinned apologetically. "Aw, come on, I was just kidding. No sense of humor."

Sarah was grim now. "One case and fifty bucks—after you show me."

He shrugged. "You pay for the gas. And we gotta go today. I got a fishing customer tomorrow." He grinned again. "At least he said that he was interested in fishing."

After Marv left the porch Sarah said to Lynn "You want to come along? It will take most of the afternoon."

Lynn nodded, pleased to have the time with Sarah and a chance to see more of the coast by boat.

Sarah said, "Get a flashlight and some bananas and fresh water from the kitchen and see if there are any left-over sandwiches from lunch. I don't know how long this will take." Then she started gathering the gear they would need, gave the supervising graduate student instructions for the dig and placed her canvas hat firmly on her head.

Lynn noted Sarah's frown. A crack in that magnificent facade? That was something to contemplate. There was more to this expedition than Sarah was telling her.

As they walked toward Marv's boat Lynn watched Sarah's sun-browned face with its sprinkle of freckles spread across her neat elegant high-bridged nose. There had been a time when she had wished those intense brown eyes would look at her with the excitement and interest that they showed toward the artifacts she studied. Lynn sighed. That was a long time ago.

Marv was waiting for them, stretched out under a tree in the shade, his hat over his face. Sarah unceremoniously stuffed the empty beer cans and potato chip bags on the bottom of the boat into a plastic bag, stowed her gear and a full gas can, jabbing Marv awake with her rubber-booted toe.

In the boat she patted the seat next to her, smiled and said quietly, "Don't worry. As far as I know it doesn't leak. At least he can handle a boat. After all, he *is* still alive."

"I heard that," Marv grumbled.

It didn't seem very practical to Lynn to be insulting to somebody they were so dependent on at the moment.

As if in answer, Sarah said complacently, but loud enough for Marv to hear, "From me that was a major compliment."

Marv laughed, shook his head, put his baseball hat on and got up.

Lynn climbed in and sat down next to Sarah.

They spent an hour in the hot midday sun cutting through clear tropical blue water, following the dense mangrove that grew thick on the coast as well as the low flat islands and hiding any sand or shoreline—a network of thick impenetrable green foliage with red brown trunks growing right out of the salt water sand and mud.

Sarah was busy making notes and studying her chart and Lynn was contemplating asking them to stop for a swim on the sliver of palm-circled beach they were just passing, when the white bow of a yacht showed up on the other side of the point ahead. "Damn," Sarah exploded, quickly folding her chart.

Marv looked at her intently. "Just my fishing customer. Told him about this cove and bit of beach."

As they came nearer the boat Lynn recognized Ed, their visitor of the morning, napping in a deck chair. As they passed he waved. Sarah smiled, politely shouting something inane about the weather. He nodded and smiled back, then watched the three of them intently until they were out of sight.

When Marv found the place, Sarah insisted they pull into the mangrove, as much out of sight as possible. Marv grumbled the whole time, but he did as she asked. The dense tangle of mangrove, one of the few land plants that could grow in salt water, engulfed the boat. Lynn watched Marv then Sarah climb nimbly over and through the dense network of red-brown, arm-thick branches and disappear into intense green shadows. She tentatively followed, fighting the mangrove, mud, and sand, sometimes sinking nearly to the top of her knee-high rubber boots.

Lynn had laughed when Sarah handed her a pair the first time. They looked a lot like the boots her mother had made her wear on rainy days as a child—the same flexible black rubber—but these where higher and with a thick sole. Now she was very grateful for them as she sunk calf deep into the sucking black mud.

Finally they came to slightly higher ground with tall marsh grass and a few trees. When Lynn stumbled over a rock, Sarah came back to look at it. "Limestone, cut limestone,"she said quietly. They used it for walls and the facing of temples."

Marv called to them from up ahead, pleased with himself. "Told you I could find it again." Ahead were the edges of more limestone blocks pulled up by the roots of trees. Marv had dug shallow holes in a couple of places, showing chips of pottery and flint.

Sarah had surveyor equipment and Lynn followed her, taking notes and helping to measure. They made a chart of the slope and contour of the ground, the location of trees, and limestone blocks. Then they dug a measured square test hole keeping track of every six inch layer, putting what they found in marked plastic bags.

Marv found a spot under a tree and hunkered down to watch them and nap.

Lynn was concentrating on her record keeping when she heard someone approaching. Assuming it was Marv, she did not look up.

"That the only hole you gonna dig? Pretty puny I'd say. Let me give you a hand." It was Ed of the super-catamaran.

Sarah frowned. "You shouldn't have followed us...you could have gotten lost in the mangrove."

The Mrs. appeared behind him with sweat and mud marring her outfit, this time in matched mauve and white including knee high mauve boots. She was out of breath. That didn't prevent her from running on with, "She's right Ed—I told you it was too dangerous what with spiders, snakes, scorpions, and—"

Ed ignored her. "Didn't want to miss out on anything exciting."

"You didn't," Sarah said dryly. "We're just doing survey. Just more potsherds, flint, and rock."

"There was a temple here wasn't there," Ed said shrewdly, pointing to the limestone. When you gonna start digging for real?"

"We don't have a permit to set up an excavation here."

Ed laughed. "That shouldn't be a problem—you got a permit

14

after all. I doubt if the government guys would worry about such a little detail. Might need a buck or two to grease—"

Sarah stood up and moved toward him, her spade tight in her fist as if she was about to hit him over the head. If he hadn't been so sunburned he would have blanched. "I was just kidding! I should know about you scholarly types and your attitude. No sense of humor."

The Mrs. sniffed. "I told you they wouldn't appreciate our help. You'd think they'd recognize our good intentions after all that slogging. You won't catch me out here again."

Thank the goddess, Lynn thought.

# Chapter 3

When they arrived back at camp it was dusk; the sky was a post-card pink behind the palms swaying in an evening breeze. A graduate student, Hank Stebbens, was at the dock getting the big wood canoe ready to take out. It was a Maya-style boat with an outboard that Sarah and her crew used for errands into town.

As they came in, Kathy came down onto the dock and grabbed the rope from Sarah. She sounded worried. "Ann went out in Teddy's kayak after you left. She hasn't come back. Hank thought he better take a look."

Hank, like Kathy, was Sarah's research assistant sharing responsibility with Kathy for the dig when Sarah was not there. Both were Ph.D. candidates.

Sarah sighed. "Did she say anything about which way she was going? She promised me—"

Hank shrugged. "I asked everybody after she didn't show up at dinner. Now Kathy tells me she took a tent and food." His tone left no doubt how annoyed he was at both Ann and Kathy. "She took a kit—shovel, specimen bags—the whole bit. Kathy was the only one saw her take off."

Kathy was clearly worried but defensive. "If you're so sure you could have done a better job talking her out of it, you shouldn't have been out in the bush looking for weird bugs and other creepy crawlies."

Hank straightened up from preparing the motor. "You could have sent somebody out to find me. I wasn't very far away."

"You couldn't have stopped her anyway. She was determined. She said the tent was just in case. She said she would be back before Sarah. She laughed at me for being worried; said she always likes to play it safe." Then Kathy turned to Sarah with a question in her eyes. "You told her she could do survey alone?"

Sarah was annoyed now. "You know better than that."

Hank wiped his oily hands on his shirt. "It was only *after* Ann left that I found out, and that was just because Kathy needed to complain to me that she didn't think it was fair for you to let Ann go out on survey when it wasn't her turn—especially not alone. I told Kathy I didn't think you gave her the go-ahead."

"Damn," Sarah said for the second time that day. "Ann knows better than to go out alone, especially so late in the day. I certainly did not say it was OK." She turned to Lynn, "Help Kathy unload the boat please, and take the stuff from today's trip up to the house. I'll go with Hank. Give me a flashlight."

Kathy handed her one and Sarah turned back to Marv. He was clearly in a hurry to get away. Instead of waiting for them to move their gear out of his boat he was putting it onto the dock himself— very out of character. She said. "After we unload will you—"

He didn't even stop moving gear to look at her, but interrupted, abruptly, snapping, "Can't. Got to get ready for tomorrow."

Sarah grabbed his arm. "C'mon Marv I need your help."

He jerked back his arm and moved back to his idling motor. Without looking at her he said, "I guess I could look around north of here...and ask in town if anybody's seen her."

"Thanks," Sarah said. She turned to Lynn "Give me my backpack please."

Lynn searched through the gear in the gathering dark and found the pack. As she handed it to Sarah she offered, "You want me to come along?"

Sarah nodded. "Sure. It shouldn't take long...if she had the good sense to take a light or light a fire. Thanks."

Kathy said, "She couldn't have gone very far in that thing; she promised not to go more than a half-hour's paddle away. It shouldn't be hard to find her. Doesn't the kit she took have one of those emergency lights?"

"If she wants to be found," Hank said.

Kathy's voice was little-girl anxious now. "I did tell her not to go alone. She said you told her it was OK. I'm sorry Sarah, I—"

Sarah switched on her flashlight. "Stop it Kathy. It is her respon-

17

sibility. I told her not to go out alone, certainly not without telling someone exactly where she was going and when to expect her back. She lied to you. You aren't her jailer—you couldn't tie her down."

Kathy squinted into the light, her voice calmer now. "She headed north, the way we went the other day on survey. I couldn't get her to tell me where she was going."

"It's OK. You did your best..."

"When it got late I told Hank we should call somebody. I was a bit worried about you too. He said it wasn't necessary...yet."

"You did the right thing. I'm sure she's fine. Probably shouldn't even bother to go out looking now. It's just that it *is* getting dark and she might not be able to find her way back. At least we know which direction to look."

Kathy looked relieved as she bent to carry the gear back to camp.

Sarah said, "Look Kathy, you are in charge here. You can handle the radio. Stay calm. Help Emma make out the grocery and supplies list for the next trip into town. I've got a radio. I'll call you right away when we find her."

Kathy smiled, gave a mock salute and said, "Sure boss."

"Thanks for coming along, Lynn. We might need you to handle the boat if Hank and I have to search inland."

They cruised slowly along the mangrove swamps along the coast and then up a small river where Sarah had done survey before. The water in the river didn't seem that different from the salt lagoon inside the barrier reef, especially after sunset in the moonlight—except that it was less clear and there was no coral. They could see only bits of the shore and water reflecting the artificial light of their lamp.

Lynn ran the motor while Hank and Sarah watched for signs of the kayak. But Lynn noted that Hank mostly seemed to be watching Sarah. It had been clear to Lynn early on that Hank had a more than scholarly regard for Sarah. In his early thirties, divorced and starting a new career, he was older and more experienced than most graduate students. He had spent ten years on a career in business in and out of Belize, which made him at the same time more useful as an assistant and more demanding as a peer. Lynn knew Sarah was recovering from a bad relationship and was in a celibate state of mind. Any amorous interest from anyone was just an annoyance. They had a tacit agreement not to discuss the subject, but Hank was

18

bad at hiding his feelings and was clearly used to getting his way. Sarah had told Lynn that she thought it was as much her unavailability as anything that made her attractive to him. Lynn thought that was probably true.

It took them about an hour before they saw the white form of the canvas kayak pulled up on a narrow, mud-blackened beach on the edge of a meandering brackish stream.

"She must have decided to camp out. Smart. She would have had a hell of a time getting back in the dark after going this far." Lynn could hear the relief in Sarah's voice.

Hank was not so forgiving. After helping Lynn shut down the motor and guide the boat closer he said, "She had no business coming this far away in a kayak."

Sarah said, "Never mind Hank; we found her."

"She had to know you would come chasing after her. That's damn inconsiderate."

They pulled their boat up next to the kayak and tied up to some mangrove branches. Sarah called to Ann but there was no answer. It was deadly quiet now, just the night insect sounds starting. Surely Ann could hear them calling. "She must have gone inland a ways to set up camp. There's no gear left in the kayak," Hank said as he reached inside it.

"You Ok here? She won't have gone far." Sarah said to Lynn. The anxiety was back in Sarah's voice.

"I'd rather come along," Lynn said, "unless you want me here."

"The boat seems secure enough. Let's go."

Further along where the mangrove turned to a grass-covered sand bar, Lynn could see bits of pottery and flint on the surface of the ground in the yellow light of her flashlight, but no test holes. Ann had not done any digging—although it was an obvious place for a test hole.

Sarah kept calling, her voice increasingly anxious. Still no answering call. Maybe Ann did not want to be found. Or maybe she had wandered too far inland and was disoriented and lost.

They found her tent set up about fifty yards in from the kayak—on a sandy knoll with some palms. Ann was not in the tent or anywhere nearby. The remains of a meal were still just outside—a cup spilled, food scattered. They called her name again several times, but still there was no answer. Lynn could see that Sarah's hand was shaking as she picked up the scattered items. "Where could she have gone in such hurry?"

Lynn tried to reassure her. "Just give it a minute, she will show up. Probably fell asleep—"

"But her sleeping bag is here!" Sarah's eyes were wide with worry. "What was she doing out here? You don't need a sleeping bag and tent for survey."

Just then Hank called to them. He had found footsteps in the sand going off at an angle back toward where they had left their boat. They followed the tracks in the dark.

Then Lynn could see a form in the mangrove as they hurried closer—Ann stretched across the branches. She didn't respond when they called to her. Lynn's heart beat in her throat.

"Jesus," Sarah whispered, "my worst nightmare." She quickly knelt next to Ann and felt for a pulse. "She's still alive," she announced, breathlessly.

When they turned her over something fell into the mud. Lynn turned her flashlight toward it. A small gray-green snake with faint darker markings lay on the mud. It didn't move. Hank poked at it with his flashlight. The snake was dead.

Sarah studied the snake for a moment and looked at Hank, "Eyelash viper?" He nodded. As she searched for a bite on Ann's upper body, she mumbled, "Good thing we have the snake. At least I know to try antivenin." As if to reassure herself she kept talking. "With pit vipers the antivenin can be more general..." Then she glanced at Lynn. "It worries me that she is unconscious. We have no way to know how long ago this happened."

After she found small punctures on Ann's wrist, Sarah rummaged around in her knapsack for her snake-bite kit, swearing under her breath.

Hank picked up the snake and answered Lynn's unspoken question. "See the scales above the eyes. Looks sort of like an eyelash. Pretty little thing—too bad Ann ran across it. These vipers are shy, not a common hazard, but usually hard to see against the bark of a tree or a branch. You'd have to brush against it or be poking in the wrong place."

Sarah shook her head as she got the antivenin ready. "Thank

god its not a Fer-de-lance or something. These little tree vipers have a lot less venom, but it's about as toxic as it gets."

Beads of sweat on Sarah's face belied her calm manner. Her hand was shaking as she tended to Ann.

Ann's face was peaceful, her hostile and hunted look gone. So young, so beautiful…

Sarah said, shaking her head. "A bite shouldn't have made her unconscious. I'm afraid she's in shock. I wonder how far she walked before—"

Hank was trying to sound reassuring. "Maybe she was drinking or something. I wouldn't be surprised. It's what I might do if—"

"The hell you would." Sarah's anxiety had turned to annoyance. You'd be in your boat trying to get back to camp."

While Sarah was administering the antivenin, Hank radioed Kathy. He told her to call for a helicopter to meet them at the dig site where it could land on the beach. Of course Sarah had worked out emergency protocol—Kathy knew what to do. They should be able to get back to camp by the time the helicopter arrived.

As Hank took one of Ann's specimen bags and put the snake in it, he said, "I can't figure out how Ann managed to kill the viper—no broken skin from a blow. Hardly a displaced scale."

Sarah closed up her bag hurriedly. "Never mind that. You can ask Ann yourself. Let's concentrate on getting her out of here."

They wrapped Ann's jacket around her and made a sling of her sleeping bag. Ann's skin felt cold, her body lifeless and too light as they lifted her.

Then it seemed like hours struggling through the labyrinth of mangrove and muck to the boat, then another eternity getting the engine started.

They went full speed back to the dig, salt water spraying and the hull slapping against the swells in spite of the danger of hidden mangrove roots, and sand bars.

Ann lay in the bottom of the boat wrapped in a blanket and her sleeping bag and covered with Lynn's plastic raincoat against the spray. Lynn shivered in the stern contemplating the huddled figure under her rain slicker. What had brought Ann out here alone? Had she been trying to impress Sarah with her exploration? Ann had to know that Sarah would be angry, that Sarah or Hank would come looking. And there was little evidence that Ann had actually done any digging—no test holes, no bag of artifacts. And why had she gone so far planning to stay over night?

Maybe if Lynn had reached out to Ann more... She had needed help. Why hadn't Lynn gone to Sarah when she suspected Ann might be in trouble. But there was still time, wasn't there? Ann wasn't dead. Lynn was sure Sarah's luck would hold and they would be able to save her.

Chilled and damp from the long boat ride, Lynn picked up Ann's jacket lying forgotten in the bottom of the boat and put it on. She put her hands into the pockets for what meager warmth that offered. In one pocket there was a folded piece of paper along with a pocket knife, a few pieces of hard candy and a pencil. She turned on her flashlight to see what the paper was. It was a fax from a Honduran address in a scrawling handwriting:

*To Annie c/o Dr Sarah Donovan*

*Will be in Belize January 14* ...then an address in Belize City and the cryptic message... *Be there! We won't wait!... BG.*

So Ann had friends she planned to meet. That date was just a day away. But why had Ann gone camping just when she was expected to meet friends in Belize City? She stuck the note in the pocket of her shorts. It sounded urgent. Someone should let those folks know. Even if she survived, Ann wouldn't be up to meeting anyone.

After they were back in camp, a British military helicopter finally arrived to take Ann, still barely alive, to a hospital. The whole camp watched as its lights disappeared into the distance. That could be any one of them being carried off. There was always the danger of coming across something poisonous in this country. But why had Ann gone off like that alone?

After Ann was gone Hank got Sarah into the camp kitchen and put food in front of her. Lynn lit the stove to boil water for tea while Sarah sat staring at the food, too much in shock to take a bite.

When Lynn sat down on the other side of the wooden kitchen table, she noted a strand of hair hanging down and stuck to Sarah's sweaty forehead. Sarah hadn't even bothered to push it back in place. Lynn reached over and tucked it back.

Finally Sarah said, her voice husky, "I've always dreaded something like this would happen to one of my workers. Ann was so young, so enthusiastic…about archaeology."

Lynn doubted it was enthusiasm about archaeology that had taken Ann out there. Finding a new Maya site was exciting. Lynn had only had one experience with survey, but it made her understand the source of Sarah's near obsession to learn about the ancient Maya. She had been at the archeological site long enough not to go digging around without proper survey and recording. There had to have been some other reason.

Lynn took Sarah's hand to get her attention. "Ann isn't dead Sarah. You gave her the antivenin in time. She will be OK."

Hank's voice sounded annoyed as well as sympathetic. "Anyway, it's not your fault, Sarah. Ann went out there alone—after you told her not to."

Sarah shook her head. "But why? Why go alone? I told her she could be part of a survey. There was no reason to go without a crew. If someone had been there earlier with the serum… I knew I shouldn't trust her—that she was down here for the wrong reasons. But it's so hard to find people who know how to work. Ann was…is such a good worker."

Sarah picked up her plate without eating anything, stared at it for a while, then picked at the food without really looking at it. After a few minutes she threw the food out, and began automatically washing what dishes were in the sink. "You know the other thing that bothers me? There were no test holes. What was she doing there all afternoon?"

Hank took a swig of tea. "Maybe she was working someplace else…further inland. That would make sense.She would be more likely to run into a tree viper."

"I don't think she—"

"Kathy said she took a trowel and sample bags.".

Sarah placed a plate carefully in the rack. "We can check when we go back for the stuff tomorrow. But I didn't see anything there. Whatever else she was, she was thorough. If she'd been digging, there would have been marked bags at the tent."

Lynn and Hank exchanged looks. It was clear neither one of them knew how to help Sarah now that her worst nightmare had been realized—one of her workers suffering—threatened with death.

Lynn said the first thing that came to mind. "Maybe she didn't find anything worth digging for."

Sarah looked at them, her eyes desperate. "Then why stay there—why not come back to camp? It doesn't make any sense. She took a tent and food with her. She planned to stay over night."

Then Lynn told them about her feeling that Ann had been trying to avoid Ed Kelly. That she had seemed more nervous than usual, even frightened.

"But Ed only stayed a little while. He was long gone when Ann left," Sarah said.

"Maybe she was afraid he would come back?" Lynn suggested.

Hank shook his head impatiently. "You're reaching for straws. Sarah has enough on her mind."

Lynn showed them the fax and said, "Do you think some friends finally showed up for a visit, or these were the people Ann was avoiding?"

Sarah said tiredly, "Hank is right, you have too vivid an imagination. We'll have to try and get in touch with them. I'm sure Ann will be happy to see them once she's better."

# Chapter 4

In the morning there were no reports about Ann's condition. The crew was jittery and subdued as they went about their work. They had all been warned about the dangers of Belize's jungle. Sarah was, if anything, overcautious as well as prepared, but she still blamed herself. She spent the morning organizing the medical supplies while Hank and Kathy supervised at the digging.

Just before lunch when they were resting on Sarah's porch, Sarah said quietly to Lynn "It's missing. I can't find it anywhere."

"What?"

"The book on poisonous snakes. Do you remember who had it last?"

Lynn shook her head. "It was on your desk when you gave me my greenhorn lecture the day I got here. I read the passage you gave me. You want me to check around?"

"No, I'll ask. I'm sure somebody has it in their tent."

All morning Sarah was on the radio trying to get information on Ann's condition. She even went into the village nearby to call the hospital by phone. All she managed to discover was that Ann was still alive but unconscious. Everyone at the hospital was too busy to to talk to her, so after lunch Lynn and Sarah took the boat to Belize City.

Later that afternoon, Lynn waited in the hospital lobby for Sarah who had managed to talk to the doctor. After a while a woman came in. Fashionably dressed, she carried herself with style and confidence. After talking with the receptionist for a moment she took the seat next to Lynn and turned her dark eyes in Lynn's direction. She said, her voice breaking slightly, "The receptionist told me...you...are a friend of Ann's?"

"I know her. Are you a friend?"

A slight shake of the head and the full eyelashes fluttered, but the woman didn't look up.

"How do you know about what happened to Ann? Are you from the newspaper?"

For an instant dark eyes studied her. Then the eyelashes fluttered again and she said, "Not just a friend...I'm...Naomi, Naomi Wilson. My sister and I...have been estranged. I came down looking for her. It was a chance to get over all that. And now— If only I had come a few days sooner."

Lynn noted now that Naomi did have the same coloring and the straight dark brows and fine dark hair as Ann—and the same slim figure. She was a bit older, the bones in her face more pronounced under the cascade of dark hair. She tried to be reassuring. "I'm sure that she will get the best treatment possible."

"I know. That's why they are moving her."

Lynn looked at her puzzled.

Again the dark eyes engaged hers. "Did you get a chance to visit her...before they took her away?"

"Took her away?"

"You didn't know? Just a little while ago some military doctor took her, put her on a plane to the States. I just missed her myself. I came down to meet her, and now this..." She pulled a lace handkerchief out of her purse and dabbed her eyes. "Now I have to get a flight back and it doesn't leave for hours. And I'm still not sure where they took her." She leaned a little closer to Lynn, the eyes intense almost accusing. "When you visited with her—did she tell you anything? What happened out there?"

"She was unconscious when we found her and I didn't see her after they brought her here. We got her out as quickly as we could. Sarah gave her the antivenin right away. I'm sure she will be all right."

"I told her it was dangerous down here. She never listens to me. I never trusted why she was here in the first place." The eyes questioned Lynn as if she should know the answer. "I never liked the people she was working with." She sniffed.

"What do you mean. What people? The archeological crew—"

"Not them. She had something else she was involved in...you

know…?" The eyes narrowed a bit. "They're the ones responsible for this." The dark eyes were a penetrating question. "Do you know why she was down here? Who she was working for?"

Lynn felt manipulated. The woman was trying to get information out of her. Suddenly the woman's grief felt fake. If this woman was a relative, no wonder Ann was running away. "No, I don't know that she was working for anyone but Sarah." Lynn leaned away defensively. "Ann didn't mention you were coming."

Naomi looked down at her carefully manicured nails. "…She…didn't know. It was supposed to be a surprise. And now…" She dabbed at her eyes and squeezed Lynn's arm. "It's such a comfort to talk to someone who knows her. Perhaps I'm wrong, but I thought she had some sort of job down here…working for…some…organization in the States? She wouldn't talk to us. She must have mentioned—?"

The woman's penetrating stare was making Lynn uncomfortable. What did she mean organization? Lynn parried with a question. "I got the impression she was running away. She seemed afraid of something…or someone. Was it you or someone else in her family?"

The arched dark brows expressed outrage. "Her family loves her—she isn't afraid of us." Naomi opened her purse and took out another handkerchief and patted her face. Then she said, petulantly, "I don't think you were a friend of hers at all. She might be a difficult person but she loved her family. Of course I knew she was here, because she wrote to let us know she was all right. She wasn't running away from us. The people she worked for—that's another story." The questioning eyes penetrated her again.

"As far as I know she was working for Dr. Donovan? Why are you asking me, a stranger."

"I have a right to ask questions about my own sister." Naomi's eyes noted something behind Lynn and she stood up, the handkerchief up to her cheek again. Lynn turned to see Sarah coming down the hallway toward the front desk. Whatever there was to be learned about Ann's condition she could get from Sarah and the doctors. She didn't care to be brokering for information from this woman any longer.

But Naomi Wilson had already turned away apparently overcome, her face covered by her lace handkerchief as Lynn hurried over to Sarah.

Sarah said, relief in her voice, "Doctor Alvarez has told me they have taken Ann back to the States for treatment. She said it probably was just as well. This is such a small place they don't have the specialists they do back home. The good news is that Ann was stable when she left here though still unconscious. The doctor has promised to contact me if she hears anything more."

Lynn turned to tell Naomi that good news but the woman had disappeared. Strange.

# Chapter 5

After they left the hospital Sarah was her old efficient self as they got a taxi. After a few more quick errands and a stop at a pharmacy to renew the medical supplies, they were back in the boat. Sarah seemed reassured and ready to go back to work. The atmosphere that night at supper was almost festive.

The next morning just as Hank and Kathy were preparing to go out in the boat to pick up the kayak, tent and equipment that Ann had taken out with her, a Belize coast guard boat appeared at the dock. Three people walked up the path, two in the uniform of the Belize City police, the third dressed in casual clothing that looked a bit too new and was a lighter shade of chocolate brown than the two police. Sarah met them on the path and took them to her house while the rest of the crew watched from the dig.

After a while Lynn thought about going up to Sarah's house with some excuse, but just then she saw Sarah coming down alone and stood waiting nervously while they all gathered. Then Sarah said quietly, a catch in her voice, "Ann didn't make it. She died without regaining consciousness. There's an investigation. The three of us who found her will have to show the place where she got...bitten; then we'll have to go with them to Belize City...probably for just a couple of days. Kathy, you'll have to run things here while we are gone."

Ann—dead. They all just stood silent for a moment staring at Sarah. In the movies the rescuers always get there just in time. Lynn had never questioned for a moment that they had saved Ann.

Lynn could see that under her cool surface, Sarah was about to fall to pieces. She put an arm around her, but Sarah pulled away, only the abrupt way she moved showed her feelings. Her voice was just a bit too strident as she said, "Thanks Lynn, for your concern...I'm OK. Just a bit in shock. The rest of you take the afternoon off; they want to ask you a few questions too. Hank, help me go over things with Kathy. Lynn, take the others up to the house to be interviewed, then you pack up what we'll need for a couple of days."

The two police were on the porch waiting for them. While the others settled down, Lynn went inside. Her suitcase was pulled apart and the guy in the casual clothes was going through it.

"What the fuck do you think you are doing?" she said, furious at the invasion. "Who the hell are you anyway?"

The man looked up at her and smiled, unapologetically. "Helping the locals with their investigation." He held out his hand. "Grant, DEA. We got called in because the dead woman was a US citizen. The Belize authorities were delighted to have us help. They don't like American tourists dying."

Lynn didn't take his hand. "Why are you interested? Your agency doesn't put out to investigate your average dead tourist."

"When their bodies are loaded up with drugs, we do. The Belize authorities tend to call us in such cases. Not good for their tourist industry." He closed her suitcase "So far you look clean."

"Drugs?"

Without answering her Grant started going through the contents of her shelf. He dumped her shoulder bag out on the bed and started to take apart her wallet. Then he said, "The local Doc who treated her at the hospital in Belize City noticed some weirdness in her tests, and called the police. They informed us that they were investigating "

"Like what in her tests?"

"Like the presence of both cocaine and heroin in her blood and needle marks as well as old scars on her body..."

"But I saw the snake."

"Yeah, the Doc had a specialist friend look at it. It was dead a while by the time he saw it. He thought it just barely possible that it was alive at the time she was bitten, just barely. It could have supplied the venom in her body—one way or the other. But the snake wasn't exactly killed. No abrasions from a blow. Biologist couldn't quite figure why it died. Could have been from being held in captivity. In other words somebody brought it there in a bag or something." He shook his head, "Lethal combination." He laughed. "Have to get the State Department to put it in the tourist advisory. Don't take drugs if you plan to get bitten by a viper."

Lynn stared at him horrified by the callousness.

He looked more serious. "Sorry, we get used to this sort of thing. A bad business; she was pretty young. That's why we need to stop it."

"She was flown home before she died. What do the doctors in the States who treated her say?"

He looked at her for a long time as if calculating what he should tell her. "Haven't got a report yet from them on specific details except that she never regained consciousness."

"The police here think somebody killed her?"

"Somebody could have put venom in her drug supply. There were bite marks, but those might have been faked. The drug combination was unusual and might have killed her anyway."

"She did seem strange that day...scared. Like she wanted to avoid somebody. You think the bite marks were faked and the snake was planted already dead?"

He shrugged. "She could have taken the drugs herself. Maybe she wanted to get attention, sympathy. Killed the snake herself then made it look like she was bitten. Put a bit of venom in her drugs to make it look authentic. She knew Dr. Donovan would come looking for her."

"Why would she do something crazy like that?"

"Addicts don't act like other people." He stopped talking and pulled a card from her wallet, waived her press card at her and shook his head. "No more questions from you!"

She snatched it and her wallet from him and started putting the contents back.

He grabbed her arm and squeezed just a little too hard. "Look, keep a lid on this for the moment."

Lynn pulled her arm away angrily. "Why should I?"

"Maybe because of your buddy, Doc Sarah. Maybe because until she is cleared this dig might be on hold."

"She wouldn't hurt a fly and she has a government permit to do archaeology here."

He smiled. "But what if she or someone working for her is

involved in the drug trade? Your friend, Ann, got her drugs some-place. We are looking for that source and we don't want that investigation jeopardized. Splash this case on the front page of your news rag, not only will it blow our investigation, but the Belize authorities will know about possible drug trade at your precious archeological site. We'll see how long your buddy Donovan can keep this site going then."

Fuming, Lynn followed Grant outside onto the porch. There Grant and the policewoman sat at Sarah's scarred table as if it were a judicial podium. The two introduced themselves to the others that had gathered there.

The policewoman asked, "Did she tell anyone she was going out in the kayak?"

Teddy spoke almost too quietly to be heard. She was clearly in shock. Ann had not been a friend before Belize, but they had shared a tent for the time that Ann had been there. "She didn't say anything to me about going out yesterday. She asked me a few days ago if I minded her borrowing my kayak. I taught her how to use it. She was kind of timid, you know…. Grew up in the city and never learned to swim, never been in a boat. Hadn't even been in a canoe before. But she did real well with my kayak. Learned to swim a bit too. I told her any time—that she could borrow it as long as she followed Sarah's rules and didn't go out of sight of camp. I was real pissed at her for taking it out so long. I didn't realize…" Her voice faltered. "…I wish I'd never taught her."

"She didn't talk to anybody but me about going out," Kathy said. "But she was kind of snappy and nervous all morning. Kept going back to her tent."

Hank said, "She was snappy and nervous all the time. I told you, Sarah, you shouldn't have let her stay."

Sarah stood leaning against the doorway, dark circles under her tired eyes. Her voice was almost a whisper as if she didn't quite trust it. "She was a good worker. Everyone else managed to get along with her."

Grant asked, "Did any of you know she was on drugs?"

Teddy's voice shook. "She was not. She told me about going to a rehab center…before she came here. She was trying real hard. Nobody here knew, but me. I would have noticed if… It was why she came here...to get out of that environment. I admired how tough she was. She'd been though some rough times. Nobody here tried to be helpful to her or understand. Sarah was the only one..." Her voice disintegrated into a squeak.

Kathy was pulling a leaf apart carefully watching each piece fall to the floor. "I think she was scared about something. Kept looking up as if she expected a boat or a plane to show up suddenly."

Hank snickered. "She did that every day. I asked her once if she was expecting visitors or something. If she was, she should warn Sarah they were coming. She just got a scared look in her eyes and said that she didn't have any friends, just enemies. I thought that was a weird thing to say, but I thought she was kidding...just being devious and rude more like it. I told her she was too young to have enemies. She laughed and said, 'You're right I'm nobody, nothing, not even worth hating.' Even though I didn't much like her I felt sorry for her then. Nobody should feel that bad about themselves."

"It didn't keep you from being mean to her," Teddy said. "None of you were very nice to her."

"She wasn't very nice to us. Moody and withdrawn a lot. It was fun around here before she showed up," Hank said.

There were tears in Teddy's eyes as she said angrily, "Well, you're all rid of her now."

Sarah looked at her, shocked, "Teddy, you don't mean that. It sounds as if you think one of us was responsible for—"

"I know Hank hated her."

"I did not. We just didn't get along. Really I didn't care. It was you, not us that cared—"

Teddy's face turned pink.

Kathy whispered, "You shouldn't have said that Hank; Teddy really did care about Ann, even if Ann wouldn't give her the time of day."

"Anna LaPlace, Anna Marie LaPlace to be precise," Grant said. "Ann Wilson was just an alias."

If he said it for the shock value, he had succeeded. They all just stared at him in silence

The policewoman said, "Did anyone know that about her?"

Teddy said angrily, "It was a way to start a new life. Be a different, better, person. That's why she was using a new name. Wilson

33

was her grandmother's name. Her grandmother was the most important person in her life. She wanted to be like her—"

"You knew her name was Anna LaPlace...?" Sarah asked.

Teddy shook her head. "She never told me that exactly. But I knew she was running away, and that she wasn't using her married name. I knew she had been in trouble and wanted to get away from her old life."

"You could have said something to me, Teddy. Maybe we could have been more helpful," Sarah said defensively.

There were tears in Teddy eyes now. "She made me promise I wouldn't tell. She *was* scared of something. She *said* it was her brother. That he would come after her and put her back in an institution. And she was afraid of an ex-boyfriend, some biker. She wanted to get better on her own. She—"

Sarah said, "Doctor Alvarez did say it was her brother that came to take her home. He's in the military..."

Grant stood up and said to the policewoman, "Don't you think it would be better to interview them all separately."

She hesitated for a moment as if caught off guard but then nodded and said, "My assistant here will be looking through your belongings while I continue the questions. I apologize in advance for the invasion."

Kathy stayed and the others went to their tents to wait.

As they walked away Hank said dryly to Teddy, "Sounds like Ann might have lied to you too."

Teddy pulled her baseball cap down over her eyes and marched abruptly to her tent.

Lynn followed her. Teddy was inside holding one of Ann's worn shirts up to her cheek. She hissed, "Leave me alone," when Lynn stuck in her head.

"The police will want to take Ann's things with them."

"They already poked their noses in here." Teddy sniffed.

"I told them I would help you pack them up," Lynn lied.

"You do it." Teddy said quietly, pointing to a pile on the other bed. The tent had two makeshift cots Jacob had put together out of rough-cut wood with thin foam mattresses. Ann's was covered with a worn madras print. She had left very little behind. It was as if she had known she wasn't coming back. A thin cotton shirt and worn jeans and a few ragged pieces of underwear were in an old suitcase under the bed. She put the few books, Mexican leather sandals and assorted half-used toiletries piled on the bed into the suitcase. Ann's passport and wallet must have been with her; Lynn didn't find them in the tent.

She asked Teddy, who answered with a reluctant shake of the head, " I don't know; they took some papers…"

Lynn took the suitcase to the policewoman who just said with annoyance, "You should have allowed us to do that."

Lynn explained about Teddy's state of mind. "I thought it would be helpful. I was afraid she might get more upset if you went back in there. Ann didn't leave much behind."

"Anna," the policewoman corrected her. "Perhaps, then, you will accompany me while I question Ms. Teddy…to avoid upsetting her further."

Lynn smiled. "Of course, I'm happy to help any way I can. Ms—"

A friendly smile lit up the policewoman's face. Now she reminded Lynn of her friend Del, a Hartfield police detective and good friend. Suddenly she missed Del and her kids, the only family Lynn had at the moment.

"Phyllis…Phyllis Thompson, Inspector Phyllis Thompson."

"Well, Inspector Thompson, Teddy was the only one here who got close to Ann. You heard her say that Ann was trying to get off drugs. It's possible that Teddy knows more, but I suspect Ann lied to her too."

Teddy was still on her bed, face down, and ignored them when they came in the tent. "Teddy, Inspector Thompson would like you to answer a few more questions." Teddy turned her back to them and curled up.

Lynn sat down on the bed. "I think you should cooperate. Don't you want to get the people that hurt Ann? Did she tell you about who might be after her, somebody she was afraid of?"

Teddy looked a Phyllis Thompson with a tear-streaked face. She turned over, sat up and sniffed. "There was this guy she told me about. The one that got her on drugs in the first place. She told me his name once when she'd had a bit too much rum. Stupid woman was still in love with him I think."

Inspector Thompson took out her note pad and sat down on

Ann's bed. "Can you remember anything she said about him?"

Teddy wiped her face on the bottom of her Lesbian Avenger t-shirt. "It was something to do with bones. I remember thinking it was a weird name, like he was a member of a rock group or something. Anyway, she sometimes called him Choc Mul after the Mayan god that has a skull face. I remember now—Skull. His real name was Scully. Bernard Gilbert Scully. Ann thought that was funny. Such an weird formal name. But really, she was afraid of him."

Teddy stared at them for a moment. "She mostly called him Skullhead. He shaved his head—a biker type." Teddy shook her head. "She was sure he was looking for her—would get her hooked again, back into the life. She seemed panicky, even terrified some-times. But I think she also got off on the excitement of it, the danger when she was in the right mood. Why else would she hang out with a weirdo like that?"

"Did you ever see him or a picture of him?" Phyllis asked.

Teddy shook her head and went on to describe how proud Ann had been that she was on her own, off drugs. How hard it had been. "She never wanted to go back." There were tears in Teddy's eyes. "Her hands shook sometimes when she talked about it."

Then Phyllis convinced Teddy to help her interview the Mayans who sometimes helped on Jacob and Emma's ranch and occasional-ly at the dig when Sarah could afford to hire them. Teddy's Spanish was excellent. She had spent much of her teen years in Guatemala, had gone to school there, so she even knew a few words in the Mayan language that these families spoke.

As they trudged up a narrow path in the jungle, Teddy explained that the Ancient Maya had known how to rotate their crops so as not to wear out the soil and that like their ancestors, they depended on tree crops as well that were less hard on the soil.

In the middle of a clearing planted with corn, squash, and beans they came upon a little house made of small upright poles tied close together with a palm leave roof. Teddy explained that the land belonged to Jacob and Emma. They had agreed to let the Mayans stay in exchange for some help on the ranch. A woman and several small children came out of the house as they approached and ran up to Teddy chattering in Mayan.

In this environment especially when she began translating, Teddy was transformed from an awkward reluctant and shy teen-ager. The woman and her children clearly felt comfortable with Teddy though defensive with Inspector Thompson.

Teddy translated while Phyllis asked questions. They had nothing to offer about Ann except that she kept her distance.

Finally Teddy said to Phyllis, "I'm sorry, I really think they don't know anything about the snake. They did say something about a healer who knew the old ways to treat snakebite, but it sounds like she is over the border in Guatemala." Then she said, appealing to Phyllis to reassure them, "They're afraid they'll be blamed."

Inspector Thompson shook her head. "Tell them Emma has told us they were working for her the whole time, clearing a new field so we are not blaming them for Anna's death."

Teddy explained to them and the woman looked relieved but still wary.

Inspector Thompson said, "Tell her to contact us if they hear anything that might be helpful."

Teddy said, anxious for them, "Are you finished with your questions?"

Thompson nodded.

As they walked back to Sarah's house, Thompson told Lynn, "Unfortunately they are right to be cautious. Mayans aren't always treated well here. Technically I should have checked their papers."

Teddy's voice was belligerent. "And send them back to Guatemala maybe to be shot? Their village was destroyed. Burned to the ground—"

Phyllis held up her hand. "It's better if we don't know the details. It's not that we're unsympathetic but we are in an awkward position. Even the environmentalists here are not always happy that the Mayans are still working the land in the traditional way because they clear the jungle for their crops and kill the wildlife for food.

"Half the population of this country lives in Belize City and they tend to participate in the British xenophobic tradition. The Maya don't speak English and sometimes not much Spanish. It doesn't matter that they've always been here. Even the Spanish-speaking people here think of them as foreigners that come across the border from Guatemala."

Teddy added, "Of course, to the Maya there is no border.

Lynn went up to the ranch house with Phyllis Thompson while she questioned Jacob and Emma.

They had very little to say about Ann. She had been distant with them too, doing her share of the cooking and cleaning-up grudgingly.

Phyllis ask if they knew anybody who might have caught and sold a tree snake recently.

They both shook their heads and smiled nervously.

When the police finished their questions, Sarah, Hank, and Lynn went with the three in the coast guard boat to look for the place where Ann had camped. Sarah remembered that there had been five tall palms on the knoll where Ann had put up the tent. They found the spot even though the white shape of the kayak was no longer there. When they came into shore they found the kayak, floating upside down in the mangrove swamp.

"Could it have been turned over by the tide?" Lynn ask.

"Maybe if it was caught on a limb, I suppose. But it doesn't seem very likely; the tide isn't very high here," Sarah said.

When they got to the top of the knoll under the palm trees, they found the tent down and everything scattered about as if someone had hastily searched for something.

"This isn't how we left it," Sarah told them. "It looks like someone came looking after we left."

The policeman took photos, Grant poked around, putting a few bits into plastic bags while Inspector Thompson took down a description of how they had left it.

Sarah said, "It was dark but the tent was intact. We just looked inside briefly before we found Ann. After that we were too busy with her...and the antivenin—then getting her to the boat."

"Couldn't some kind of wild animal after food, even a couple of bush rats, or monkeys have scattered stuff around like this?" Hank suggested, puzzled.

"Then why is there food still here, some of the packages still unopened?" Mr. DEA Grant asked, pointing to a potato chip bag, still half full. There were ants on everything. Half a peanut butter sandwich, now covered with insects still sat in its wrapping of plastic on the sand.

Hank found a disposable hypodermic needle in the bushes and the policeman carefully bagged it.

Sarah studied the sand. "Nothing but bird and people tracks. There are ours and Ann's boot tracks. All the rubber boots we wear on the archeology team have the same tread. They were bought at the same time. We all had them on, including Ann, when we found her.

"So those shoes." Sarah pointed to a fresh set of footprint in the sand that left a round regular pattern. "...belong to someone else. And I don't remember seeing them when we were here before."

The tracks ran off at an angle into the mangrove. Where they disappeared there were broken branches as if someone had been in a hurry to get away. Had they interrupted someone just now—a human scavenger perhaps?

The policeman took off in that direction. He came back after a few minutes and told them that a boat had recently come in on a beach just beyond the screen of mangrove.

# Chapter 6

Sarah, Hank and Lynn went into Belize City that afternoon in the camp's outboard canoe. Lynn left Sarah and Hank at the police station to call her editor, Gayle, at the Hartfield *Chronicle* and give her a verbal report on the event—and that the DEA man, Grant, had told her to keep quiet.

"I'd like to find out why Anna Marie LaPlace, alias Ann Wilson, was in Central America. If her name or names show up in any news reports. You know, criminal prosecutions—drug cases especially. Get my office-mate Bill on it. He's good at it. There has to be a reason Grant is so interested in Ann. Interested enough to threaten me, interested enough to want it kept out of the papers."

Gayle laughed. "Sounds like this guy Grant got under your skin, hon. I do remember some drug case, fairly big time, some woman informer turned state's witness. I think her name was something like LaPlace. We'll get on it for you. There's been nothing on the wire about a suspicious death of anybody air-lifted out of Belize. We'll check around. Do you know what hospital they took her to here in the States?"

"I don't know. Her brother is in the military. He came to get her. I'll try to find out."

She called the hospital. The doctor who treated Ann was not there, and the woman who answered the phone finally said, clearly annoyed at being bothered, "That information was not released to us. You will have to contact the U.S. authorities."

She would have to ask the Belize police or Grant or maybe Sarah knew.

Meanwhile she wanted to find the people who had sent the fax to Ann asking—demanding to meet her. It seemed just common courtesy to tell them what had happened and she was curious. She had given the fax she found in Ann's pocket to Phyllis Thompson after copying down the address, but Lynn decided to look them up herself anyway.

Lynn was grateful that Belize was chiefly an English speaking country. Though in theory she thought it a good thing to learn other people's languages, she never had managed to function adequately in anything other than English.

Before the British threw out the Spanish and set up their coastal logging operations, Belize had been part of the Spanish empire, but the Spanish had never fully conquered it. It was one of the few places where native Mayans had defeated the Spanish for a time, and even now was a refuge for people from politically repressive Guatemala and other parts of Central America.

Sarah had told her that Belize had been a refuge for pirates and that when the British had taken over from the Spanish they had stayed in a few places on the coast to log off the valuable timber and had brought in Blacks to do it. Then British Honduras—now Belize, it was currently one of the most peaceful, relatively prosperous, relatively democratic countries in Central America.

Belize City had not been built for its good location or congenial climate. In fact it was built on a swamp so that it flooded often. Convenient perhaps for the British to move logs onto the ships, not so convenient to live in.

To avoid the flooding, the small wooden houses of the local people were built on stilts. Underneath the small houses was a general work area usually adorned with newly washed clothes hanging out to dry. People seemed to managed to live an orderly happy life even though it was hot and steamy and the pervasive smell of the canals let one know that the sewage problem was never fully under control.

Lynn got directions that took her down a residential street not far from the main canal. She finally stopped in front of a two-story stucco house not built on stilts with a small flower garden and patch of grass behind a low wooden fence. Parked inside the gate in the shade of the tree was a rusty vintage 1970s red Volkswagen bus fully fitted out as a camper with the tent top up and flowered curtains in the back windows.

A milk chocolate child in a red brocade dress with spotless white socks and patent leather shoes was hanging on the fence watching her.

Lynn said, "I'm looking for someone with the initials BG. The child stared at her with a 'who me' look in her wide beautiful eyes. Lynn asked "Is your mother home?" The child ran up the stairs and leaned over the banister pointing at the bus with a slightly disgusted expression as if she had expected Lynn to read her mind and thought Lynn was incredibly stupid for not doing it.

Lynn went through the gate and stood by the door of the bus feeling a little foolish. She couldn't see anyone inside. She looked back at the child who pointed again and smiled. This time the idiot got it—Lynn knocked on the door panel. After a moment a striking-ly pretty sunbrown face surrounded by fuzzy, sun-bleached redbrown curls appeared at the window from below, sleepy and puzzled. Then it disappeared and the door opened.

A slim tanned woman in shorts and a tie-dyed t-shirt stepped out. Two very green eyes peered at Lynn sleepily from under delicate long golden brown lashes. *"Qu'est-ce que?..."*

"I'm sorry," Lynn said, disconcerted, "I was trying to find some-one with the initials BG."

The green eyes squinted suspiciously. "She was supposed to come herself. Where is she?"

Lynn decided on a half truth, hoping to get some information. "Ann...couldn't come herself..."

The woman checked out Lynn's damp somewhat grubby shirt and shorts, her hair, stringy from being washed in salt water. "Who are you?"

"My name is Lynn Evans. I...work with Ann."

*"Eh, Michelle, viens ici,"* the woman called back into the van. After awhile another sleepy face appeared. This one was surrounded by an abundance of straight shiny black hair. Two intense brown eyes under oriental-shaped lids stared at her. Chinese?

"Inuit," she said to Lynn's rather impolite stare. "My mother was Inuit, my father, French, French Canadian."

Green eyes said, "She says she works with Annie. She said Annie can't come."

Michelle was suddenly more alert. She looked at Lynn suspi-ciously, then at her bag. But green-eyes was the one to ask, "So, did she give you something for us or what?"

42

Another face appeared—a man with long stringy gray hair care-lessly tied up with a rubber band. He snarled, "Shut up Ivette," to green-eyes. He gestured at Lynn, "Get in," and pushed the door a lit-tle wider, then unceremoniously pulled her inside when she hesitated.

Green-eyed Ivette crawled into the back which was one wide bed and lay on her back propped up on pillow, staring at Lynn. Michelle stood next to the door watchfully.

Lynn was crammed onto a sticky yellow plastic seat next to a sink/stove combination with unwashed coffee cups and left-over lunch. Gray-hair grabbed Lynn's bag and dumped the contents onto the linoleum-covered floor. He grabbed Lynn's wallet. Fortunately she had her identification—her press card, passport and travelers checks—in a money belt inside her shirt.

Lynn peered through the dusty window. Should she yell for help? Maybe the little girl in red would go and get her mother.

Gray hair threw Lynn's wallet on the floor. "*Merd.* Just a drivers license and a few Belize dollars." He rummaged around in the con-tents of her pack. "Nada. Nothing here but groceries, fruit, and tooth paste."

"I'm glad she decided to dump us," said Ivette. "She needed to take care of herself, not us. Let's get out of here. Forget about Annie. She's better off alone."

Gray hair made a fist. "Shut your trap, Ivette, before I shut it for you."

Michelle put a hand on gray-hair's arm. "Take it easy BG."

"I never wanted that stupid broad with us in the first place," he said spitefully at Ivette. So this was the BG of the fax.

"It's my bus," green-eyed Ivette said, petulantly.

Michelle leaned against the door and smiled at Lynn, cool and casual now. "Don't mind them, *cher*. Their brains got fried driving through Honduras. So what happened to Annie? Why can't she come? Did she decide she didn't want to leave with us after all?"

Lynn took a deep breath. "She can't go anywhere right now." That at least was true.

BG was furious. "Shit. She can't expect us to wait. We got to eat."

Lynn contemplated the three. What had they expected her to be carrying in her bag? Drugs? Money? They thought Ann was going to

43

bring them something. She wanted badly to find out what. She risked another bit of deception. "She can't get...anything for you...now." She was answered with silent stares.

Then Ivette said, "I'm sick of waiting. So? Did Ann go off someplace by herself? Back to the States? Her family—"

BG threw one of Lynn's bananas at her. "I told you to shut-the-fuck up."

Ivette wiped squished banana from her face with an injured look. Lynn wondered why the women put up with him? It was hard to imagine any of them as lovers. She suppressed her Saint George impulse. Green-eyed Ivette had to take care of herself.

So it was money they expected. Were they planning on selling drugs to Ann or...? Where was Ann going to get money. Was that why she went out in the kayak to make a deal? And got killed instead. Maybe Grant had been right that she was involved in drug dealing through the site. And that was why she had been so standoffish. And why she had lied to Teddy? At least now she had an idea which way the transaction was supposed to go. They expected cash or something that would bring it.

But it was time to get out. It was getting very hot in the bus with the windows closed and it smelled of rotting lunch. She could see the little girl up on a balcony watching them. Did she report to some invisible adult inside? Should Lynn wave frantically hoping she would get the girl's mother? BG followed the line of her eyes and saw the little girl. Now, behind the child there was an older face looking from behind the lace curtain.

BG climbed into the drivers seat. "We're getting out of here. I don't trust that old woman."

"They were nice enough about letting us rent this space." Ivette said.

"Yeah and they made us pay for it—up front."

Lynn thought about diving for the door, but Michelle stood firmly in front of it. Her bare brown arms showed the muscle definition that indicated that she was a power lifter.

"Look I just came to tell you Ann isn't coming. I don't know anything about any money. I've got to go now, people are expecting me back on the boat. I—"

Unfortunately Lynn had left the gate open. As they drove out into the main street, BG said, "So if Annie can't come to us maybe we'd better go to her..."

Michelle said to Lynn, "You'll just have to come along *cher amie*, to show the way."

Ivette climbed over the seat putting herself between BG and Lynn. Her tentative smile said, "Don't worry, I won't let them hurt you." What did she think BG was going to do? Lynn was touched by the gesture even though it didn't make her feel any safer. She was amazed at how she could feel fear and sexual attraction at the same time.

Meanwhile Lynn's sensible side, the one that had told her not to come at all said, hey, why do I think you got yourself in over your head again? She decided even though it was a bit late, it was time to tell the whole truth. "Really. I just came here to tell you that Ann... the reason she can't meet you..." They all turned to look at her. "...is dead."

BG stopped the bus on the narrow street driving up on the curb to get out of the traffic lane. "What the hell—?"

The other two were staring at her in shocked silence. Lynn explained about the snake bite.

Ivette's green eyes were wide with horror. "What an awful way to die. We saw her just a few weeks ago. She was so alive." A tear started to run down one cheek. "I told her not to stick around. That it was too dangerous—"

BG raised his hand to slap her. "When will you learn to shut up?"

Michelle grabbed his wrist. They stared at each other silently for a few seconds then BG turned his back to them. Michelle said, "*Merd*. Talk about *me* over-reacting."

Lynn felt a little better about Michelle now that she seemed to be defending Ivette. ...And maybe even a little jealous. They probably were lovers.

Michelle leaned toward Lynn, her voice confidential, almost friendly. It was clear to Lynn that Michelle didn't believe Ann was dead. "BG...liked Annie. We all did even though we didn't know her very well. He is just upset because we are running out of money— haven't had a decent meal in two days. Annie promised to pay for gas and food if we took her home with us—back to Montreal. Of course it was stupid to get ourselves into such a fix. One disaster after another. First the bus broke down. That took all our cash to fix. Now this."

This was obviously not whole truth. Did Michelle think Lynn was stupid enough to be taken in by this condescending niceness. She returned Michelle's polite smile. "I'm sorry to upset you all. I really don't have anything more to tell you."

BG said without turning, the anger palpable in his voice, "Fucking bitch. You're lying. I don't believe she's dead. She gave you money and you're keeping it."

"If you don't believe me you can call the Belize police. I'm sorry. I should have told you right away what happened. As far as I know she didn't have much money. The police found her passport and a few dollars with her, but she didn't have cards or travelers checks. Certainly there was no package addressed to you."

"How would you know? You a cop?" BG asked.

Lynn shook her head. "Teddy, one of the workers at the archaeological site, was her tent mate—she packed up Ann's stuff. Teddy would have told me if there was anything like that."

Ivette whispered, "She was so beautiful and alive."

Lynn touched her shoulder. "I'm sorry about her too. It's a shame when someone's life is cut off so suddenly." She wanted to get Ivette away from these two...somehow. She liked Ivette. More than just her seductive green eyes and pretty face. Ivette was genuine. She really had cared about Ann.

Lynn didn't think it likely that these three were involved in Ann's death, but they might know who was. It would be useful to ask some more questions. She turned to the others. "Look, I've got to get back. My friend Sarah will wonder where I am. I'm meeting her at a hotel that has a decent restaurant. I'll buy you all lunch."

BG's laugh was abrupt and harsh. "Why don't you just give us the package Annie gave you for us and quit lying."

Lynn sighed. "I found your fax in a pocket of Ann's jacket...after we found her. I thought you should know—"

BG leaned closer. "You show that fax to anybody? For instance the cops?"

"Why should I do that?"

Michelle rescued a banana and sat across from Lynn to eat it. "Telling us Annie sent you; what was that all about?"

Lynn was sorry she had indulged in that bit of deception. The truth would probably have worked as well. "Sorry, I wanted to be sure you were the right people...before I told you. I had no way of knowing if you were the ones that sent the fax. It did sound urgent, and I thought you should know."

Michelle didn't look convinced but BG started the bus and pulled into the traffic lane. "Where's this hotel? I could eat a horse."

Lynn left them in the dining room and went to see if Sarah was back. The man at the desk told her Sarah had checked in. What had happened? They had planned to go right back to the dig. She found Sarah lying on a bed turned toward the wall. She didn't move when Lynn came in the room.

Lynn sat quietly on the other bed and Sarah said in a whisper, "I'm awake." Sarah's voice was a hoarse whisper. "I can't believe this is happening to me. It has to be some sort of horrible mistake." She turned over, her eyes red and swollen. "The police suggested that...I might be responsible for her death."

Lynn was shocked and outraged. "That's ridiculous. Anyway you were with me all day. We weren't even in camp."

"They think somebody set it up earlier. Put the snake in her pack, put venom in her drug supply—or supplied her with the tainted drugs."

"But why you? Everybody else at camp had access to Ann's stuff—to her tent."

"They haven't actually charged me. They are focusing on me, I suppose because I'm the one in charge of the dig. Drugs are always an ongoing problem in Belize. Because we are in such a remote area the DEA and the police have suspected for awhile that there was somebody at our camp involved in drug dealing. I do have a little morphine for emergencies as part of my medical supplies. They know I went to talk to a biologist in Belize City about tree snakes last month. You know, I try to keep up with the hazards down here. After all I am responsible for my crew. It's my job."

"But why would you kill one of your workers even if she was a drug dealer? It's absurd. You hardly knew her. And, to be crass, you need all the workers you can get."

Sarah sat up and began pulling tufts of cotton off the worn chenille bedspread. After a while she said, her voice still a hoarse whisper, "They found out Ann was my brother Bobby's girlfriend for a while. Several months ago, after they broke up, she called me at the University and asked about Belize—said she was taking a long vacation to get her head together. I encouraged her, if only as a favor to Bobby. So I wasn't too surprised when she showed up here from someplace south, Honduras I guess. I knew she had been in trouble, that she had a drug problem. Bobby told me. I don't think he was every really into drugs, you know, but he does seem to have an odd set of friends sometimes. I thought if I helped her she would stay away from him."

Oh, yes baby brother Bobby. Sarah's father had remarried a woman with a young son. Lynn had met him when she and Sarah were in college. Smart enough but a spoiled and difficult teenager. He had hated being called Bobby.

"But you never mentioned any of that to anyone, even me." Lynn was a bit shaken. Suddenly true-blue Sarah had secrets she hadn't shared.

Sarah went on, a bit more defensive now, "I thought it wouldn't have helped her or anyone if I told people she was recovering from a drug habit. I've had enough trouble with suspicious officials; it certainly would be bad for us if they knew I was harboring an ex-drug addict. And I thought it wouldn't help Ann for people to know. But I should have done something when I saw she wasn't getting along with the crew. And I knew she was worried, anxious. If I had sent her away—"

"She did have Teddy to talk to. And whoever killed her would have managed to do it some place else. If she left the camp in the kayak to meet someone, perhaps to get or sell a supply of drugs, she had to have trusted that person or persons enough to risk being out in the bush alone with them."

"She was nervous before she came, anxious to get away from the States. I thought she was just a bit neurotic, and worried once she got here because, after all, I am Bobby's sister. She must have known how I felt about her involvement with him. Stupid. I should have wondered how she was able to travel for so long...alone."

"Did you know about her being Anna Marie LaPlace like the DEA guy said?"

Sarah shook her head. "And I'm sure Bobby didn't know that...if

48

it's true. She had a passport with the name Ann Wilson on it, and it had her photo. I saw it myself."

Lynn made a mental note to see if she could find out how the DEA had identified her as Anna LaPlace. "Still none of that's evidence against you."

"Inspector Thompson said nobody else had enough knowledge about tree snakes and their venom. I told them somebody took my snake book. Of course they haven't found drugs or drug money, not in my bank account or anywhere else, and Ann apparently didn't have one."

Lynn was horrified. "That's all circumstantial."

"That's why I haven't been arrested...yet. But it's likely they will stop me from working at the dig. Take away my permit."

"That's all so crazy. If you and she were into drug dealing why would you kill her anyway. You would just share the profits. No motive."

Sarah stared at her, clearly shocked that Lynn would even entertain the idea of her guilt.

"I mean Inspector Thompson is an intelligent woman even if Grant might not be," Lynn added.

"There's more. Ann was some sort of police informer back in the States. She was hiding out here from the guys she testified against. Members of a drug ring. The police apparently believe a lot of the drug money was never located. The dealers that were convicted are still in jail. The DEA thinks Ann knew where the money was."

"No wonder she was so edgy all the time. So you are supposed to have killed Ann for the mythical millions she had? If Ann had all that money why wear rags and dig up old bones out in a swamp?"

Sarah laughed, the absurdity of it even too much for her. "The police suggested that even if I wasn't after the millions...I'm supposed to be some sort of assassin for the drug dealers or something."

It made sense—not Sarah, of course, but as a motive for somebody. "Ann was scared that last day. If she wasn't going to meet someone, seems to me that could very well be why she took off in the kayak—to hide. How much money is involved?"

"They think a couple million, more or less."

"And they gave you, a murder suspect, all this information?"

Sarah sighed. "No, my local friend Abigail found out. She was outraged at the idea that I was a suspect. She knows people in the government and asked some questions. She says they aren't taking me as a suspect too seriously. I'm not so sure. Grant is probably behind it."

Lynn looked at Sarah for a long moment. How well did she know this woman? Could she kill for her great passion—archaeology? A million dollars would buy a lot of trowels. Sarah who couldn't bear to crush an ant? No. Sarah couldn't hurt anyone even for her work.

Lynn moved over next to Sarah and took her hand. "What can I do?"

Sarah sighed. "I'd hoped not to get you involved. Of course anybody could have gotten that snake from one of the local people. They kill them when they can. The snakes are a hazard to anyone who is working in the jungle—farmer, cattle rancher, logger. The police haven't found anyone who admits to selling a live snake. I doubt if they did much of an investigation. If somebody could go and ask questions... I know there are people who make a living selling live animals. I think Jacob has done some of that in the past. It's illegal so no one would admit it to the police. I suggested that more thorough investigation could be done, but I doubt they would follow up."

"I'll ask some questions. But you shouldn't worry. I'm sure this will blow over."

"But why the snake? A drug overdose—"

"Would alert the authorities to the drug dealer's presence in the area. An accidental death by snake bite would not. It was just the doctor's vigilance that revealed the presence of drugs in her blood. She was smart enough to realize that Ann wasn't responding fast enough to the antivenin. And I'm sure the killer didn't expect us to find her in time to get her to a hospital. Without that it could well have been declared an accidental death with no need for an autopsy. Do you know by any chance what hospital they took her to in the States. They don't seem to know at the hospital here. Gayle could check on what happened there. She says there are no reports of her death on the wire."

Sarah shook her head. "I didn't ask." She got up and washed her face and from the depths of a towel said, "You're probably right, I shouldn't worry, but in any case I have to stay in town a few days till something gets resolved."

Lynn told her about the three Canadians. "They said Ann was going to give them money to finance their trip north. Maybe Ann's trip out in the kayak was to raise the money she promised them. Maybe she was going to sell somebody drugs—Maybe they killed her instead of paying up."

Sarah shook her head. "I don't believe Ann was a drug dealer. And I even think she was honest enough to have told me if she was planning to leave so soon. Anyway she was determined not to go back to the States. I know that much. You're as bad as that cloak and dagger DEA guy. Go tell him about your Canadians. I think you're letting your imagination run away with you. You and the police."

"I think being Canadians, they are out his jurisdiction."

"Not if they plan to bring drugs through the US."

"Somebody was responsible for Ann's death. I think they know something about why somebody might want to kill her." Lynn sighed. "I'll go back to the dig try to help keep things going and ask some questions."

"You don't need to do that. I sent Hank back in the boat to help Kathy and he can do some asking around about the snake. I want to keep things going, get as much information as we can until they officially shut us down. I have to go up to the capital, Belmopan, this afternoon." Sarah smiled bravely. "I'll be OK. I have friends here. You probably should go someplace fun in the few days you have left. Go to the beach. Or...you haven't been to Tikal..."

"Don't be stupid. I'm not leaving you here to face this alone. Do you have a lawyer yet? "

Sarah tried to smile. "Abigail is a lawyer and her family is important here. I just don't know what to do. If we could only figure out who might have done it."

"Those three downstairs know more than they're saying. They expected money from Ann. They said she was going to pay them to take her with them. First thing is I'm going down and see what else I can get out of them. Maybe I'll pay them to take me back to the dig in their bus and get the rest of my things. I'll ask a few more questions down there too. Do you mind if I do an article on the situation? I promise to wait till you and your dig are off the hook to publish it. You know, a sympathetic look at the plight of archeology in Belize, along with Ann's story. Might even bring in some donations to help you finish your research."

Tears came to Sarah's eyes again. "God knows we could use a little help. Everybody loves to know about the past, but not enough to fund legitimate archeological research. Thanks Lynn. You've been a real friend though all of this. I don't know what I would have done without you. Just be careful."

Lynn went back to the hotel desk. There was a fax from Gayle at the *Chronicle*. Some information about a trial—an article from a Miami paper with a indecipherable picture of a woman with her face covered by her handbag in front of a court house trying to escape the press. There had been a conviction of three drug dealers based partly on the testimony of an Anna LaPlace. Not much useful information. The authorities had been disappointed that the resources of the three felons did not reflect the size of their operation. A suggestion of hidden money. At the bottom of the fax Gayle had scrawled a note asking Lynn to write an article on Ann's death. If Gayle wanted a real article, she would have to wait until Lynn found out a lot more.

Her friend Del, being a police detective, might get some answers for her. Lynn made a call from the hotel office to Del.

Del was always glad to hear from her. "You okay, Hon? We got your postcard. It's still snowing up here. We miss you, the kids especially." Lynn spent a lot of time with Del and her two kids. If it weren't that Del was straight…

Lynn told Del about working at the dig. "It's been more fun than you can imagine, although I've been covered with dirt more than I have sand." She went on to describe some of the archaeological work she had been doing. Then she asked, "Can you get me some information about a drug trial. A woman name of Anna Marie LaPlace was involved. She didn't go to jail; she was a state's witness. I need any info you can give me." She told Del what was in the article that Gayle had sent.

"What's going on down there? You sticking your nose where it doesn't belong again, Sugar? I thought you were on vacation?"

Lynn sighed. "I know you won't believe it, but I did come down here for a vacation. A young woman, the police and the US DEA guy say her name was Anna LaPlace although we knew her as Ann Wilson, one of the crew working for Sarah—died—of snake bite and drug overdose. The police think she might have been murdered—and

52

that somehow Sarah is involved. She was taken out of here by the US military. Apparently her brother is an officer. I haven't been able to find out what hospital she was taken to in the States where she died."

"I'll do what I can, Hon—for Sarah. But you try to stay out of it, at least this once."

"I am worried about her. Sarah feels so responsible for the people who work for her. She is worried about losing her permit."

"Uh, huh, and of course you the white knight are going to rescue the fair princess Sarah."

"You're jealous Del!"

Del laughed her wonderful infectious laugh. "Only of all that hot sun and sand and blue, blue water. Then she sighed. "I got to muck through this city's gray ice and snow and—"

"Feeling sorry for ourselves are we?"

"Girl, you are too cruel. Go ahead get in trouble so I have an excuse to come down there and pull you out of it like I did last time you were stupid enough to—"

It was Lynn's turn to laugh. Del had gone to Nepal to help her trap some international antiquities smugglers. "Don't worry, I learned my lesson—I'll leave the arrests to the police. I'm only gathering information for an article and to help Sarah clear her name."

# Chapter 7

After she said good-bye to Del, she went back to the lunch room. The three were still sitting at the table. Lynn could tell even from across the room that the BG and Michelle were arguing, probably in French, but she could hear nothing over the noise of other diners anyway. Ivette sat staring teary-eyed at her unfinished food. The other two shut up when they saw Lynn. She sat down at the table and started munching on left-over rolls. "Are you going to Guatemala on your way north?" Lynn asked. "Sarah says I should see Tikal."

"We can take you. We're going through Flores. That's nearby the ruins," Ivette said, eagerly. "I haven't seen Tikal either. Annie said…" She looked down, the tears welling up again.

"Would you like to drive me down the coast to the archaeological dig first? I need to pick up some stuff. You could see more of the country and—"

"It's all swamp down there. We came through there on the way here from Honduras," BG protested.

"How much?" Michelle asked abruptly.

Lynn calculated her vacation resources. She hadn't spent much since Sarah had been housing and feeding her. She wanted to keep an eye on these three. At the same time she wanted to get back to the dig and ask a few more questions. "It's not very far. They say it takes a bit over an hour by car if it's not raining. Fifty dollars US plus gas money."

The three looked at each other silently for a moment. Ivette said to BG, "I want to go. I've never ever seen an archeological dig."

BG swallowed the last of his beer. "Stupid idea. Nothin' down there, but rain and bugs."

Ivette had begun tearing apart a paper napkin rather methodically into tiny squares, but she persisted with, "It's my bus. You said you don't need to be in Guatemala 'til—"

BG lifted a fist.

Ivette stared at him defiantly.

Michelle turned to Lynn calmly and stared at her for a moment. "One-hundred US...plus gas and food."

BG frowned. "If the bus breaks down on those damned dirt roads...I gotta buy spare parts, just in case before we go."

Lynn stared back at Michelle. "One hundred US... and gas and food, if you take me with you to Guatemala."

Michelle took a sip of her cold tea stoically.

Lynn turned to BG. "Jacob can fix anything. He even has welding equipment. And you can all eat with crew down there. Emma is an excellent cook."

Michelle nodded a curt assent and BG said to her, a bit whiny now. "How long we got to hang around down there?"

Lynn said, "I just need to collect some of my stuff and report back to Dr. Donovan about how things are going there. Should only take a day or two."

Michelle was already standing.

Once they were outside the building Lynn said, "Before we go maybe you should take a minute and tell the police what you know about Ann. Inspector Thompson—"

"No way, José," BG said, laughing mirthlessly and shaking his head. "You think we're crazy. We'd never get out of this dump. They'd be questioning us for days."

Michelle said too quickly, "We really don't know anything that would help. Annie was a tourist that we exploited for a while—for travel money. She didn't talk to us about herself. The trip North was strictly a cash proposition."

BG interrupted impatiently. "That's what she said, anyway."

Lynn debated whether she should try to find a way to check in with Inspector Thompson. She should have called while she had a chance. She decided it was just as well not to. BG was right for once. She had been told not to leave town herself. She would make time once they were back in Belize City to call Phyllis Thompson before they left for Guatemala and maybe by that time she would have more to report.

The road that would take them to Jacob and Emma's ranch was

a largely unpaved track that skirted coastal swamps and was longer and muddier than Lynn had imagined, especially the last little bit of narrow muddy track through a banana plantation and Jacob's cow field. Getting there in Sarah's outboard was slow too, but much more pleasant in spite of the salt spray and smelly motor.

Ivette had insisted that they not leave the bus at the small village nearby and take a boat to the ranch the way that Sarah always did when she went into town by the road. "I'm not taking any chances she'll get stripped again like in Honduras. Too hard to get parts here."

Michelle was cursing in French by the time they came to a halt next to Emma and Jacob's small wooden ranch house. Clearly Ivette was disappointed. She must have imagined something grander in the way of ranch and archaeological site. Something more like Tikal or Chichen Itza. When she saw the excavation her only comment was, "It's just a big muddy hole."

Lynn tried to explain. "It was originally a mound. It's being investigated one layer at a time. People lived here for a thousand years more or less. There is evidence that this was a stop on the trade that still existed when the Spanish came—big dugout canoes went from Mexico to Columbia along the coast inside the barrier reef. Dr. Donovan is more interested in how people lived rather than the ruling elite with their monuments—"

Michelle had already headed for the pristine beach through the palm grove beyond the tents and excavation, stripping off her cloths along the way. Fortunately Emma and Jacob were not in sight. They had somewhat more conservative views of proper bathing dress.

No one was actually digging. Kathy was sitting on Sarah's porch painting labels on pottery pieces. Kathy told her that Teddy was out fishing for supper with Jacob.

Lynn found Emma with one of the Mayan women in her tomato patch behind the house, clearing away the weeds. Lynn watched them work for a moment. The older, stouter black women was stooping from the waist and uprooting weeds with a leisurely motion of her hoe. The small, quicker Mayan woman shaking off the dirt and piling the uprooted weeds in a neat pile. Each worker paced herself to make a graceful rhythmic dance.

Emma leaned on her hoe while Lynn explained about the extra guests. "There are just three and we stopped at a grocery before we left town and brought some extra supplies." Emma agreed to cook for them too for a small extra fee though she clearly disapproved of guests who did not work. The bus and its occupants were of a class of tourists that she did not approve, and now she made it clear that she thought Lynn was one of them. Then she expressed her opinion on the weeds and the work lost its leisurely grace.

Lynn could understand her distrust. She was a loyal friend to Sarah as was Jacob and was very worried about Sarah's situation. Belize was a small county and there was bound to be talk among the local folk. Foreigners rarely got killed in this peaceful safe country.

Lynn retreated to carry the groceries into the kitchen from the bus leaving Michelle and BG to contemplate new noises that had developed in the engine.

Then she found Hank in the artifact tent meticulously painting numbers on to a collection of potsherds and flint chips. It was a never ending, tedious task that they were always behind on. Before she could speak he said, "Where'd you find that riff-raff."

Lynn explained that they were taking her to Tikal and she had come back for her things.

She didn't tell him that they knew Ann and had planned to meet her. "I might decide to fly home from Guatemala. Anyway there's no reason for me to come back here even if I come back to Belize City before I go home."

"You could have radioed; I probably have to go back into town with the boat tomorrow anyway. Sarah—"

"Has to stay in town for a few days. They seem to be holding her responsible for Ann's death."

Hank was clearly upset. He lay down his brush. "That's absolutely ridiculous."

"We know that, but the authorities seem to need somebody to blame. Did you know that they have suspected someone here at the dig of being involved in drug running for some time?"

Hank said angrily. "If anybody bothered to check they could find plenty of illegal substances almost anywhere on this coast at one time or another. But that doesn't make Sarah a drug dealer or a murderer."

Lynn looked at Hank. His outrage seemed genuine. But how did he know so much about illegal substances? "So you think somebody could be using the dig to make drug connections?"

Hank looked out to sea. "It's true that a lot of people go through here one way or another. Tourists, researchers, workers. Lots of curious folk. Some of them could be dealing or trading. No way to tell."

"How do you happen to know about all the illegal substances? From people in the village here?"

He laughed. "I read it in the papers." He shook his head. "It's common knowledge, especially among the Americans who live here. You'd hear the same if you spent much time here. I've had a few beers with the locals; I like the people in this country. I certainly haven't seen anybody with that kind of cash. Like everywhere, teenagers get into trouble mostly when they go to Belize City. People here are poor and hard working when there is work." He put the tray away. "I'm worried about Sarah. You should have stayed in town with her."

"She sent me off. Said she doesn't need me. Her friend Abigail is a lawyer and has some influence."

"I hope you and your motley crew are leaving soon."

Lynn nodded. "How come nobody ever mentioned Sarah's brother Bobby?"

Hank dipped his brush. "You'd have seen him if you stayed around long enough. He comes down here all the time. But he doesn't let anybody but Sarah call him that. Rob is what he goes by. He helps her with the management side of this operation—when he's around. Pretty good at fund-raising and schmoozing with the tourists. Useless as a worker in the trenches though. Wouldn't want to get dirt under his fingernails or on his designer silk shirt."

"What does he do for work?"

Hank shrugged. "Takes people on tour sometimes. Fishing, looking at orchids in the rain forest. Other places besides Belize as well. I guess Daddy supports him some of the time."

"A candidate for drug dealer?"

"Don't let Sarah hear you say that!"

Lynn decided not to mention that Ann had been Bobby's girl friend. Sarah had told her in confidence—Sarah would have to decide if she wanted Hank to know.

After Jacob and Teddy came back with a couple of three-foot barracuda, Jacob stayed on the beach to clean them and Lynn went down to talk to him.

She sat on the sand while Jacob deftly filleted the long narrow fish with wicked looking teeth. Jacob smiled at her pleased with his catch. "Very tasty fish. Emma will cook it up nice in coconut oil."

"I wouldn't want to meet one of those out swimming." Lynn said, shuddering.

He smiled and shook his head. "Wouldn't bother you. Minds his own business eating small fishes. Just don't wear a lot of shiny stuff he might mistake for ballyoo."

"Jacob, you have any ideas about what happened to Ann?" He shook his head. "They say she was involved in drugs. Do you think she might have gotten them around here?"

He looked away. "I told the police lady. I know nothing."

"I know, but it's getting serious for Sarah. We need to help. The situation is causing her a lot of trouble. They are blaming her. They might even close down the dig—take away her permit."

He rinsed the fillets in salt water and put them on newspaper. Then he wiped his knife carefully. Lynn admired the strength in his broad brown and callused hands. She had gone out once in his home-made sail boat with him, seen him pull in a four-foot barracuda with those strong hands, clubbing it with one accurate blow before it could sink those dagger teeth into his fingers

Those hands had built the small sailboat he used for fishing as well as the small wooden ranch house he shared with his wife and several children, now grown. But he and his wife were growing too old for the hard work of farming. He needed the money that Sarah paid them. He didn't want to move into town to live with his children. He liked the entertainment and the company of the crew. And Lynn knew he especially liked Sarah.

He handed her the fish. "*Some* people got too much money lately…swaggering drunk…noisy like a parrot. Take these to Emma and come back. I will show you."

When she got back, he was getting the boat ready to go out again. He gestured for her to get in, then he pushed off the sand and got in himself.

It was a small sailboat, the elegant simple homemade traditional design of his family. No expensive brass hardware; everything was wood and rope, hand carved and stitched, and it sailed like a dream. No evil gasoline smell, no thudding motor. It just slipped silently on white wings past the mangrove and warm sand beaches. Lynn loved to sail. Boats had been the salvation of her childhood. She had lived near a salt pond and had her own small boat. When things got too tense at home and when the weather was decent she could console herself battling wind and waves instead of the storms and silences at home. It was why she went into the Navy after high school. She had learned about boats, but of course it wasn't the same.

They finally sailed into a little cove on one of the nearby islands inside the reef.

And there was Ed Kelly's catamaran As they got closer Lynn could see Marv stretched out in the lounge chair on deck, his eyes closed, his feet propped up on the rail. There was no sign of his boat anywhere nearby. And he was hardly recognizable with neatly clipped hair, clean shaven and newly outfitted in crisp white.

"I want to go aboard—to talk to him for a minute," Lynn said quietly.

Jacob shook his head but pulled up to the catamaran's ladder. Jacob turned his boat to drop anchor, while Lynn climbed aboard.

No one but Marv seemed to be about. She could see into the luxurious main lounge with its leather and teak furnishings and into the main cabin with neatly made beds. The boat was so neat it could have been sitting on a sales lot unlived in.

Marv did not budge as Lynn went over to him quietly. He was fast asleep, or passed out. His legs supported by a low table, his feet displaying a pair of soft leather designer shoes held on with elastic across the top—a French label. She studied the pattern of the tread, and drew in a breath. As far as she could remember, it matched that in the sand near Ann's tent. She gently pulled off the shoes.

Marv sat up drunkenly. "What the hell."

"Where'd you get these shoes?"

Marv looked around frantically to see how she had gotten there. When he saw Jacob's boat with no one but Jacob on it, he relaxed visibly. "Ed gave them to me. They were tight on him. He was going to throw them away."

"When?"

Marv shrugged and yawned. "What you want? Ed and his wife ain't here."

"You working for him now?"

"What's it to you?"

"What did you find in Ann's stuff? Money? How much did you get? Looks like you've been doing a bit of spending. I hear you've been making quite a scene in town. You'd have been smarter to lay low for a while."

"I had nothing to do with that woman. I was with you and Dr. Donovan all day."

"But you went back later, after Ann was taken to the hospital."

He shook his head.

Lynn waved the shoes at him. "Did Ed send you back to snoop around Ann's camp after we got her out, or did you do that on your own?"

Marv grabbed at the shoes. "Lots of people got shoes like that."

"Not around here. There's probably not another pair like that in the whole country of Belize."

Marv stared at her sullenly looking for a chance to grab back his shoes.

"Did Ed pay you to get Sarah out of the way the day Ann went off in the kayak?"

He turned red. "Where'd you hear that? Jacob tell you that? He doesn't know shit."

"Who paid you?"

"I don't have to talk to you. You better leave now."

Lynn stuffed the shoes in her pack.

"Give me my fucking shoes, bitch," Marv hissed, trying to grab her arm. She shoved his hand away. He was too drunk to keep his footing and went down with a thud on the deck.

"I took those shoes out of the trash yesterday." Marv said from the deck, rubbing his shoulder. "I ain't taking no rap for Ed. He paid me to get Dr. Donovan out of camp. Said he wanted to take a look around the dig without her hanging over him. He was convinced she was hiding some sort of treasure horde. At least that's what he said. He's got his eye on that property."

"I'm sure he has his eye on a lot of property. You're the one who's getting him Mayan antiquities to sell in the States? Is that how he got so rich?"

Marv got up defensive now. "He's legit, a real businessman. Real clever too. Gonna build hotels that look like Mayan temples. He knows his stuff. Knows all about them Mayan gods."

Marv sat wearily back down in the chair. "He hired me to run this boat. His other crew ditched him. Didn't like his old-south colonial attitudes, I hear. Pays me good enough, but I don't do nothin' but run the motor. I ain't no sailor. Just give me back my shoes. I don't need trouble with the cops."

"What about the fancy duds and the hair cut and shave?"

"The Mrs.—she made me wear them. Said she wouldn't have me hanging around smelling like a locker room. Made me wear Ed's old stuff. See, it's way too big." He pulled out his shirt and showed her how big it was, the pants gathered at the waist.

"Where are Ed and the Mrs. now?"

"They're in town till late. Some sort of yacht party."

"I'll just look around a bit then. While I'm here."

Marv stood up again slowly. "Can't let you do that. I'm suppose to be guarding this tub. They'll have a shit-fit if—"

"Don't worry, I won't touch anything. They don't need to know I was here."

He thought about that. "You better not touch anything. I got my eye on you."

Lynn nodded. "I've never been on one of these—catamaran isn't it? Must be awkward to maneuver in a harbor."

He didn't answer. His attention was back on his cooler of beer.

The master bedroom was locked, but everything else was open. Kitchenette neat as a pin. The two crew cabins were cleaned up, one with a few possessions. Marv was living on the boat. She wondered what he had done with his own boat.

The guest bedroom, bigger than the crew bunks with its own bath was simply furnished but neat and not occupied.

She peered through the porthole into the locked master bedroom. It was also neat but fully occupied. Cosmetics on one dresser top. On almost every other surface there were Mayan artifacts or facsimile, ornate bowls and figurines, even a knife with a volcanic glass blade and a bone handle. That was right beneath the window. Next to it was what must be a replica of the skull Ed had mentioned, a clear glass or quartz, carved and polished. Sarah had told her the originals were a hoax, probably manufactured in Germany. The sun refracting through it cast a rainbow shadow on the opposite white wall.

Strange all this breakable stuff on a sailboat. They must have to put it all away every time they went into open water. Or maybe it was glued down to the shelves. In the main cabin, she picked up a bowl. It was beautiful with three delicately molded legs. Some of the potsherds she had been digging up must have once been part of a bowl like this.

Once Marv had a fresh beer in hand he had followed her, mumbling. "You put that thing down and get out of here."

"You must have to wrap these all up and put them away before you head out to sea?"

Marv didn't answer so she turned to repeat her question.

"Give me back my shoes and I might tell you something."

"Where does he get that stuff? Is it real? Is he some sort of antiques smuggler? Is that how he makes his money?"

"Ed's a legit businessman. He's a collector is all. It's his art collection. He likes to have it with him."

"To show off to his potential customers?"

He shoved her against the wall and tried to grab her bag with the shoes. Lynn pushed him over and got away barely hanging on to the bag. Marv was going for the boat hook. No time to climb down the ladder and wait for Jacob to get close enough for her to jump onto his boat. She jumped overboard.

Jacob was chuckling when he pulled her into his boat. "I told you not to go on board."

Lynn smiled not minding the cool water dripping from her clothes. It felt good. She was pleased with herself. The contents of her bag had stayed dry because the bag floated on the surface when she jumped. The only problem was how to get the shoes to Phyllis Thompson. Maybe she could get more out of Mr. DEA if she shared this information. She just had to get them back to Belize City to the police.

Jacob turned the boat and aimed it directly at the catamaran. She observed the look on Marv's face when it looked like Jacob might mar the lily white side of the catamaran. Marv gave her the finger as, smiling to himself, Jacob pulled away at the last possible moment showing his exquisite control of the sails. He certainly didn't like Marv.

Marv shouted at them as they sailed away, "Ed has friends in this country. You'll see."

When they got back, Ivette and Michelle were swimming nude on the beach splashing and screaming in and out of the water just beyond the camp. Lynn sat admiring their even golden tans, Michelle's just a shade darker. Her body was lean and muscular, her breasts small and firm, beautiful but not Lynn's type. Ivette, on the other hand, had that narrow waisted slimness that exaggerated her feminine curves. Lynn felt the speed of the boat pick up and noted that Jacob, deliberately ignored the two women on the beach with a long-suffering look on his face.

"Sorry Jacob. They're leaving soon. They don't mean to offend."

He didn't say anything, just beached the boat and began to put it away for the night. Lynn helped as much as she could, then went to find Kathy and Hank. She showed them the shoes and asked if they could help her get them to Phyllis.

"Let's make a photo of the sole," Kathy suggested. "Then you can send the shoes on the next boat into Belize City from the village and you still have a copy—just in case.

"Yeah," said Hank, "I've got errands in the village in the morning. I can take the shoes in before the next supply boat is due—they'll deliver it to the police for you. Kathy's right. If you have a snap-shot then when the boat goes down at least you'll still have a copy."

After they took some pictures, Lynn wrote a letter, wrapped it up with the shoes and gave them to Hank. By then Emma had the fish cooked and they all assembled around the big wooden homemade table on the verandah of the ranch house. Ivette oohed and awed over Emma's cooking. BG and Michelle ate in silence. Teddy had taken some of the fish to the two Mayan families. Kathy explained that since Ann's death Teddy had decided that she wanted to become an ethnographer rather than an archeologist. "She says she wants to work with live people rather than the bones of their dead ancestors."

"I can understand that," Lynn said.

"I think she is just trading in her skateboarder image for a hippie granola one. Next week she'll be Star-Trek or punk or something," Hank said.

Kathy make a face at him. "Not only are you fashion-dated, but you're wrong about Teddy. Under that fake cynical teen-ager facade she is a sincere person, just young. She still is capable of ideals."

"Preserve me from the young and ardent." Hank shook his head and bit into another tender morsel of fish.

All evening Teddy and Michelle argued heatedly about whether representatives of 'Western Culture'—meaning Teddy—should try to help native peoples like the Maya —meaning Michelle and her Inuit mother—maintain their cultural integrity.

All afternoon and even during dinner Ivette had flirted with Lynn, even while she asked questions about Mayan archaeology. Hank and Kathy had tried to answer her questions while Ivette's wide green eyes and brushing touches devoured Lynn.

Lynn who still believed herself in love with Marta, a woman who had left her for the rigors of life in Nepal, was shocked at how much she was attracted to Ivette.

After dinner Ivette curled up in her sleeping bag on Sarah's bed and told Lynn about her childhood on a small farm near Montreal. "I was in love with the movies. I papered my walls with the stars until I fell in love with Mrs Johnson, my swimming teacher—then it was swimmers—Diana Nyad..." Ivette smiled with nostalgia. "I even got into Ester Williams movies. For a long time my friends...and lovers were swimmers. That's when I met Michelle—years ago at a swim meet. She was a competitive swimmer from another school. Fortunately for everyone I gave up that obsession when I left school. I was never really fast and I haven't kept in shape. She has stayed fit even though she doesn't compete anymore."

Then Lynn told her a little about herself. How much she liked her job. How her obsession with it had ruined her relationship with Shirley, a long-time lover. Then they spent an hour discussing the absurdity of Lynn's loyalty to the woman in Nepal, Marta... and the virtues and defects of monogamy in general. Ivette finally said with sleepy annoyance in her voice. "I'm not HIV positive and not nearly as promiscuous as you might think."

Lynn felt herself flushing. She admired people who could be so straight forward, not so easy for her. "That's not it, Ivette. I am very attracted to you. It's just—"

Ivette turned over in her sleeping bag, her back to Lynn and covered her head with the mosquito netting.

Lynn lay awake for a long time contemplating her own reluctant nature and feeling even more drawn to the woman sleeping quietly in the next bed—torn between wanting to sleep and the urge to crawl in next to her.

Ivette was gone when she woke the next morning.

# Chapter 8

In the morning after Hank left, Jacob reluctantly agreed to take the Canadians out to the reef to snorkel. BG said he needed to work on the bus. Ivette insisted that Lynn go snorkeling too. She told Lynn that she didn't trust Michelle to stay with her in the water. "She'll go off on her own. She's done it before. She's a stronger swimmer than I am. I nearly got swept out to sea in Honduras because she insisted on swimming to the outside through a channel in the reef."

Michelle looked at her disgusted. "*Merd. Ma pauvre petite,*" she said sarcastically. "A little current. You were in no danger." Her laugh teased. "Anyway, the current would have brought you back in when the tide changed."

"Yeah, drowned." Ivette threw a ragged towel at Michelle.

Lynn was not reluctant to go. Ivette intrigued her more and more.

Lynn warned Michelle and Ivette that Jacob would not go unless they were more modestly attired than the day before.

Ivette shook her head and said, "You think we're crazy. I'm wearing sun block and a long sleeved shirt."

"I want to be evenly tanned, not fried," Michelle contributed.

"And suits," Lynn insisted. "Jacob won't go if you don't."

They both nodded solemnly and Ivette said, "In deference to the traditional customs of the local natives..." and burst out laughing.

Jacob took them out to a little island right on the reef where he knew some fishermen. He sat in the shade under their wooden house visiting and drinking orange soda while the three women swam out to the coral. It was a calm morning, still early, and there was little current. Michelle, as predicted, took off on her own, swimming around the island. Ivette and Lynn floated at a leisurely pace watching the parrot fish chomp on the coral garden down below—a forest of purple and green fan coral, against the bright yellow of stinging coral. Plant-like sponges, and colorful soft coral waved in the gentle current like miniature trees while a bewildering variety of colorful fish ignored them. It was an alien world so quietly exotic and magical, Lynn always felt her kinship with her aquatic ancestors strongly. Maybe people weren't actually descended from fish, but some primordial grandmother of hers had swum or paddled or oozed through just such a sea.

And next to her Ivette was a seductive slim brown life form, her blue fins and a tattered red bathing suit only accentuating her sensuous, erotic shape. Lynn imagined what it would be like to make love, floating in this warm blue water, surrounded by soft velvety coral and sea sponges. She imagined their lips meeting, two kissing fish.

Too soon she heard Jacob's shout above the sound of the surf. She looked over to see Michelle on the beach, her swim complete, waving at them to come in. On the beach they snacked on the luke warm orange soda and crackers Emma had packed for them.

On the way back the three of them sat in the front of the boat huddled against the fresh morning breeze. Then Lynn almost liked Michelle, and more than liked Ivette who snuggle against her and shared her big beach towel.

After they got back Lynn dressed and went to help Kathy, Teddy and some of Mayans who were digging up the hardened clay floor to look for more floors from earlier construction. Several different-sized children played nearby staying remarkably well out of the way.

Teddy explained to Lynn, "They can use the money. I know Sarah can't afford it but, it's important to finish up this project before—"

"I know Sarah is worried, but do you really think the authorities would close down the dig?" Lynn asked.

Teddy was furious. "After you left for Belize City, that asshole Ed came by in his fat boat and said, smug as a bug, that Sarah was under suspicion and the authorities—he made it sound like they were his personal buddies—were going to shut her down. He implied he might get an archeological permit for the region. He thinks he can buy anything."

Kathy sighed and moved over for Lynn to help uncover a burial while she did some sketching. "You shouldn't let him get under your skin Teddy. He just heard some gossip in town and was trying to impress us." She said to Lynn, "Sarah radioed from town after you left. Sounds like her lawyer, Abigail, has things under control. She was the one who suggested that we go ahead and hire help so I can be freed up for some of the recording and analysis we need to get done. Of course Hank had to rush off to her rescue. He is useless when she isn't here."

Teddy put down her pick for a moment. "That asshole Ed tried to buy the ranch from Jacob. Fortunately he's too cheap to give him a fair offer, or Emma would have insisted on taking it. She's wants to live in town with her kids." She laid into the hardened clay floor with her pick as if it was all the real estate speculators in the world.

After a while Ivette came over looking sleepy but pleased to be there without Michelle and BG. Lynn took Ivette on a tour of the site, and then Ivette settled down with Teddy and the Mayans, content to scrap away at an old fireplace collecting bits of charcoal that would be used for carbon dating.

In the afternoon Teddy disappeared with the Mayan families and Lynn and Ivette washed themselves and went for a swim. Lynn was liking Ivette more and more. She had turned out to be a good worker, curious and enthusiastic, asking intelligent questions that Teddy or Kathy who had a fair grounding in Mayan archeology, tried to answer. And she had not given up on her flirtation with Lynn.

BG showed up asking where Michelle was. Nobody knew. After he went off down the beach looking for her, Ivette said quietly to Lynn, "I'm beginning to be sorry I hooked up with him. Michelle is OK by herself."

"Why did you?" Lynn asked bluntly.

Ivette shrugged. "He's rather good at fixing the bus. I feel safer with a man around. I don't get hassled by the local macho types as much."

"It looks like he is pretty good at that himself. Besides Michelle could handle the macho types well enough. I'm sure she would be happy to be your protector."

"You think we are lovers don't you?"

"You and BG, or you and Michelle?" Lynn asked dryly.

Ivette concentrated on her washing and did not even look up as she said, "You can be really stupid. Is that why you gave me that song and dance about your precious Marta and Nepal last night? You think I sleep with him?"

Lynn felt herself flushing again. "Your the one being deliberately stupid. I didn't say that. I—"

Ivette gave her a look so cold it stopped her words. She wanted to apologize—to make it all right again, but she was afraid of the intensity of what she felt and turned away.

She carried the day's finds, lots of potsherds and flint chips and a pottery bird whistle to Sarah's porch. Only Kathy and Lynn were there to wash the artifacts in buckets of rain water. Hank had not come back yet. He had told Kathy that after he checked in with Sarah he wanted to do some surveying down the coast on his own with the boat.

Kathy confessed to Lynn that she had found the snake book in her tent. "I'm sure it wasn't there before when the police were searching, and I know I didn't borrow it from Sarah. I'm phobic about snakes. I don't even want to read about them. I'm in complete denial about wiggly things. That's why I chose archaeology—nothing moves on its own."

Lynn was puzzled. Anyone from the camp borrowing it would know to put the book back on Sarah's shelf where it belonged. "Teddy said that Ed of the catamaran was snooping around. Do you think he could have put it there?"

Kathy snorted. "He's got the mentality for a trick like that and he doesn't like me. I had the temerity to ignore him both times he was here. And he knew of my feelings about live things because Hank found a scorpion in his shoe and was teasing me with it when Ed was hanging around the last time. Men!" Kathy turned to Lynn suddenly wide eyed. "Do you think he—? But Ann didn't even know him. Why would he...?"

Lynn frowned. "Ann seemed nervous when she saw him. Called him an SOB when I talked to her. Maybe she did know him. According to the DEA guy somebody doctored Ann's drug supply or injected her with poison. If the murderer knew she had drugs here, he would have to get into her tent to mess with them. Ed could have taken the snake book from Sarah's shelf when he was here the first time, but I don't see how he could have gotten into Ann's tent without being seen. He was never alone that day."

Lynn nodded. "It's just as likely somebody she went out to meet or who found her out there, her gave her contaminated drugs and dropped the snake in her pack. "It seems to me nobody here in the crew disliked her *that* much."

Kathy nervously adjusted her scarf. "It would have been easy to have done it here at camp. After all the tents aren't visible when we are all working down in the dig and nothing is locked up. Lots of people come in and out of here. There are times during the day when anybody could have walked into camp and nobody would notice. They could have gone into Ann's tent and dropped the snake in her pack. It certainly would have been easy enough to put the snake book in my tent to make me look bad. They could have just put it back on Sarah's shelf." Kathy frowned. "Why didn't I notice it there sooner?"

"Sarah's shelf is a more public place. They might have been seen. But maybe it was Hank who put it there—to tease you."

"I asked him how he thought it got there. He was as puzzled as I was. I don't think he would deliberately lie to me, especially about that, right now. He's too worried about Sarah. He has a stake in keeping this dig going too, not to mention his feelings about Sarah."

"How well do you know him? Could he have been jealous of Sarah's success and wanted to get her in trouble? He certainly didn't like Ann."

Kathy shook her head an emphatic no. "He adores Sarah. And he couldn't even kill the damned scorpion. Took it with him to let it go down the beach. If I hadn't had hysterics over it he probably would have kept it as a pet."

"He didn't by any chance have a pet tree snake?"

"Humph, that doesn't even deserve an answer."

Just as they were cleaning up the table and emptying the wash buckets, Teddy stormed up on to the porch. "Your asshole friend B. Gilbert Scully was snooping around my tent. I caught him going through my papers."

BG of course. Why hadn't she thought of that out herself. "How do you know BG is B. Gilbert " Lynn asked chagrined.

"When I found him in my tent I asked him what the hell business he had snooping around in my stuff. He said he was looking for something his girlfriend, Annie, had left for him. Asked if he meant Ann and he just grinned. So I asked the asshole point blank if he was Ann's old biker boyfriend, the one she was running away from. He looked confused at first—maybe he wondered how I knew, but then he smiled, a real nasty smile and said, 'How'd you guess, Hon? Annie been talking? What she tell you about me?'"

"Did he take anything?"

"No, but he accused me of sleeping with Ann. Waved my magazines and my Avenger shirt in my face. Goddamned greasy pig. Why'd you bring them here anyway?"

"To keep an eye on them. I think they know something about Ann that might help me figure out—"

"What? You a goddamned detective now? Ann's dead. All your digging around isn't going to bring her back. And now I have to think about her and that asshole." Tears were streaming down her face. Lynn tried to put an arm around her but she pulled away. "Just get them the hell out of here."

"No problem, *chére*. We're leaving today." It was Michelle leaning against the bottom of the stairs. Lynn had not seen her come up to the house. How long had she been there? What had she heard?

*"Votre charriage, se préparer, ma petite."* Michelle said to Lynn, with an exaggerated smile and a courtly bow.

Ivette came up just behind Michelle, a bit breathless. She was obviously annoyed "But you said we could stay here a couple of days," she said, plaintively.

Michelle shrugged. "We're leaving now. *Venez ou ne venez pas.*" Then, her tone more apologetic, she said, "If we leave now we can be back in Belize City for a late supper." She smiled at Teddy and handed her a book. "I believe this belongs to you. Sorry BG is such a shit."

Teddy grabbed it blushing and said to Lynn, defensively, "Ann gave it to me. It's the only thing of hers I have." Lynn could see it was a book of poems in French.

Michelle wiggled her fingers at Teddy to come with her. Lynn was surprised to see Teddy obey and they walked away down the path arm in arm. Michelle threw back at Lynn without turning her head, "One hour, then we're gone."

Ivette turned away toward the beach without another word and

Lynn went to gather up her things. It was likely she would not be back here. She had told the crew she was due to go home in a few days, back to her job at the paper so she would fly home from Guatemala. She was determined not to leave until Sarah was cleared, but no point in telling *them* that.

As she was taking a last look around she noticed one of Sarah's rain spattered site notebooks under a shelf. She picked it up. It was not like Sarah to leave it here. Hank and Kathy would need it to keep up the daily log. It was usually kept in the main tent. The last entry was the day before Ann's foray out in the kayak. She read some of the recent entries. She was puzzled; it was a daily log but not entirely about the archeological dig.

She read:

*November Eleven. Everybody up early. Kathy finished the drawing of burial number three. Some rain damage this morning—need to get it recorded and bagged. Enough charcoal finally for a carbon date for this level. Bobby arrived at eleven with the new survey equipment I requested. Awkward until Ann went off on survey in the boat with Hank. Ann must really want to avoid Bobby to be willing to accompany Hank.*

Bobby, Sarah's brother Bobby, the one who had been Ann's boyfriend in the States. Was it Bobby that Ann had been afraid of?

The police had found out that Ann had been Bobby's girlfriend and confronted Sarah with it. Maybe Sarah was afraid Bobby was involved in Ann's death. She read on:

*Bobby didn't stay. Sent the charcoal samples back with him to be sent home for analysis. Trying to avoid Ann too I guess. Is he ashamed of her? Is that why he told me not to tell the others he knows her?*

Suddenly she realized that this must be a personal diary. But how could she have known this wasn't just field notes? And there were no recent entries. Either Sarah had started a new one or stopped writing a personal diary altogether. Why? She put it carefully back, feeling like an intruder.

She checked in the main tent. The daily site diary was there with Hank and Kathy's entries up to date, so the other one *was* a private diary. She was tempted to read further but it really would be an invasion of privacy now. She had too much respect for Sarah to snoop, however tempted she was. Still, she would have to ask Sarah more about Ann's connection with her brother. It was clearly why Sarah had put up with Ann in spite of her difficulty getting along with the rest of the crew.

It was two hours later when Michelle and Teddy showed up at the bus. BG was furious but he didn't say anything, just sat in the driver's seat slowly pounding on the dented door.

Ivette sulked in the back of the bus while Lynn said her good-byes. Teddy pulled her aside just before she got in the bus. She whispered quickly, "The Mayans said a white woman was buying live snakes last week. They didn't know who she was. Not anyone they had seen before."

"Thanks Teddy. I'll see if I can get Phyllis Thompson to follow up on it."

Lynn climbed in back with Ivette, but couldn't talk to her without shouting over the noise of the radio. Finally Michelle turned it off, but Ivette still refused to talk to Lynn. Lynn didn't feel that she deserved quite this much punishment. She wanted not to care. Was she really falling for the woman or would these feelings disappear once she was on her way home to the States?

They stopped just before dark when the engine overheated. While BG took a walk the three of them sat on the edge of the road staring across marsh grass and ocean at an incredible orange and purple sunset.

"So Ann and BG were lovers back in BG's biker days?" Lynn asked. Both of the women looked at her blankly.

"None of us ever met Annie before Costa Rica." Ivette said. Then she turned to Michelle. "Did we?" Michelle did not deign to answer.

"BG, B. Gilbert Scully. He has a US passport too doesn't he? He was snooping in Ann's tent. What was he looking for? What was it she promised to bring you in Belize City?"

Ivette stared at her and laughed. "That's not his name. It's—" She looked at Michelle again.

Michelle stared complacently at the sunset. "If we know, why should we tell you?"

"Maybe I know something that you want to know? Ann talked a lot to me."

Michelle's eyes narrowed. "You're lying. Annie wasn't like that. She didn't talk about herself. And she certainly wouldn't talk to you."

"Why else would I know about her and B. Gilbert the biker. He sent the fax demanding that she meet you. I know Ann was scared of somebody. I know she came to Central America to hide from someone. Was it BG? Was she traveling with you before she came here or were you following her?"

Ivette said, "She was planning to meet us; that shows she wasn't scared of us. Why would she tell us she was going to be at your archaeological dig if—"

"BG told Ann to meet you, but that doesn't mean she was going to do it. The fax just proves you knew where she was."

Michelle laughed and shook her head. "You actually think we might have killed her. Assuming we got ourselves out there somehow, why in hell would we bother to do that?"

Lynn took a chance. If Ann was the mysterious Anna LaPlace as Grant claimed maybe BG or all of them knew about the drug case and the mysterious missing drug money. She asked, "Your Annie had a lot of money?"

Ivette was looking nervous. The pink light exaggerated the green of her wide open eyes. "What money is she talking about, Michelle?"

Michelle didn't answer. She stretched out on the sand and closed her eyes.

"There is a rumor that Ann knew where some convicted drug dealers hid a million or so," Lynn said.

Ivette stared at Michelle waiting for her to say something.

Michelle sat up. Her face still told nothing but her voice was sarcastic. "That's all very interesting. Now that I know about Annie's resources we'll have to think back. Maybe she did accidentally give us some information." She looked at Lynn but her face was in the shadow created by the setting sun. "*Merd*, now we know about all that money, we'll be sure to keep an eye on you to see if you know where it's hidden..." She laughed again. "...since Annie took you into her confidence." She got up and went off down the road presumably looking for BG.

"You're making that up about the money, right? ...To get a rise out of us," Ivette said.

"How do you think she was able to travel for so long and even give money for expenses?"

"She told me she had a small divorce settlement, on a house. She didn't even have any clothes. Just worn-out stuff from the Goodwill for crissakes."

"Best way to keep from being robbed...or found. Nobody pays attention to somebody so obviously poor."

"I don't believe it?"

"Where was she going to get the money you said she promised you three?"

BG and Michelle were coming back down the road with a bucket of water between them. Her back to them, Ivette whispered fiercely, as if she were angry but a little afraid, "Annie said she had a friend at the dig that owed her. She *was* going to meet us. She wasn't afraid of BG." Then she climbed into the van.

BG started up the van and they were back on their way over the soggy rutted road. Ivette curled up in the back again refusing to talk to Lynn.

# Chapter 9

Lynn woke up back in Belize City where Michelle was parking the bus next to Sarah's hotel. BG was gone and Ivette was still asleep. Michelle got out of the bus and stretched, then started doing push-ups in the parking lot. When Lynn got out Michelle said without a break in her routine, "We leave in the morning...early and we're going to put breakfast in the hotel on your tab."

Lynn stopped at the desk for messages. There was a fax from Del and two from the *Chronicle*—both from her office mate, Bill, who had done some of the research she had asked for. Bill had faxed several pages crammed with newspaper articles, but no pictures. None of the articles mentioned an Ann Wilson, although there was quite a bit about Anna Marie LaPlace. She carried it all upstairs to Sarah's room to study.

Sarah was out, but there was a note from her. It just said that in case Lynn got back Sarah was having dinner at her friend Abigail's house. There was a telephone number.

Del's fax was one page with a badly printed copy of a photo of someone that looked a lot like Ann. Anna Marie LaPlace had been a major witness for the prosecution in a drug case. She testified that she had heard one of the defendants talk about their drug operation. She had been a key witness in their conviction. No wonder Ann had been afraid. Apparently there were others involved in the ring who had not been caught. Maybe it was one of them who found Ann and killed her. The police were still looking for some missing money.

Lynn remembered how Ann avoided getting close to people and was always looking behind her—how edgy she was when Ed Kelly showed up in his catamaran. Could he be one of the convicted drug dealers referred to in the article, or somebody in the operation looking for the missing money?

She tried to call Phyllis Thompson, but couldn't reach her. They wouldn't give out her unlisted home phone. She had to talk to somebody before she left the next morning. With a bit of persuasion she got Phyllis's home address from the desk sergeant claiming she wanted to write to her. Then she left through the opposite side of the hotel from where the bus was parked.

After she found the house and knocked, an older woman came to the door and told Lynn that Inspector Thompson was just sitting down to a late supper, but please come inside. Everything about the house, inside and out, spoke of caring—couches and chairs with hand crocheted covers, family pictures on furniture made of local hardwood. Phyllis and her family—two teenage children, her mother, who had come to the door, and her husband—were in the dining room. Inspector Thompson introduced Lynn to her family while her mother set a place for her.

Lynn apologized for disturbing them and said she would wait until they were finished. But they insisted she sit down and share their meal of native fish, vegetables and fried plantain served on white china, set carefully on a hand-crocheted tablecloth. For a moment she felt envy of such family comfort like a beggar staring through the window at the warm lighted room of a special Christmas feast. But their genuine interest and friendliness soon made her feel welcome.

After eating she and Phyllis took their coffee into an office-parlor Phyllis shared with her husband, a lawyer. Lynn showed her the fax from Del and the articles that Bill had sent.

Phyllis looked them over carefully. "Thank you for showing me these. I believe we have much of this information from your government. It's very interesting, but of course it does not prove who might have intended to kill her. Can you leave these with me?"

"Yes, I'm going to Tikal with the three people who faxed Ann to meet them before she died. They claim Ann planned to travel with them through Guatemala and Mexico...and that she traveled with them before in Central America. I gave you the fax they sent. They may not be implicated in her death but I think they know something about her that might help."

Lynn stirred her coffee. "Surely you don't believe that Sarah is really responsible in any way for Ann's death."

Phyllis sighed. "I am sorry about that. I personally don't think so, but there are others here in authority...they see all foreigners as the enemy. They want to blame our drug problem on them. Of course there is some justice in that point of view, but Dr. Donovan..." She shook her head. "You should not worry overly much. We are still working on the case. I'm sure her name will be cleared."

Lynn told her more about the bus crew. "I think BG is a B. Gilbert Scully, Ann's ex. That's what Teddy thinks. Ann told her about him. She confronted him with it when she found him snooping around her tent and he didn't deny it. Ann told her a B. Gilbert Scully was looking for her. The Canadian's claim Ann was traveling with them, but they may have been following her. Michelle and Ivette refused to confirm that Ann and BG have a history, but they didn't deny it either."

"Theodora—a reluctant child. Very protective of Ann and the Mayans. I thought she might know more than she was willing to tell us."

"Anyway, it's possible Scully has been following Ann. Teddy said she was afraid of him, afraid he'd show up. But even if BG is Scully, I don't quite see how he could have been at the scene of the murder. Although Michelle and Ivette probably wouldn't tell me if he had been away from the bus on that day. Of course he could have laced Ann's drug supply while they were still traveling together. The snake is another question. From what I understand there is no way it could have stayed alive more than a few hours trapped in a backpack."

"I will check at that boarding house where they parked the bus here in Belize City and see if they were there at the time the woman died. And Mr. Grant of the DEA could check the man's passport— find out if he is your Mr. Scully... "

"Even if he is Scully, we don't have any evidence that he was involved in Ann's death. Give me a day on the road to see what I can find out. Whatever they are into I think Ivette is just a bystander. She happens to own the bus. Although she knows more than she's told me. I think she's a little scared now and will talk."

Phyllis sipped her coffee. "I will do a little research on your Mr. Scully. If your Mr. Scully has been involved in illegal activities in the past, Mr Grant will be able to find out. Then we might have sufficient justification to question him."

"Teddy talked more with the Mayans. She's gotten them to trust her. They said a white woman was buying snakes a few days ago."

"I'll follow it up as best I can. It could have been Ann herself. I doubt if they will admit to knowing anything." Phyllis smiled, "I got your package with the shoes. How did you manage to get them?"

Lynn didn't answer right away. She took a deep breath. "That guy, Marv, the one who took Sarah out the day Ann died. He works for Ed Kelly now. He was wearing them. He claimed that Ed gave them to him. I—"

Phyllis held up her hand. "Never mind; you don't have to tell me how you persuaded him to let you have them. I've questioned the Texas man, Edward Kelly. He and his wife are not very hard to find. I don't think they are involved in anything that is obviously illegal. He's that type of foreign businessman that we have to deal with all the time here. We're a last small frontier—a place where entrepreneurs think it's easy to take control. Sometimes they do.

"The shoes did match the prints we found and we found traces of dirt in them that could be from the area where Ann was camped. Again it would be difficult to prove who actually wore them there. However, Edward Kelly confessed or rather bragged that he visited the murder site after Ann was taken away. His explanation is that he is interested in antiquities and thought she might have uncovered something. A rather difficult man. Of course he has an alibi for the time of her death."

"But the whole thing could have been set up ahead. The murderer didn't have to be there to kill her—if she took the drugs herself. And the snake could have been planted in her bags."

Inspector Thompson nodded. "But what would be Kelly's motive?"

"Teddy said Ed has been trying to buy the ranch down there. Intimidating Jacob and Emma. A treasure hunter. Maybe he wanted to get Sarah in trouble with the authorities so he could—"

Phyllis interrupted with an understated, "A rather extreme and unnecessarily risky method I would say."

"But Ann did seem to know him and be afraid of him. It seemed to me she was avoiding him."

"Both he and his wife denied ever seeing her before."

"Can he dig for stuff legally?"

Inspector Thompson nodded. "If he gets a government permit there is nothing we can do."

"Is that possible?"

"I doubt it. But if he hires somebody with credentials to be a front, I suppose it is possible." Phyllis took a sip of her coffee. "I still would like to question your Canadians in the morning before you leave the country. Do you think you can persuade them to come in to my office voluntarily?"

"I already suggested that and they declined." Lynn shook her head. "I'll suggest it again. They'll claim they weren't even in Belize yet when Ann died."

Inspector Thompson sighed. "But once they cross at the Guatemalan border..." She shook her head. "I am sorry, but I will have to have them stopped at the border and questioned. It will ostensibly be routine. I'm sure they are used to that. We will not let them know it has anything to do with the death."

Lynn sighed. "That doesn't give me much time on this side—unless the bus breaks down. If I find out any useful information I'll call you even from Guatemala." Lynn took another sip of her coffee. "Do you know where they took Ann in the US for treatment?"

Phyllis shook her head. "They sent us information on the death, but not the location of the hospital. Why?"

"Was it the US authorities that alerted you in the first place that the circumstances around her death were suspicious?"

Phyllis shook her head. "The doctor at the hospital called us because of the presence of drugs in her blood, while she was still at the hospital. We contacted the DEA right away because she was a citizen of the US."

"My boss at the paper says there is nothing on the news wire about her death."

Phyllis smiled. "Perhaps she is not famous enough."

# Chapter 10

Sarah arrived, laughing as she opened the door to their room. Lynn was happy to see her cheered up.

A young man, in neat white rayon slacks and batik shirt followed her through the door. Sarah said, "You remember Bobby, Lynn, my little brother—my step-brother actually, but..." She looked at him dotingly, "...dearer than a blood relative."

Lynn thought Sarah had probably had a little too much rum, something Sarah never indulged in while at camp. She put out her hand and said ,"Hi Rob, nice to meet you...again."

He didn't look at all like the petulant, skinny teen-ager she had once met. His wide dark eyes evaluated her unapologetically as he squeezed her hand too seductively and sat down next to her on the bed. "Lynn Evans," he said with a smile on his handsome face that Lynn couldn't interpret but made her uncomfortable. "I've been hearing how much help you've been. I can't thank you enough for supporting my big sister. But don't worry. Now I'm here, we'll get it all straightened out. After all, I owe her. She's been like a second mother to me, especially lately. She's a saint. Look how she tried to rescue Ann."

He turned and patted Sarah's hand. "It's really my fault. I should have warned you about her." He shook his head. "I really believed she had changed—that there would be no more of her tricks." He sighed. "This one got her, though." He fell silent and reached in his jacket pocket to pull out a cigarette. He started to light it then stopped and looked up at them. "Do you mind?"

They both shook their heads. Then Lynn remembered; they had to sleep in that room, and they had already turned off the air-conditioning and opened the windows. She thought about turning on the fan. She could do that after he left. Instead she asked, "What do you mean? You think she did this to herself? On purpose!"

Bobby concentrated on his cigarette for a long moment. "She was always doing it—faking suicide, getting into jams...to get sympathy...to get attention. That whole fiasco of the hidden drug money." He shook his head. "It's ridiculous. She barely knew the guy. You know, one of the ones that're in jail now. Had just met him after we broke up. But she sort of liked the publicity of it—the police believing she knew where the money was. Led them along a bit until it got out of hand and they really wouldn't believe she didn't know anything. I'll never forgive myself. I introduced Ann to that crook. Me! had no idea what he was into." He shook his head and took another drag on his cigarette.

"You know the drug dealers that went to jail?"

He shrugged. "I knew that one." He looked at her as if amused by the obvious conclusion one might make. "He was an old school buddy of mine actually. I never met the others they put in jail. I guess Ann knew them."

"The police don't think it was suicide. And Ann certainly wasn't just being dramatic. It's likely a combination of drugs and poison would have killed her even if we'd gotten to her sooner."

"I'm sure she didn't know that. All she knew was that Sarah or Hank would come looking for her when she didn't show up for supper. It surely did get their attention!" He shook his head. "Stupid chick."

Sarah said, "Bobby, she's dead!"

This guy didn't act like somebody whose exlover had just died. Lynn didn't like him, or his attitude, even if he was a relative of Sarah's. "So you don't think Ann had the money or knew where it was?"

"Come on, I would have known. The woman couldn't keep a secret. I could read her like a book."

Somehow the Ann he was describing didn't match the reticent, tough Ann that Lynn had known at camp.

Bobby took another drag. Sarah handed him an ash tray and he knocked the ashes off slowly and thoroughly as if to give himself time to think. Then he said, "Sorry, Sis, but I got tired. If somebody wants to do herself in, in the end you can't stop her."

Lynn waved away some smoke and leaned closer. "I suppose you've told all this to the police. Maybe they would leave Sarah alone if they thought Ann had done it all herself."

The pair of intense brown eyes drilled into hers again for a long moment. She felt a chill in spite of the close hot room. Then he smiled and patted her hand before she could pull it away. "Don't worry about them. You can go on home to the States confident. All is well here. I can take care of my big sister."

"Did you know her as Anna LaPlace or Ann Wilson?"

He shrugged. "We called her Annie. LaPlace was the name in the papers. She made a deal with the cops."

"Bobby never told me her last name when he warned me she might call."

"Sorry Sis, I warned you she was trouble, if you recall."

"You also said she needed help."

Bobbie's voice was petulant. "I didn't know she had actually contacted you until after she showed up at the dig."

"You saw her when she was there." Lynn asked.

He shook his head. "I stayed away once she got there. Better that way."

"Do you know an ex of hers BG or Scully. He used to be a biker, real name B. Gerald Scully?"

He looked puzzled and shook his head.

"But you said she told you everything."

He got up. "She lied a lot too. Anything to get attention." He put a brotherly arm around Sarah who was looking sleepy and annoyed at Lynn's questioning.

Lynn was embarrassed by the devoted look on Sarah's face as he said, "See you in the morning, Sis."

After he was gone Lynn turned on the fan.

"Sorry," Sarah said, "I should have done that before."

Lynn asked, "Did Bobby, or you, tell the police what he knew about Ann? They will want his state—"

Sarah broke in impatiently. "Oh Lynn, let up. Of course he will—if he hasn't already. He knows people down here better than I do. He's been helping me with them for years, ever since I started the dig."

"He comes down every year?"

Sarah nodded. "He's been in the country for a while this year.

He stayed away from the dig because Ann was there. He's not much good at digging, better at administrative detail."

Sarah said the last words slowly, slurring her consonants. Then she lay down on the bed and closed her eyes not even bothering to undress, or wash, or even brush her teeth. Very unSarah-like. Even in school she had been meticulous. This whole affair had exhausted her. Maybe Bobby *was* just what she needed to get her through this bad time.

"I'm leaving early in the morning," Lynn said quietly in case Sarah was already asleep. Sarah looked over at her inquiringly.

"You know those three Canadians that knew Ann. I still can't help thinking they are involved somehow, that they know something. One of them may be the old boyfriend I mentioned to Bobby. I'll try to get back to Belize City before I go home."

"You're not really going to travel with them? Why don't you leave the detective work to the police?"

"You told me I had to see Tikal."

Sarah sighed and sat up. "Take the plane."

"Heck, that wouldn't be any fun."

"Anyway, you don't need to worry now that Bobby is here. He's promised to stay for a while. I can't help but think Ann might not have...if I'd gotten them together while she was there instead of letting them avoid each other."

"But you told me you let her stay there to keep her away from him."

"Maybe I was wrong."

"He doesn't seem to think so."

"He encouraged me to let her stay when I told him she was there, but I think he didn't like it. He knew she was hiding out and was afraid for me."

"But he didn't tell you the truth about her."

"A difficult conflict for him. He is so loyal. I feel really bad that he had to learn about her death...the way he did. I had to fax him when she was in the hospital. He was in Mexico—across the border in Chetumal. Taking some tourist to see the ruins there. He never saw her alive again."

Sarah covered her face with the pillow for a moment. Then she sat up and started to undress slowly. "Anyway, you don't need to go chasing off with some Canadian tourists in a decrepit old Volkswagen bus to clear me. It looks like I'll get to keep my permit, though they still suspect me of something. They would like to get some drug runners if only to keep the DEA happy. That tourist Edward Kelly isn't any help. He's been gossiping about how my camp might be a drug pickup."

"Teddy heard Ed say the government will give him a dig permit once you're out of the picture. He even tried to buy the ranch. He found out Emma wants move in to town nearer their kids. Jacob was not interested. He wants the land for his grandkids. But Teddy was afraid Jacob wouldn't hold out if Ed actually came up with a fair offer."

Sarah shook her head. "I'm not surprised. Ed has illusions of grandeur. Abigail told me he has been hanging around Belmopan for a couple of days spreading money in the wrong places. I don't think anyone really takes him very seriously beyond a few bar drunks."

"And Teddy found out from the Mayans that a white woman was buying live snakes recently. They wouldn't say if they knew who it was. I told Inspector Thompson."

Sarah frowned. "It could be a coincidence. Another foreigner trying to make an illegal buck trading in exotic animals. I hope the authorities follow it up."

# Chapter 11

Early the next morning Lynn was awakened by a banging on the door. Predictably, it was BG standing impatiently outside. "Ten minutes and the bus goes."

Lynn washed quickly, picked up her bag and gave Sarah a quick hug.

"Be careful and try just being a tourist for once. Belize and Guatemala have some of the most exciting archeology in the world not to mention the birds, untouched forest and orchids," Sarah said as Lynn hurried out the door.

"I want to stop at San Ignacio," Ivette announced as they were getting in the bus. I'm ready for some hills." There was a freshness about her unapologetic curiosity when she was an enthusiastic tourist.

Lynn had to admit to herself that a good part of the reason she was on the bus was Ivette. It had been a while since she had been so attracted to someone. She said, "That sounds like a good idea. I've heard it is beautiful there. I read that you can do a rafting trip all the way to the sea. And you can go up into the hills where there is a totally different landscape, even pine trees."

Ivette ignored her. Lynn wondered if her coolness was because Lynn hadn't responded to her flirting back at the camp. Ivette had seemed to understand about her feelings of loyalty to Marta even if Lynn didn't really understand it herself. After all it had been Marta who had broken off their affair.

After she and Ivette were safely packed into the back and Michelle had revved the engine and put it in gear, Lynn said to Ivette, "You still mad?"

Ivette settled back onto her pillow and adjusted the window to get just the right amount of breeze. Lynn admired her ability not to answer a question immediately, but to take advantage of the poised attention of the speaker and to make her suffer awhile. It was a talent she had admired and hated in an ex-lover Shirley too. Lynn could never stand not to answer right away. Dramatic and emotional encounters were not what she enjoyed in life. She always felt an obligation to move the drama along. A distinct disadvantage in love relationships.

"I wasn't ready to leave the beach yet," Ivette finally said in a breathy petulant voice. "I liked it there. Jacob was going to take me fishing. You could have made them stay longer; you're paying for the gas."

"I didn't want to be left behind." Lynn said defensively.

Ivette lost her dramatic pose and snickered behind her hand. "That Michelle can be intimidating. Right? Even you do what she says."

Lynn was annoyed. "Why didn't you insist on staying yourself? After all it is your bus."

"Never mind." Ivette dismissed the whole affair with a wave of her hand, signaling that the scene was over. Now she was all attentiveness and concern for Lynn's welfare. "I hope they didn't ruin your plans. Did you get done what you needed to down there?"

Lynn nodded and asked, "How come you're suddenly so interested in stopping in San Ignacio? You never mentioned it before."

"I'm tired of them deciding what we are going to do, making me leave places I like. I decided it was time to take charge. You're right. It is my bus." She looked at Lynn then with what could only be described as seduction in her eyes. "Besides you're more fun than they are." She waved her head at the two in the front seat. "We'll send them off somewhere. We'll have a good time. Right?" She touched Lynn's cheek with the back of her hand.

Lynn could feel her face flushing. She found herself smiling and saying yes. And then Ivette's lips touched hers soft and warm—a promise.

By the time they drove into the foothills, Lynn had fallen asleep. She woke to Ivette shaking her. All around her the flat pasture and swamp land had given way to rich, tropical, hill farms. Massive trees replaced the grass, palmettos, and low growth of the coast. BG ignored Ivette when she demanded that they stay in San Ignacio, but when they got to the small town in the hills not far from the

Guatemalan border, he parked saying he wanted a beer anyway and they went into a local bar-restaurant.

Lynn and Ivette left him there with Michelle to walk around the tiny town. On the way back a familiar Texas voice hailed her. It was Ed Kelly. Lynn reluctantly introduced him to Ivette.

He, in turn, introduced the two men with him—Carlos Garcia, a short stocky El Salvadoran and a younger man from Guatemala named Renaldo Schmidt who looked only partly German. All three wore Levi's and designer shirts, and sporty hiking boots.

"We're business partners," Ed explained, "Came up here to look over some real estate. Seen several nice pieces today. This place has got more Maya ruins..." He shook his head. "Can't hardly find a piece of land without 'em."

Ed was clearly baiting her, but Lynn couldn't manage not to respond. "So you've given up on Jacob and Emma then? Dr. Donovan will be relieved."

He shook his head. "Need some beach front too, sweetheart. But the Doc can have her piles of potsherds and rock. They got major temples, whole cities buried up this way. We'll build the hotel down on the beach, out of her way." He chuckled.

"When you build your big tourist resort up here, I'm sure you'll preserve anything you find as an attraction for the tourists. You could incorporate the temples into your golf course."

He looked at her without blinking for a moment. "No, I think I'll stick to ranching. Sell off the timber, burn the bush and grow grass for cattle. Then when it gets overgrazed I can sell it off to the golf course guys. You know, since it's already all grass they'll be half way there." His two companions chuckled with him over that one.

Unfortunately, Ivette accepted their offer of a drink and they all went inside. BG and Michelle were still at the bar with some locals. Ivette convinced Lynn to order some food.

Over their beer the three men went on in Spanish about their plans for the land they were going to buy. Lynn tried to follow, but her Spanish was too bad. Ivette stayed with the conversation while Lynn gave her full attention to her tortillas and beans until Ed said, smirking, "How's about you all stick around tonight. There's a hot Mariachi group here over from Mexico. The restaurant'll be barbecuing a pig and chickens." He leaned closer to Lynn and dipped his head toward the El Salvadoran. "Carlos here's taken quite a shine to you."

Lynn tried to be polite. "Thanks but no thanks. We're on our way to Guatemala." She looked at Ivette pointedly.

Ivette blinked coquettishly. "I don't think we are in a big hurry."

Lynn was actually relieved when BG and Michelle came over and she happily gave up her seat and retreated to the bus.

In a little while Ivette came out to the bus. Lynn pretended to be asleep when she climbed in the back. Ivette shook her. "How would you like to spend the day here tomorrow? We can check out the river trip, maybe get a taxi to takes us to the pines."

Lynn didn't answer. She wasn't sure how she felt. "Depends on who is in the party."

"Your friend Ed solved that for us. BG and Michelle are taking off with them tonight. Some scheme they are hatching." Ivette touched Lynn lightly with the back of her hand and said softly, "Just you and me."

Lynn turned to look at Ivette. The pupils of her green eyes were almost black in the reflected sunlight. The pink neon of the restaurant sign flashed on and off exotically on her cheek. Lynn could feel blood pumping in a vein in her throat. Was it just the afternoon heat? Lynn took a deep breath as Ivette leaned over to kiss her lightly on the lips.

# Chapter 12

"We're going to leave you two here tonight." Michelle said settling herself in the drivers seat.

BG climbed in next to her and snickered. "Yeah, you two babes have all day tomorrow to admire the view, drown in the river. We got business."

"What did you do that they are suddenly so willing to let you stay here. I thought they were hot to get to Guatemala," Lynn whispered to Ivette.

Ivette snuggled down into her pillows. "Now that we don't have Annie to get us through to the States, and I insisted on staying in what he called this dump, BG said he might as well hustle a bit."

Lynn didn't really know, but she nodded knowingly anyway. Then after Michelle got the motor going Lynn asked, "Where are BG and Michelle going? Ivette glanced up at the two in front, then whispered in Lynn's ear, "You know—to do a deal." She leaned back trying to look cool, a seasoned drug dealer.

"So Ed Kelly and his friends are buying drugs from them?"

Ivette suddenly gave a nervous glance at the two in front. "Its better you don't know too much; then you don't have to get in trouble—in case you should get asked. Actually, that's what they told me. Anyway, what they said was they are going to meet Ed and his buddies again. You know, to see the land he's found. BG likes him. Then we go back to Belize City."

"So if they're doing their deal here, why go back?"

Ivette said, "It's part of the deal. Don't worry you'll get to Tikal." She glanced to the front again. "Anyway, Michelle decided to keep a date with Teddy." She smirked with satisfaction like all good gossips the world over when they have an exclusive.

90

Michelle and BG left them at a small stucco hotel on an opposite hillside from the little town.

Lynn registered while Ivette found their room. Then Lynn went down the street to find them some drinks and a little food for an evening picnic down by the river.

Approaching the little hotel with the late afternoon sun just touching the edge of the green hills above, Lynn felt she was entering a tropical paradise. She stepped into the Spanish tiled patio with its dark wood paneling against white stucco walls and neat, orderly tropical plants, newly watered—magic, like stepping into a thirties movie of the tropics. She remembered a photo she had loved as a child. Her favorite aunt, the one who had never married, in a flowing silk paisley dress lounging on a day-bed, her beautiful long dark hair parted in the middle and wound tight against her head and coiled over each ear, one hand gracefully draped over the oriental rug. Behind her were the dark low beams and stucco walls of a Spanish hacienda with palm trees just outside the window lit up by the California sun.

Lynn stood in the doorway to their room. As her eyes adjusted to the shadowy interior, she noted the pattern of palm leaves on the red tile floor made by the golden evening light slanting through the paneless windows. A bare brown foot rested against the darker wood of an interior doorway. Her eyes traveled up a smooth calf to the edge of a terry cloth towel. Above, long damp hair rested on the cloth and the swell of soft breasts moved gently beneath the towel.

Lynn stepped into this picture to the sweet scent of bath soap, lotion, and steamy woman. She moved even closer and a warm hand reached out to pull her face near.

The next afternoon Lynn waited near the river where golden light brightened a stretch of cropped grass, not cut by a mower but champed close by a donkey and a few skinny tropical sheep and goats. Nearby the river wound through huge, shiny-green tropical trees with white and orange flowers high up and scattered on the grass.

She walked down to the river's edge to pick up one of the flowers that had fallen—the orange of a hot flame, thinking how it matched last night's lovemaking. She held it in her hand, saving it to give to Ivette, and climbed back up a steep grassy slope to sit on a rock watching children dig in the sand near the river. Next to the children, their mother washed out a few clothes in the shallow edge of the river and then spread them to dry on the grass.

Two soft hands covered her eyes from behind. "Michelle?" Lynn teased. Ivette laughed and handed Lynn a sandwich "You better thank the goddess it isn't—yet."

Lynn didn't care for the tone of the remark. "Thought you weren't lovers with either of those two," she said still trying to sound joking.

"I'm not," Ivette said defensively and bit into her own sandwich. "They have a relationship...with each other...of a sort." She laughed, and looked out over the hillside. "...But it doesn't mean they haven't tried. I told them I wasn't interested in you so they would leave us alone."

"And what if they find out?"

Ivette sighed and took a wilted piece of lettuce out of her sandwich, wrinkling her nose with distaste. She threw it to some birds and then looked at Lynn with the same expression on her face. "Are you scared."

"Should I be?"

Ivette shrugged. "I am just traveling with them. At home I hardly even see Michelle. She brought BG along. And he is more noise than anything. He does intimidate people sometimes. That makes him a useful traveling companion...mostly. Unless he is on drugs. I was glad you didn't have any when you found us."

"Is that what Ann was bringing them?"

"I suppose. They didn't tell me what Ann was supposed to have. Just that it would cover the expenses of the trip. She must have offered them *some* money because their market is north, not here and they didn't have enough to get home."

"I understand Ann was trying to get off drugs."

"So are they. Or so they say. Even before we came they admitted they were planning to deal. But just enough to get by. And just the harmless stuff. You know mushrooms and stuff—no cocaine or heroin. Anyway, whatever Ann may have had certainly wasn't for our use. It was supposed to be an investment. Cover the expenses of the trip. Maybe even give us a stake when we got home."

Ivette broke the rest of her sandwich into little bits, thoughtfully and threw it to the birds gathering around the lettuce leaf. Her voice was sad as she said, "I never even thought about doing anything like that before. I guess it's a message, huh, that I should stay away from that sort of business."

Lynn nodded. "Kind of hard isn't it, if you keep traveling with them?"

Ivette smiled and said dryly, "Thanks for pointing out my problems. I wouldn't have figured that out for myself."

"Sorry, but its hard not to be concerned when—"

Ivette squeezed her hand. "Let's not talk about that now, *chére, amie.*" She put a banana chip in Lynn's mouth and kissed her and the world took on an even more surreal golden glow.

# Chapter 13

Lynn woke up. It was still pitch black. Against the window she could just make out the silhouette of someone standing at the foot of the bed. Damn, she should have locked the door. A thief? She should probably pretend to be asleep—let them have her money and her passport—but that would be such a drag. Traveling was hard enough with a passport and money. She didn't see a gun. She heard her own annoyed voice say, "What do you want?"

"Get up. Now."

Ivette sat up, rubbed her face and said calmly, "What's up?" The silhouette reached over to pull Ivette out of the bed. Lynn grabbed a wrist, twisting and pulling the figure down, pinning whoever it was face down under her weight.

Somebody turned on a light and Lynn found herself on top of BG...naked. Michelle was standing by the door looking bored and tired. She laughed at the sight of them perched on the bed.

Lynn climbed off BG and the bed and grabbed her clothes.

BG got to his feet grumbling and rubbing his shoulder, "Jesus, stupid broad. You could of broke my arm."

Michelle tossed a newspaper onto the bed. Ivette looked at it while Lynn got dressed. Then she leaned over Ivette's shoulder. Lynn's picture was on the front page standing next to Ann at the dig. It looked like one she remembered Teddy taking. How had the newspapers gotten it. From the police?

Ed had been in Teddy's tent. Maybe he had sent it to the papers to embarrass Sarah. The caption under it was *American Reporter at Scene.* Next to it was a feature article about Ann's death.

Ivette asked. "Who's that next to you?"

Lynn took the paper from her. Then she looked at Ivette puzzled and said, "Ann of course."

"That isn't Annie."

Lynn looked again closely. It was definitely Ann. "That *is* Ann — the woman who died. The police said her name is Anna LaPlace."

"Well it isn't the Annie we know." Ivette. said. "That means Annie isn't dead?" Ivette had a wild look in her eyes.

Lynn was confused. "But you sent her the fax from Belize City— addressed to Ann—" She looked at BG. "And Ann told Teddy that you, B. Gerald Scully—Skullhead—had lived with her. She—"

BG actually began to laugh. Then he stopped abruptly. "You got that one wrong, dead wrong, sweetheart. And so did that baby-queer. She was so sure she was right, I wasn't into straightening her out. One way or the other. Stupid broads. both of you."

"See, I told you Annie couldn't be dead." Ivette. said.

BG tossed Lynn his Canadian passport. Lynn read the name, Henry J. Burling.

"He used to like the Bee Gees. You know, the music group," Ivette said.

"Used to is right, but who wants to be called Henry." BG said.

"Annie told us she was going to be at that dig. Said she had a friend there that would get her some money. But I guess she was lying," Michelle said.

"Are you sure—maybe it's just a very bad picture."

Michelle said, "You think we're that stupid. You made the stupid mistake, not us."

Lynn read the article. It referred to the woman next to Lynn in the picture as Anna Marie LaPlace. It mentioned the drug case she had testified in. No mention of her using the name Ann Wilson.

Damn, if she only had kept the picture of Ann that Del had sent, bad as it was, instead of giving it to Phyllis. She thought about it. She had thought it was of the Ann she knew, but now she couldn't swear to that. But now, even though the fax was bad, it might have helped to clear this up.

She asked Ivette, "What was her whole name—the woman you were traveling with?"

"She never told me. She just said to call her Annie. I never saw her passport."

"Annie never gave you the name of her friend at the dig either?"

Ivette shook her head. "She told us Dr. Donovan was the archeologist—to tell the hotel to give the fax to her or her crew."

"When did she leave you in Honduras?"

Ivette yawned, "I don't know. Maybe four weeks ago. My bus broke down and we were hanging out at the beach in Honduras, waiting for the parts for at least three weeks. Before she took the public bus north she said just to fax her at the hotel in Belize City, once we knew when we would get there, the one you were staying at. She said they would get the fax to her through her friend at the dig, and then she would meet us. She said that her friend there was expecting her. Can't all this wait till morning?"

Lynn turned to the other two. Michelle shook her head slowly. BG said, obviously still mad about the arm twist, "Fucking newspaper reporter, I'm not telling you shit."

Michelle said, "All we know is the woman in the paper sure as hell isn't the Annie we were traveling with."

Ivette sat up suddenly the sheet still wrapped around her tightly. "Shit, maybe Annie showed up looking for us in Belize City after we left."

BG snickered, "How could she know to meet us if she wasn't the one that got the fax?"

Suddenly Lynn said, "Is this some sort of stupid joke?"

Ivette was the only one who shook her head. Lynn looked at the picture in the paper again. Did she believe these people? But why lie? What possible advantage could there be for them? Nobody reassured her that it wasn't some sort of weird joke. Ivette crawled back under the covers. Michelle went into their little kitchenette looking for food.

Maybe there *were* two people. Maybe the Annie these three knew decided not to go to the archaeological site and took off somewhere else. Maybe she was even one of those tourists that Sarah decided not to let stay. Just a stupid coincidence. Two people with the same first name. But who was the friend and why was their Annie so sure that friend would get the fax. Was it Ann. She had the fax in her jacket pocket. Would she have kept it if she didn't know the woman it was meant for? Why hadn't Lynn thought to asked anybody else at the site if they had seen the fax or brought it to Ann? She had been so sure it had been intended for the Ann who Lynn knew.

Lynn said, "What are you going to do now? Did you have a contingency plan for meeting Annie if you didn't reach her at the archeological dig? I still want to get to Guatemala. I don't see why this has to make any difference in our plans."

Ivette opened her mouth but shut it again at a look from Michelle.

There was a look exchanged between BG and Michelle and they both disappeared out the door.

"Come on Ivette. What are those two up to?" Lynn said sitting on the bed.

Ivette pulled the covers up around her head and stretched. "Don't be so paranoid Lynn. They're OK. They'll come around. They play a little with stuff like psilocybin mushrooms and cannabis, but, like I told you, they aren't heavies. BG just likes to play act big time dealer, but that's a joke. He gets a little cash trading sometimes and gets paranoid and skittish. After all you didn't tell us the truth about who you are. They're pissed they missed the boat with Annie. And they want to blame you. You can still help us get to Guatemala if you're coming along." Ivette touched her hand. "And I say you are. It's my bus. They can do what they want. We'll go to Guatemala by ourselves."

Why not. The business about Ann was just making her tired. Sarah was right; let the police and the DEA deal with it. She would go to Tikal with Ivette, look at ruins and orchids and birds through her sweet, enthusiastic eyes. She gave Ivette a kiss and Ivette pulled her down onto the bed.

But Michelle came back in with a bag of chips and parked herself on the floor with her back against the wall near the door. She said, "Sorry lovebirds but BG wants to sort this out. Really we don't give a shit if you are a reporter. We were just pissed you didn't square with us. We still need to get to Guat City."

BG came back in a minute later with a beer and dropped into the only chair. There was no sound for a few minutes but the crunch of chips against teeth.

"You're making me hungry," BG said, in an almost conciliatory tone that made Lynn nervous. "Come on. Let's go out to the bus and warm something up...and talk this over."

"I'm not hungry. Why can't we do this later?" Ivette said, annoyed.

BG's eyes narrowed for a second, but he smiled at her. "You just close your pretty little eyes then and leave this to me."

Ivette yawned. "Don't be so fucking condescending BG. I am staying in here and getting some sleep. As far as I'm concerned there is nothing to discuss anyway. Lynn is going with me as far as she wants to. End of discussion."

But Lynn decided to take him up on it—a little diplomacy wouldn't hurt if she had to travel with these two. She followed BG and Michelle out and climbed into the bus. While he heated up some soup, Lynn said conversationally. "So you never met your Annie before this trip?" BG stayed busy making himself a sandwich, but he said, rather cheerfully—for him, "Like you heard we met her on the road. She was hitchhiking out of Panama. Ivette made us stop because she thought it wasn't safe for a woman."

She wondered why he was suddenly so friendly. She watched him slice bread and tried not to wonder if she was next. Then he handed her and Michelle a bowl of soup and a piece of bread nicely buttered. "Wanna beer."

"Thanks."

Michelle didn't eat hers. She continued to munch on the chips. "Don't thank us. You bought it."

She accepted it all in the interests of diplomacy. The soup was delicious—a delicate mushroom in chicken broth with vegetables.

She complemented him and he said, "Michelle made it. It's the one thing she bothers to cook."

"Your French grandmother's recipe?" she asked Michelle.

BG laughed. "Not hardly."

"Look, writing is my job, but I had nothing to do with the article about Ann's death. I still don't intend to write about you three. Anyway, it looks like you didn't even know her, although your Annie probably was a friend of the woman who died."

"It's no skin off my back." BG said, "When push comes to shove, I got nothing to hide. Just spell my name right and no pictures. Send it to my Ma in Poughkeepsie. Then I don't have to write her this year and remind her I'm still alive."

"What about you, Michelle?"

Michelle didn't answer.

BG took another bite of his sandwich. "What about her?"

"One of you was pissed when you found out I was a reporter, And...about me and Ivette."

He shrugged. "We don't like people trying to put stuff over on us. Anyway, Michelle, she doesn't like you. She had her eye on Ivette. She doesn't like people getting in her way."

Michelle dumped the bowl of soup BG had given her back in the pot "Shut up BG," she said and turned to Lynn. "I wasn't mad about the article, but they claimed that that woman in the picture was Anna LaPlace. It wasn't. I saw Annie's passport. Anna LaPlace was her name. I don't know what shit is going on, but we figured you might know. We got enough troubles without the police." She took another chip. "As far as I'm concerned, you're welcome to that tramp, Ivette. But if we had another vehicle I'd say bye-bye right now. Get us to Guatemala City and she's yours, bus and all."

Lynn was confused. Annie was Anna LaPlace. Ann Wilson, the woman who died was not? Somebody was lying. Maybe it was Grant, but why? Was Michelle just saying that to confuse Lynn, because she was pissed?

Lynn took another sip of soup. "I'll have to fly home from Guatemala City, especially if we go back to Belize City before we go to Tikal. Anyway, what about Teddy? I thought she was the one getting eyeballed by you."

Michelle bit into her chip. "BG is right, Ivette talks too much."

BG was smirking. "Teddy's a snack, just one little bite. Ivette is a meal—right?"

Lynn hated that she was flushing in front of them, and BG was getting off on it and on watching the fireworks between them.

Michelle sighed. "Now that this is all settled I'm getting some sleep. We're taking off as soon as it gets light." She got out of the bus, no doubt going to take Lynn's place in the bed. Lynn wished she had stayed there. She would go back soon—she didn't trust Michelle

"And what's in this for you? How come you hang out with Michelle," she asked BG defensively.

He shook his head slowly. "Don't like whiny, powder-puff, females. Had enough of them. Michelle doesn't put out, but I like to watch her style." He put more soup in her bowl. "Eat up. You're too skinny by half."

She took another sip. It really was delicious. "What about your Annie?"

"What about her?"

"Who's lover was...is she?"

"You don't get it do you? I don't fuck with people I travel with. Don't get involved. If you talk to the people you fuck..." He shook his head. "I was married once. She talked all the time. Weepy, whiney. She wanted me to get a steady job. Lasted a whole month. Couldn't wait to get away." He dumped the dishes in the sink.

"Ivette said we are going back to Belize City first. How come the change of plans?"

"Ivette sure as hell talks too much."

"You going to look for Annie now you think she is still alive?"

He just watched her. She tried to get up to go back and join Ivette, but she was so sleepy.

BG watched her for a long moment as if he was expecting something. She tried to think of something to say, tried to look alert interested, but her eyelids felt remarkably heavy.

Instead of saying anything else he got out of the bus. So much for talking things over. Maybe she would just snooze here until they left. She curled up.

She was actually glad for the chance to go back to Belize City before they went to Tikal. She wanted to tell somebody about this new development. And to ask around if anyone had seen the fax BG had sent before it had been delivered to Ann. Maybe somebody at the hotel.

And who had sent the picture to the paper? In it she and Ann had been standing next to a low wall of limestone they had uncovered. For once Ann had a smile on her face. The Newspaper had printed it in color, a rather bad reproduction, the shadows too dark the greens too bright. Ann looked like any pretty young woman, her features hidden and exaggerated by the stark shadows of the trees above her; hard to tell who she was. How could they be so sure it wasn't the Anna LaPlace they knew?

# Chapter 14

She felt the van moving. Why were they traveling in the dark? Were they going in the right direction? It was hard to tell at night with black tree shadows in the moonlight falling across the bus. She was so tired, so many strange dreams...

She felt herself being lifted, falling, the jar of hitting the ground, then its unevenness and prickles. Still dreaming? Everything had that misty strange quality of a dream, a yellow light shifted through her eyelids. Bits of twigs and stone dug into her back. As in lots of dreams she couldn't move. It was as if heavy stones were on her chest slowing her breathing. Lynn tried to call out, but her lips still wouldn't move.

The dry, silent darkness swallowed her up. She tried again to open her eyes—to sit up, open her lips, but she couldn't move and no sound came out. A light flashed through her eyelids again. Was this some sort of awful nightmare? The sound of footsteps breaking branches. Each tiny sound invaded her brain with a burst of light behind her eyes as if it were an explosion.

Then she heard voices, a long way away—BG's voice. "She can walk back to the pavement, the bus stop's right there. She's still got her money." She didn't like this dream.

Michelle's voice was angry. "Real generous of you." She started swearing in French. Then she said, "I thought it was cute you gave her the mushrooms. She'd have a trip while she waited for the bus. But she's out cold. What else did you give her anyway?"

Ivette's voice wasn't there. Lynn was confused—could you hear conversations while you were dreaming? Suddenly she was afraid. It really was BG and Michelle. They had given her some sort of drug. She tried to call out. Ivette must be somewhere, but still no sound came. What had BG given her? —something to kill her or just scare her to death?

BG sounded smug. "Never you mind, sweetheart. Just get back to the bus. She'll manage fine. Sleep if off by dawn." He laughed. "You can call somebody once we're back in Belize City. Leave a message at her hotel with that digging buddy of hers if you're so worried."

"Ivette's going to be really pissed," Michelle said sullenly.

BG was angry now too. "You think I care?"

Then the crunch of leaves and branches and the slam of doors and an engine revving...

Then it was silent and dark; even her fear couldn't keep her conscious.

She dreamed herself as soil dampened by the rain. She dreamed of lying beneath a tree frozen in time as the world changed and she was invaded by roots, chewed by insects.

She was her own Welsh grandmother...English...Afro-American ...Indian...self. A dark woman—beautiful in the secret seductive way that most attracted her. She followed the woman, that was herself, but she was always too far away, always beyond reach. Then the woman stood before her, her feet buried in the ground. She looked down at her own tree roots growing from her feet. On each gnarly root the face of another woman grew, dark-eyed and beautiful. Then the faces began to change, to become grotesque distortions of people Lynn knew. Then those too faded and she was tired and old. She slowly fell to the forest floor. There was a fire and she began to burn and burn, then lay, a blackened hulk.

She heard voices, men's voices whispering in Spanish, but almost familiar. Again the crunch of footsteps, a bright light...Someone pulled at her roughly. She could feel ropes being tied around her wrists and ankles. She still couldn't open her eyes.

A touch. Something soft tickled her forehead, her arms, settled over her. She tried again to open her eyelids. In a moment she would wake up...find herself lying in the back of the bus next to Ivette.

She was suddenly lifted and carried by rough hands. She could see nothing but the shadows of trees moving above her. Her eyes were open but it was dark except for the quick flash of light. In the flashes she saw that she was covered with feathers—A cloudlike black and white feathered cape. The soft feathers brushed her skin as she moved along. It tickled but she couldn't lift a hand to brush it away. Another nightmare that felt too real.

A light in the distance a little above her, a small flickering light—another star through the trees? Was it another dream inside her mind or really in the trees? She moved her head back and forth, But the light stayed in one place, a tiny yellow glow, often hidden, but always reappearing as she was carried along. Always there, the same tiny yellow flicker slowly getting larger.

The men who carried her were silent shadows; with the help of the distant flickering light she could just distinguish the hooded man at her feet. His hand gripping her ankle was the only evidence that he was human.

Then she noticed an acrid burning smell. Was it burning pitch, the trees on fire? Sarah had told her that Mayans burn the resin as an offering to their gods. Surely?...

Now the fire was a glow reflected by the trees. Those who carried her began climbing a steep boulder-strewn slope. The remains of a Mayan temple? They put her on hard cold stone. Then it was still and silent again.

The next time she opened her eyes a procession approached from the dark forest with lighted torches. A Mayan woman looked at her and covered the face of her children. She still couldn't move...Tried to remember some Spanish words. All she managed was a whispered apology. *"Permisso...Ayuda me."*

Then the woman turned to several people who followed her and they spoke in whispered voices Lynn could not understand. A man came toward her; she could see a blade reflect the torch light. He placed the knife next to her skin and pricked it as the knife slid under the ropes that bound her, cutting them.

A circle of Mayan faces looked at her silently in the light of the small fire. The fire's heat was all that told her this might not be just another drug-induced hallucination. Then she was surrounded by the murmur of voices drowning out the forest sounds. She understood nothing of what they said, but all the feeling was clear in tone, all the pain and frustration of their lives, the quiet complaints and appeals to their gods and goddesses. They too needed help.

Everything was blurry. A Mayan dressed in traditional embroidered homespun of the region held out a piece of wood with acrid burning pitch on it to her. She shook her head trying to clear her vision. The heat and the acrid smell of the burning pitch helped.

Each of the people now had a piece of wood or clay with smoldering smoky bits of resin burning on it. Opposite her was a large white limestone altar. Next to the altar lay a bundle of feathers moving—a chicken with its feet tied. A circle of faces watched her patiently, expectantly. A low murmur of voices she could not understand.

Smooth brown faces reflected in the fire-light watched her expectantly. What did they want. Who was she? Was she someone who could help them. Was that why she was here?

Suddenly she *was* a Mayan noblewoman. She must remember her dignity. Her back straightened. It was not proper to lie. She stood, shakily. The feather cape fell around her in a swirl of black and white. What did they want from her? What was she supposed to do to help them? She felt a great sadness and guilt. She had not done enough. She had failed. The dryness of the forest around her was her fault, her responsibility. They needed rain for their crops. She had failed them somehow. Someone had not made the necessary sacrifices in the past and now the people were suffering. These people needed rain. Without her intervention they might starve.

She placed the burning incense on the altar where there were others. Someone picked up the chicken by its bound legs. There was a brown hand holding a sharp black blade of volcanic glass. A quick blow with the blade to the feathered sacrifice and blood spattered onto the stone. She watched the glistening red drops begin to turn brown in the heat of the fire.

Such a small sacrifice. No god would be appeased by such a small gesture. No rain would come. Such trivial sacrifice would only bring the gods' contempt and rage and the drought would continue. Without the rain crops would fail, many might starve. There would be sickness in villages. Responsibility for their plight hung heavy on her shoulders. They had come to her to appeal to the rain god, Choc. She must make the necessary sacrifices.

Black and glistening, the obsidian blade lay now in a clay bowl by the fire. She took the black glass in her hand. The pain would be nothing compared with the pain of guilt at the plight of her people. The knife still had a crust of the chicken blood. She wiped it away on the white feathers and passed the blade three times slowly through the cleansing flame of the fire to burn off the chicken blood. Then she carefully made the three long ritual cuts on her arm with the razor sharp glass and watched the blood flow freely on the white stone, a river to feed the god and bring the rain.

Then she took off the feather cape and put it on the altar and fell to the ground, flowing too. The last things she saw before her eyes closed were blood spattered feathers.

Then she was lifted...again...this time gently carried as falling rain cooled her.

She opened her eyes. She was alone in the dark, lying on damp ground. Her clothes were damp, the feathers gone.

She felt something pressing against her arm and reached out. It was her bag that someone had dropped next to her. That little bit of care comforted her.

But something screeched nearby, a sad animal distress sound. Something getting consumed—a late supper? She forced herself to open her eyes. She thought she saw movement—a flicker of motion nearby or in the corner of her eye, just an instant and she was afraid.

It was all she could do not to scream. She became super aware of small sounds. Was it leaves rustling? A mouse chewing?

She remembered Hank's lecture about snakes. He had said most of them were shy and didn't attack humans. But some of them did live on the ground and were dangerous. What was it that she had heard about...the Barba Amarilla, the Fer-de-lance. Hadn't Hank said they hunted at night. She hoped that they were all in their burrows right now. They did sleep underground didn't they? She imagined a little gray-green snake on her hand like the one that had bitten Ann and she did scream. An uneasy sound that hurt her throat. Now something would come after her, would know where she was.

Then she took a deep breath. She imagined Del's voice saying to her, "Get a hold on yourself girl. That snake image is in your mind. You couldn't even see it in this darkness. But she felt the snake crawl across her hand and buried her hands under her arms to control the images.

She thought about screaming again if only to relieve the tension building up in her body. But that would help the snake or whatever it was she had seen move—locate where she was. In case something was stalking her, she sat silent, frozen for a long moment. Then the sound came again, the distant cry. It was not near her. Nothing moved or made a noise near her. She breathed and got up slowly. Then she reached out tentatively and touched...a tree trunk. Nothing bit her.

Absurdly, she was comforted by the tree's solidity. With the reality of the living tree and its rough bark to orient her she looked around and tried to distinguish shapes in the dim predawn light. She could just make out branches against the sky and cloud shapes. Hadn't BG and Michelle left her near a road? She tried to remember. She had heard the bus drive away. Had someone really carried her into the forest? She was lost. She huddled against the tree for a long time, fighting the images, the rising panic that assaulted her. She told herself again and again that the vivid garish monstrous shapes she saw were drug induced.

Staying still frightened her too much. She started to move slowly from tree to tree, stepping carefully on the underbrush in between. She had to do something or her brain would explode. Then she felt the dirt of a path or a road.

And if there was a path, a dirt road, surely there was a house. Where there was a road people lived didn't they? She sat down for a moment, and fell asleep, her head on her bag.

She woke again. There was more light—she could see the trees. She realized it must almost be dawn. It hadn't been just nightmares. BG and Michelle really had dumped her. But she did feel better; things were beginning to look normal again. Whatever BG had given her was wearing off. She sat up. Her head felt huge, swollen.

Perhaps being carried into the jungle—what she thought had been a Mayan ritual—all that had been drug induced nightmares. But it had felt so real.

BG had said she would be able to walk to a bus stop. Or had that been a dream too? He had probably been lying to keep Michelle quiet.

In any case she had lost her chance to find out what they knew...about Ann's death. She had failed, failed Ann and failed Sarah and she wasn't even sure she could save herself.

But right now she just wanted to sleep. Once it was really light she would figure out what to do. She closed her eyes again.

# Chapter 15

She felt wet and cold. She opened her eyes—it was light. Through fuzzy vision she saw two sturdy walking shoes and nylon clad legs emerging from a neat gray skirt. Had she fallen off the swing again and Miss Garnet was coming to rescue her?

A soft voice asked, from what seemed a great height, "You all right, Sugar?"

Lynn looked up to see a smooth brown face looking at her with kindly concern from under a large black umbrella.

The woman bent closer. "The bus will be here soon; you might want to clean up a bit." She dug in the big leather purse slung over her shoulder with one hand. "I have a box of tissues here someplace that I keep for the children...runny noses—you know."

Lynn sat up suddenly embarrassed. She felt her hair. Full of twiggy bits. Her bag was still over her shoulder. Did she still have money for a bus fare. She rummaged in it and found her wallet with money still in it. She felt suddenly for her money belt. It still held the reassuring bulge of her passport and cards.

The woman held out a small package of tissues sympathetically.

Lynn took the package...and saw that her own hands were covered with sticky brown pitch from the trees or resin from...? And she remembered. Had she really been at a Mayan ritual? Had she spent the whole night in the ditch beside road or...? Her memories of those moments and those faces was as vivid as the welcome sight of a comfortingly full-bodied and well-dressed woman in front of her. Sarah had told her that modern Mayans burned resin during the ceremonies of the Mayan religion they held at the old temples and other sacred sites. She wanted that part to have been real.

She dipped the tissue in the puddle beside her and did her best to clean up. While she worked she explained to the woman that she was a tourist and had gotten lost after wandering off in the previous evening from a local ruin. "A Mayan woman told me where to find the bus stop," she lied.

The woman nodded. "That's quite a ways from here."

Lynn asked, to change the subject, "Do you live out here?" The woman smiled. "No. I live in Belize City. I'm a school inspector. I've already been to a local school just by here."

Lynn rummaged around in her bag for a comb. "You don't travel by car?"

The woman chuckled. "On these roads? We are a very rural country and the villages are very far apart, and the roads." She shook her head. "Today I will travel to three more schools by public bus. We are a small country but we have a good bus system. One can get anywhere," she said proudly.

When they got on the bus, all the black and Indian faces looked at her with concern, but the two tourists sitting in the back turned the other way, clearly uncomfortable at her condition. No doubt they assumed her to be down-and-out, a hippie tourist out of money, or a drug addict down on her luck, and were embarrassed that a fellow American should have been brought to such a state.

# Chapter 16

Back at the hotel she found that Sarah was out. Lynn took a shower and called Del. "Is there any way to do a search to see if there were really two people? Drivers license, Social Security, so that we can get pictures. I know Anna Marie LaPlace has a police record. The stuff you sent me was about her. Did you find any reference to an alias for her of Ann Wilson? "

"Anna LaPlace? I found no reference to her having an alias. Who told you she had an alias?"

"The DEA guy here, Grant, said that Ann Wilson was really Anna LaPlace. An article in the local paper on her death referred to her as Anna LaPlace. Somebody sent a snapshot of Ann and me to a local paper calling her Anna LaPlace. No mention of the name Ann Wilson, although Sarah says she had a passport under that name. Grant of the DEA said it was an alias."

"She could have stolen it."

"Of course that's possible. Could you check up on an Ann Wilson? "

"Fax me what you know. I could use a copy of the Ann Wilson passport. I'll need a picture of the woman who died so I can compare it to the one I have of LaPlace."

"Maybe I can get a photo from the stuff that Phyllis Thompson of the Belize police collected at the dig. If she still has it."

"The woman that the Canadians say was traveling with them, what did they say about her? Did they know her as Wilson or LaPlace?"

"They claim they didn't know her last name. It makes sense that she wouldn't travel under her real name if she was hiding from someone. They just knew her as Annie. Ivette told me she always seemed to have money even though she didn't have nice things—no car, no fancy duds. Ivette said this Annie wore funky clothes like she shopped at the Goodwill. Never carried much with her—did without or bought what she needed locally. Certainly the Ann I knew mostly borrowed what she needed when she was at the dig...or scavenged what other people left behind. She never went into town to buy stuff, not while I was here. Everybody is supposed to take a turn shopping for the camp. She never would even though she didn't have to spend her own money. The Canadians said they met the Annie they knew hitchhiking out of Panama into Costa Rica. They traveled with her to Honduras where their bus broke down. She paid for gas and food while she was with them. When they got stuck she took a public bus and was supposed to meet them in Belize City—pay them to take her back to Canada with them. That's Ivette's story anyway."

On the other end of the line Del sighed. "I thought you'd be safe down there—stay out of trouble with your academic friend to watch over you. What is it? You got a trouble magnet implanted last year?"

Lynn laughed. "It was just a minor operation, just under the skin. It was a bargain the week I was doing the tough hide transplant."

It was Del's turn to laugh. "I'll see what I can find out, Hon. You just try to stay out of trouble long enough for me to get back to you with the information...if I find anything. I'll try to fax you some more pictures to see if we got two people or one."

Lynn hesitated for a moment, then she said, "Del, do you believe in out-of-body experiences?"

Del laughed again. "This from you, Ms. Skeptic extrordinaire? All that sun gone to your head? Some Mayan princess step out off a wall and join the sisterhood?"

"Something like that." She told Del briefly an edited version of the experience in the jungle. No need to worry her. While she lied to Del she realized how scared she had been and still was. If somebody went to such lengths to scare her or... what would keep them from coming after her again. Still she said reassuringly to Del, "I think it was just BG's weird idea of a practical joke or something. I don't know. He was probably more pissed than he let on about me being a newspaper reporter. I'm not sure now what was hallucination and what was real because of the drugs. I think there were Mayans with some sort of traditional Mayan ritual, but I was so out of my head...

Fortunately, I think they carried me to the road so I could find my way back here in the morning."

Del sighed. "I'm just glad you got out of there alive. Do me a favor take the hint and get on a plane."

Sarah came in while Lynn was still on the telephone. She stood looking at Lynn shaking her head. When Lynn put down the phone Sarah said, "You look like a truck ran over you. Did the bus break down or run into something?"

Lynn said defensively, "I took a shower." She held up her hands. "It's some sort of pitch from a tree...you know." She looked up at Sarah, "resin, the stuff the Mayans burn at their rituals."

"Why the hell aren't you in Tikal or on the way home? What have you been doing?"

"Why are you so angry?" Lynn asked, petulantly.

Sarah shook her head. "I'm not angry. I'm just scared for you. In some ways Belize is a real frontier. There are a lot of cowboys and outlaws out there running drugs and god knows what else. I don't want you getting hurt."

"I'm not hurt. I just..." Lynn rubbed her eyes. She *was* exhausted.

Sarah said, "That woman, Ivette, called worried and angry. She said you took off. I was actually relieved. I thought you had finally come to your senses and gone to Tikal on your own. She seemed to think you owed her an explanation and left a number here in the City. I don't know. I don't think you should trust her."

Maybe Sarah was right. Could Ivette have known about the whole thing? But when could Michelle or BG have told her about it?

Sarah grabbed her arm. "What's that?" She pointed at the long gashes just beginning to scab over.

Lynn looked down at her arm. So it had been real—at least that part of it.

While Sarah cleaned up the cuts for her, Lynn told her about the mushroom soup and what she could remember after that.

"They drugged you and just dumped you out there?"

"It was BG. I don't think Michelle would have done it by herself, even if she was jealous about Ivette. They left me my bag, my papers. Didn't even take the cash."

"And what about your little Ivette with the sweet green eyes?"

Now Lynn regretted that she had told Sarah about her attraction to Ivette. "Ivette was asleep in the hotel, She couldn't have know what was going on. I'm sure they lied to her about it later."

Sarah shook her head. "Probably was in on it too. How'd you get out of that mess?"

Lynn felt herself flush. "I'm not sure. I might have been hallucinating, but I think I was at some sort of ritual. The drug makes it all so unclear. I think some people, men, carried me into the jungle. There was a feather cape and obsidian knife and... I thought I was a Mayan noblewoman and they needed rain. I did cut myself...and then it rained and some Mayans at the ritual carried me to the bus stop. I...*think* I made those cuts myself. I think—"

Sarah sighed and went to look for her first aid kit. "Maybe you did run into some Mayans worshipping. They might even have been asking for rain. Certainly they would have helped you—even carried you to the bus stop. They would figure that's where you came from and where they knew you would find help in the morning. They wouldn't have contacted any authorities. Some Mayan have come over from Guatemala because of the repressive genocidal government there, but are considered illegal here. Although as far as they're concerned, there are no national borders; they've always been here and traveled freely through the forests." She laughed. "We better make sure to send you home soon before they find you and deify you for getting rain for them."

Then more seriously she said, shaking her head, "I worry about you sometimes. It's one thing for the evangelists that plague this country to think that they, the white northerners, need to come here and 'save' the natives from their heathen way, but I didn't expect those kinds of delusions in someone like you—even under drugs. I'm afraid with you it's just your feeling guilty for everything that goes wrong in the world and thinking you have to fix it. You were like that in college—world hunger, the environment, stopping all the violence in the world—"

Lynn flushed. "So were you."

Sarah frowned. "But I've focused in on a smaller part of the task. I'm only one person. I can save just a little. A piece of human history, a few artifacts and the information they can give us..."

"You're right, I did imagine it was my fault that there was no rain. After all, you did tell me about how the Mayan nobility and priesthood made blood sacrifices, cut themselves, to appease the gods. I was just doing my job as I saw it at the moment."

Sarah smiled, "So now it's my fault you tried to pass yourself off as a priestess or something?"

"I'm sure the Mayans saw me as a wild-eyed, crazy US tourist that didn't even have the sense to stay on the pavement or out of the sun."

Sarah finished up her bandaging. "Let's hope so."

Lynn smiled too, in spite of her exhaustion—at the thought of herself, a skinny, washed-out, hallucinating white woman in the forest in the middle of a Mayan ceremony. They had indeed been very forgiving and kind. She wished there was some way she could pay them back for their kindness.

She lay down on the bed and closed her eyes. Sarah was right. She would love to believe she had brought the rain, rather than that her being there was just a coincidence. Of course thinking that she was personally responsible was just like her. Del would have said the same thing that Sarah had. Lynn did have to quit blaming herself for everything in the world that went wrong. Every bad thing that happened was not her personal failure. In fact to think so was very self-centered as well as absurd.

She was so tired. She should call Phyllis Thompson and tell her about the two identities. Instead she told Sarah. "The Canadians saw the article in the paper. They said that Ann was not the woman they knew. So it probably was a waste of time to go with them. But I—"

Sarah interrupted quietly, "I'm sorry, Lynn, I have to go. Bobby is waiting for me. We had a service here for Ann this morning. Her brother came. He's in the military; he's the one that got her airlifted out. The whole thing was nobody's fault. No charges, no investigation. Ann was a troubled woman. She made her own choices. So it's all over and I want to get on with my life."

"What's her brother's name? He a general or something? Wait a minute; was her sister there?"

Sarah looked puzzled. "Ann didn't have a sister."

"There was a woman sitting next to me when we went to the hospital after they took Ann back to the States. Well-dressed, in black? She *said* she was Ann's sister, Naomi."

Sarah shook her head. "I don't know anything about that. Maybe you misunderstood her. In any case, Ann's brother was the only relative there. We gave him all the rest of her things. I'm just glad it's all over."

"What is her brother's name?"

Sarah was getting impatient. "I don't know. I didn't actually talk to him. Bobby was the one that arranged it all."

"The DEA guy Grant claims—"

"What does it matter what she called herself. Ann was Bobby's lover and a friend and she's...gone now. If the authorities identified her as having some other name what difference does it make?"

"Do you know who sent the papers that photo of Ann that they published?"

"It was one that Teddy took. She must have given it to the press people. There were a couple of them out there after you left."

Sarah sat down next to Lynn on the bed. "Lynn, you know you don't have to rescue me from the clutches of the authorities any more."

Lynn sat up. "Sarah, that's not fair."

"You're right. I did ask you for help. But now I need you to stop."

"I promised my boss I'd do an article. There are some things that still don't make sense to me."

"Tell the police what you have found out and let them deal with it. I'm sorry but I have to go. I have to get back to the dig." Sarah got up slowly and pulled her pack out from under the bed.

"Teddy might not be there."

Sarah turned to stare at Lynn. "What do you mean?"

"Well Teddy made a...date—with Michelle. Here in Belize City."

"Great. Lynn, Teddy is just a kid. Why didn't you tell me before. I am responsible—"

"I thought because Michelle was leaving the country, going to Guatemala, it was not going to happen, but Michelle was obviously lying all along. I think they always intended to come back here. They were lying to Ivette too. While we were in San Ignacio they took off to do some sort of deal. Drugs, I think. They probably just used me to finance their trip that far. Then, when they found out that I was a newspaper reporter in the article about Ann being killed, they dumped me in the jungle."

"That is supposed to reassure me?"

"Once they've finished their deal here I'm sure they'll take off north, if they haven't already gone."

"And will Teddy get drugged and dumped someplace like you did or worse?"

"I don't think they meant to kill me."

Sarah shook her head, "Sometimes I think your optimism verges on stupidity. So where is Teddy now?"

"I don't know. I left her at the dig. I don't even know if she is in town. If she is, I imagine she's with Michelle; otherwise she would have shown up here already. Don't worry. Teddy can take care of herself. She'll be back at the dig in a couple of days."

Sarah let Lynn know how she felt by the way she stuffed clothes into her bag.

Lynn lay back down on the bed and covered her eyes. Then she said quietly, "I might not see you again. I guess I might as well sit on the beach someplace."

Sarah shut her bag. Her voice was calmer now. "Just let me know when your flight is leaving. I'll come down and see you off."

Lynn didn't say anything. She still felt she had failed Sarah...and Ann. She was no nearer to understanding what had really happened to Ann or whoever she really was. If Ann had a brother so high up in the US military that he could get her out of the country, why had Ann or Anna had to hide out in Central America. Had she been hiding from him? And who was the mysterious woman who had claimed to be her sister?

# Chapter 17

Del sent her more information. Anna LaPlace had a Canadian passport under the name Anna Marie LaPlace and a green card under the name Ann Marie Wilcox because she had married a US citizen who had subsequently divorced her. She had gone to a drug rehab center after the drug trial where she was a witness and met one Ann Louise Wilson. A nurse at the rehab center had remarked that they had looked enough alike to confuse people there. And they had spent a lot of time together. Anna LaPlace or Anna Wilcox had a record. Heroin addiction with a history of petty crime. The court had helped her get in the rehab center. Del couldn't trace Anna LaPlace after she left the center. That could be because she was in a protection program. They had an address that was apparently her mother's, but they told Del when she called that the mother didn't live there anymore. Maybe Anna's mother got a new identity too because of the court case.

Ann Louise Wilson apparently had no criminal record. She had voluntarily entered the rehab center. There was no record of her whereabouts after leaving the center.

Lynn called Del, who said, "I don't find any official record of the death of either Ann Wilson or Anna LaPlace. Of course the information might not have gotten into the system yet."

"That doesn't seem likely unless the military is covering up. Maybe her brother pulled strings to keep it quiet. Maybe because Anna was not the woman who was killed, and is still be hiding out, possibly under another assumed name."

"But your DEA guy said they had identified the dead woman as Anna LaPlace," Del said rather impatiently.

"And the Canadians say she wasn't."

"The DEA has the means to make a positive ID. I can't think how they could make a mistake like that."

"Maybe Anna LaPlace took or traded for Ann Wilson's passport. Then the woman the Canadian's were traveling with was Ann Wilson traveling under Anna LaPlace's passport. Maybe the real Ann Wilson—"

Del practically shouted into Lynn's ear. "Wait— " When Lynn had stopped talking Del said patiently. "Lets see what we have here. Your Canadians say the woman who died was not Anna LaPlace. Your DEA guy, Grant says she was. A photo is the only way I know how to establish her identity from here seeing as how I can't get access to the body or the DEA files. Fax copies of photos aren't good enough. Did you mail me a photo yet of the woman who was at your archaeological dig?"

"I still don't have a picture except the one in the paper of the two of us, and its not good enough. I'll have to get one from the police or someone at the dig. I'll get it to you as soon as I can."

There was silence on the other end of the line for a long minute. Then Del said, "Why don't you just go to the beach like you planned to. This will sort itself out."

"Didn't they have pictures of Ann Wilson or Anna LaPlace at the Rehab center?"

"Curiously no. They usually do have them on record but in this case they were missing. And, as I said, I couldn't find any trace of Ann Wilson after she left there. Unfortunately the clinic had no forwarding address for her either. Of course she was there voluntarily, just a patient. I'd guess from what the nurse said, she took some sort of overdose, possibly a suicide attempt. It's common enough. There was no indication in her file that she was addicted to heroin. She was a bit overweight when she came in. Her treatment seemed to be mostly psychological—for depression. Also, strangely, the rehab center had no record of a social security number for her. Ann Louise Wilson has no criminal record that I can find. Both could be under a married name. That happens fairly often."

"At least I know for sure there were two people, Ann and Anna. Now all I have to figure out is which one of them was killed."

"That shouldn't be hard once you get me a picture. Your DEA guy was sure it was LaPlace. He isn't likely to be mistaken."

"If he wasn't lying."

"Lynn you see conspiracies everywhere. Go to the beach. Now!"

"Thanks, Del. I'm sure you think being drugged and getting dumped into the woods— "

"A very bad joke, or punishment for sticking your nose—?"

"I will send a picture."

Del sighed. "Sure hon. Now go out there on that beach and have a good time, or... I can't think of anything to threaten you with." She laughed.

"How about no more steak dinners?"

"Doesn't quite do it."

After Del hung up Lynn tried sorting through the information she had so far. Maybe Anna LaPlace did take Ann's place at the dig. Maybe that was why she made such an effort to avoid Sarah's brother Bobby while she was there. Maybe Ann traded places to help her friend who was being threatened by the criminals she had testified against...and it hadn't worked. Sarah had said she hadn't actually met Ann before she showed up in Belize. So where was the real Ann Wilson now?

# Chapter 18

Lynn called Sarah's biologist friend; she wanted more snake details. She needed that for her article anyway. She went out to his 'research center,' a small wooden house on posts like many Belize houses in the middle of what once had been a small farm. He showed her his collection of snakes—kept in quarters that made his house look shabby. As Sarah had warned her he immediately began giving her more information than she could possibly remember.

After giving her the latin name of the snakes that she could see behind mesh screen of the cages he said, "Most snakes are shy and rather delicate. They don't deserve their bad reputation. That one over there. That's like the one that bit your friend. The eyelash viper, Bothrops or Bothriechis schlegeli, possess raised spinelike scales over their eyes, supraocular scales. It gives the eye a hooded appearance." He looked at the snake affectionately and continued, "Most vipers are heavy bodied and terrestrial; however, some have become adapted to life in the trees and are multicolored, polychromatism a unique feature, some are blue and gold as well as rust and gray—with prehensile tails like this one."

He leaned closer to the snake. "As you can see if you look closer, a small pit in front and just below the eye. It's a heat sensing organ that'll allows them to hunt and strike with great accuracy even in total darkness."

"Are they very dangerous?"

He laughed and shook his head. "They won't come after you, if that's what you mean. But they do have movable front fangs. The fangs fold back into the mouth until they are ready to use them. It's what makes these snakes dangerous to work with. They can grab on to your hand like a cobra would, but they can also open their mouth almost 180 degrees with the fangs extended straight out. They can strike at any portion of your body; it's more of a stab than a bite."

Lynn looked closer. The small snake was almost invisible against the branch and behind some green foliage in its cage. "They said Ann died of a combination of narcotics and venom. Do you think that's possible once she got the antivenin?"

"Venom is modified saliva. It's primary function is to capture and kill the prey and it also helps to digest. Some venoms are referred to as hematoxic which means that they primarily affect the blood. Almost all American pit vipers fall into that category. A hematoxic venom destroys tissue and is very painful but most people don't die. I haven't read of any cases where narcotics were involved."

Interesting information but not much help. "Could the snake have survived in Ann's baggage for a time?"

The man nodded. "If it was in your camp it might very well crawl into something like a knapsack—a quiet dark shelter. Snakes are more fragile than people think. Even if someone had picked up the pack the snake might have been all right if it wasn't knocked about too much and kept cool with enough air. The snake I looked at had definitely had been dead a while when I got it. But it didn't die violently. She could have smothered it in her bag after she was bitten, I suppose."

"According to the police and the doctor at the hospital there was venom in her drugs. It was probably the combination she died from."

The man sighed and shook his head. "It was a fine specimen. Too bad she killed it. It would have been a nice addition to my collection."

Lynn could see that he had more sympathy for the snake as a victim of human evil than for a dead drug addict.

She thanked him for his help and promised to mention his work in her article and started back to town.

What were the possibilities? If someone had planted the snake as well as putting venom in the drugs, they might very well have expected her to die at Sarah's camp, not out in the bush. Did someone really want to kill her or was it a plot to incriminate Sarah and stop her project? Ed Kelly would want to get Sarah in trouble. He had ambitions to take over the property, but would he go to that length? He had had the opportunity to get into Ann's tent, but so did everyone else. Maybe there was some other reason that Ed had wanted to kill Ann-Anna. Lynn remembered the day he visited the site. It had looked like Ann was afraid of him; she had certainly been trying to avoid him. Or was he involved with the crooks that were after Anna and had acted as their agent?

Phyllis was not in her office, but Lynn learned from another officer that the Canadians had not yet crossed a border. He took the information Lynn had gotten from Del but was noncommittal. He claimed that there were no pictures in the files. That they must have been returned when the case was closed.

"The case was closed?"

"There wasn't sufficient evidence to pursue it as a criminal case. Her family...her brother agreed it appeared to be self-inflicted. Officially the woman died after she left Belize; your government has taken over the case. It may be that the photos went to the appropriate office there along with other evidence."

"So the photo of Ann and me in the papers came from here?"

He shook his head and smiled in a patronizing way. "Why would we do that?"

As she left the office, Lynn remembered Bobby's comment about Ann's suicide attempts. Would she have bought the snake herself? Teddy had known her best at camp. She was certainly hostile to some people, but suicidal? Her anger had seemed to be on the surface. Lynn had suspected it of being an act, a cover-up. Still the woman that Bobby had described did not match the Ann she had known. And Bobby had not visited Ann in the hospital in Belize or seen her at the archeological camp. Maybe the woman who died was not the one he knew either. If she could just find a decent picture of Ann.

The next day Lynn went to confront Mr. DEA Grant. He was in the middle of an air conditioned office with several computers, all of them on. He leaned back in his chair and stretched. "As far as we are concerned the case is closed. She is where she belongs with her family now." He smiled at her. "Nobody is being charged. You can relax and go home."

"But I have evidence that the woman who died might not be Anna LaPlace. The Canadians I was traveling with said that the Ann in the newspaper photo was not the woman they knew. BG said that the woman traveling with them had a passport under the name Anna LaPlace."

"Well he was mistaken...or lying."

"It's true they acted like people who had something to hide. BG got real pissed off when he found out I work for a newspaper. They gave me some sort of drug and dumped me in the jungle."

He smiled slowly, amused. "I'm sorry you had a bad experience, but all I can say is you should leave the detective work to professionals. Inspector Thompson did tell me about your Canadians. We are interested in their activities and will follow up on your information about them. But they were mistaken about...the woman who died. We identified her by more than a bad photo. There are medical and police records after all."

She told him about Del's research. That there was an Ann Wilson and that Ann and Anna had been friends at the rehab center in the States.

He listened patiently but he didn't seem particularly surprised or interested. He sat back in his chair and put his hands behind his head. "You know, a lot of women look alike to me. But you certainly have done your homework. It could be Anna borrowed the identity of an old friend. After all she was hiding out. She had refused our help. In fact, her brother identified her even before we got her to the States."

"Was it you who gave that photo of Ann and me to the papers?"

He shook his head. "Why would I do a stupid thing like that? How would that help an investigation. At that time the police thought it might be murder. If they happened to be drug dealers, that would sabotage any chance I might have of catching them."

"And have you made any progress in that investigation?"

He patted her hand condescendingly. "Now sweetheart, you know I can't tell you anything about that."

"So you are telling me that the woman who died was Anna LaPlace. Then who was traveling with the Canadians with Anna LaPlace's passport?"

He shrugged. "I don't know who your Canadians might have

been traveling with, but Anna LaPlace was at your camp under the alias Ann Wilson." He shrugged. "Maybe there is a real Ann Wilson and, like you said, Anna looked enough like her to pass. Let me throw out this scenario. Maybe Anna stole Ann Wilson's passport in order to have a new identity. It would make sense considering who might be looking for her. Or maybe after they left the rehab center they traded passports."

"Her brother's name is LaPlace? Sarah thought it was Wilson."

Grant didn't respond.

"So where is the real Ann Wilson? If we could find her, maybe she could shed some light on—"

"I haven't time to waste searching for look-alikes."

"Where is Ann Wilson's passport. I would like to see the picture on it."

"I've no idea. All personal effects were returned to the family when the case was closed. If Ann Wilson does exist she'll just have to apply for a new passport. I'm more interested in your Canadians—in what they might be trying to deal. we've been following their activities for a while."

"They were on their way to Guatemala when they dumped me."

"They haven't crossed any borders...yet."

"Ivette said they changed their plans after meeting some guys in San Ignacio—some sort of drug deal back here in the City."

"So the last thing they needed was a newspaper reporter for a passenger—and witness, and dumped you. You should really confine your research to the news wire, the telephone, the library, and the TV." Grant couldn't help smiling at his bit of vindictive humor. It was clear he was ready to see the last of her. "Are you sure they didn't go to Guatemala because you told them the police have plans to stop them at the border?"

"I certainly wouldn't have told them that."

"You don't know what you might have said when you were drugged."

Lynn flushed. She didn't like being out of control. To think she might have said or done something without being able to remember it...

Grant turned to his computer. After a few minutes he said to her, "You're right, they have been back in the City. The police stopped them today for illegal parking and checked the bus and their papers. There were only two of them, though—Henry J Burling and a Michelle Arneau."

"You have access to Belize police records?

"Not directly of course, but they are very cooperative about sharing information."

"So, the police didn't decide to hold them?"

"What for? Unfortunately there was nothing illegal in the bus. The bus was not stolen; they had some possessions of a Miss Ivette Devereau. Said she was traveling with them. We had already established that your Canadians where still in Honduras when Anna went out in the kayak."

"I could have told you that. So what did you find out about them?"

Grant frowned. He had clearly quit trying to be charming. He growled. "I can't give out that kind of information especially to the press."

"Oh come on. I may know something about their activities you might be interested in."

He took a minute to decide, tapping impatiently on a file on his desk. Then he pulled out some computer printouts from a stack. "Henry J Burling has a US passport. Some arrests on possession over the years from the sixties on. Hasn't spent much time in jail—a small-time dealer. But maybe he's ready for the big time now. We'll be watching him. The woman, Michelle Arneau, didn't show up on the records. Do you think they have other names they work under? Any ideas?"

"It's too bad you aren't interested in asking him who it was hired him to drug me and dump me in the jungle. If you're right that it was because I was snooping, it might have been the drug dealers you are looking for."

He didn't say anything just stared at her for a long moment. Then he said "Ok, what have you got."

"BG and Michelle met up with three guys in San Ignacio. Ed Kelly and two potential business partners, somebody named Carlos and another named Renaldo, Renaldo Schmidt."

Grant typed the names into his computer.

"Ivette Devereau doesn't show up either. No arrests."

"I really don't think Ivette or Michelle—"

"—Have been caught," he finished for her. I'll check out those other two. What's Carlos' other name?"

Lynn thought for a minute, "Garcia I think. He was from El Salvador. Schmidt was Spanish-speaking, but partly German."

"Did you say where Devereau is staying?"

"I...I'm not exactly sure. She isn't a drug dealer. She was just traveling with BG and Michelle."

Grant smiled. "I think you have been taken for a ride in more ways than—"

Lynn changed the subject. "What do you know about Robert Donovan. He's Sarah's stepbrother. He knew Anna—introduced her to the drug dealers she testified against. I think—"

"He's clean. Of course he was the first one we checked out when we found out his connection to her. Don't you think its time to let go of this one. After all the case is closed."

"I know somehow you got the local police to turn the case over to you, but the evidence—"

"The evidence points to self-inflicted. The local judge agreed with us. We checked thoroughly into her past. She was a drug addict with a history of dramatic suicide attempts... This time she succeeded."

"But we found tracks, the place had been trashed. Why snake venom? It doesn't make any sense. What about the people who she testified against? What about the hidden money?"

"You have been doing your homework. They're in jail thanks in part to her testimony. We have evidence that she was the one who bought the snake. Inspector Thompson found that out."

"She couldn't have bought it. She never left camp...until she took the kayak out. The people she testified against have friends probably even here in Belize. Like you said, she had reason to be afraid...if she was Anna LaPlace."

He stood up and smiled, his charming official self again. "We appreciate your concern and your efforts, but, frankly, why don't you enjoy your vacation and leave this kind of work to us? After all your friend Sarah has been exonerated. We appreciate your information. Please let us know if anything else—"

"What about kidnapping and attempted murder?"

"I'm sorry about your ordeal in the jungle, but frankly it wasn't very wise of you to be traveling with such questionable characters. You were traveling with them voluntarily. I'm sure Henry Burling wasn't trying to kill you. It seems to me now more like a rather crude joke. A little risky, but not meant to be fatal. A message that you ought to mind your own business perhaps? I'm afraid I rather agree with him."

He walked to the door and opened it pointedly. "If you do get in touch with Miss...Devereau please let her know we would like to have a word with her." He smiled dismissively.

# Chapter 19

Lynn went back to her hotel room and sat staring at her worn nearly white chenille bedspread. The knots of white cotton made a pleasing pattern though some were almost gone. She could imagine its symmetrical beauty when new.

Life didn't have that symmetry but there was a pattern. A flow of events and consequences that could be traced and unwoven.

Names were knots in the pattern. Ways to trace the pattern of the weaving. She suddenly felt profoundly sad. Did a name really matter? Did it matter that the woman who died was not Ann Louise Wilson, but Ann Wilcox, alias Anna Marie LaPlace as Grant claimed? A woman was dead, and Lynn wasn't satisfied with the explanations. Somebody *was* responsible for Ann's death.

And why had Grant made such an effort to get the case closed? Were they covering something up? Why? She didn't get Grant's agenda, and she certainly didn't trust it. Somehow he had gotten Phyllis and the Belize police off the case. What information had he given them that he hadn't told Lynn? She needed to talk to Phyllis Thompson. What kind of pressure had she gotten from Grant and why?

She had several days before she was to fly home and somehow didn't feel like spending them with Sarah at the dig. She was glad Sarah was no longer under suspicion, but... Anyway Sarah had made it clear that she really would prefer not to have Lynn there.

Might as well do some research for the article Gayle wanted her to write. She certainly wasn't going to be put off by Grant, or BG for that matter.

And Sarah had not even seen the mysterious military brother. There might well be more than one officer in the US military by the name LaPlace—or would it be Wilson? Or maybe it was a brother-in-law. Who could she ask. She didn't trust Grant to tell her the truth and the only other relative that had shown up was Naomi, the woman in the hospital who had said she was Ann's sister.

If Naomi was a relative why hadn't she been at the memorial? Maybe she should ask Del to follow up on her. Naomi LaPlace, or Naomi Wilson. Or maybe she was Naomi Wilcox an ex-sister-in-law. She should have asked. She hadn't noticed a wedding ring. Even if Naomi wasn't lying about who she was, it would be hard enough finding her

She pulled out the fax that Del had sent her with the picture of Anna. It had the stark black and white flatness of an image too often reproduced. A bad reproduction of a pretty dark haired woman. It could be Ann or a dozen other women she knew. Lynn sighed.

She still needed to get a photo for Del so she could confirm the identity of the dead woman. She would call the village near the dig—have someone radio to Jacob to leave a message for Kathy. Somebody there must still have a picture. If Grant or Phyllis hadn't gotten them all.

How could Ann have been the one who bought the snake? After all she had not left camp any time in the week Lynn had been there. She wouldn't even go in to town on the food runs.

When Lynn called Phyllis' office they said she had gone out of town. When she called her home number Phyllis' mother said that the family had gone out to their house on one of the keys for a rest, they would be back in a week and there was no phone on the island. It looked like Phyllis had accepted that the case was closed or she wouldn't have left town.

Back in the hotel Lynn wrote up her notes and just as she was dozing off the phone rang.

It was Teddy. "Can I come up?"

"Of course. But Sarah has already left, if you need a ride back to the dig."

"I know. I waited till after she left to call. I'm not ready to go back."

Lynn could see when she opened the door to her room that Teddy had been crying. She knew about the intensity of those first relationships. It would do no good to tell her that one did recover and life went on. In a way Lynn almost envied her the simplicity. So much easier to be totally in love and all poetic and sentimental.

Teddy clutched the little book Ann had given her in one hand and a backpack in the other as she came in the room and lay down on Sarah's bed. "Sarah knows doesn't she? About Michelle?"

Lynn nodded.

"I don't know if I can ever go back."

"Of course you can. Sarah will understand."

"I know you think I am weird going with Michelle after...what happened to Ann."

Lynn shook her head. "It's not that unusual a response to the death of someone you care about—to do something life affirming right away. It happened to me when my mother died. Instead of grieving, I fell desperately in love for a month. Then I realized why. It's being desperate to hang on to life. I think it's an affirmation that my mother's life meant something. And Michelle was safe; you knew she meant it to be just a flirtation. She's disappeared already hasn't she?"

Teddy snorted through her tears. "That does sound very wise. You think I'm smarter than I am. I didn't think I liked her because she was going to leave. She never told me she was just flirting."

"She never told you anything, did she?"

Teddy shook her head slowly.

"Best thing is to go back to work and forget about her."

Teddy's voice was very light, wistful. She fingered a new leather backpack—a present? "Michelle said to come to Montreal. She said to meet her there in September. You think she didn't mean it?"

"Did she leave you an address?"

Teddy voice was petulant, defensive now. "No. She didn't know where she was going to be living. I gave her my parents' address and phone number. She doesn't have an apartment right now. She said she would call when she gets settled again. You don't think she will call do you?"

Lynn shook her head.

"You think she won't even write."

"Don't hold your breath."

Teddy slowly put the book into her pack, then lay back staring at the ceiling. She covered her eyes and shook her head. "I don't understand getting so involved with somebody new that I don't even know."

Lynn sat down on the bed across from her trying to think of something to say that might help.

Teddy curled up. "I know; I'll get over it. It's just that, well, Ann died and I felt so bad. Even though we weren't lovers you know, I really cared about her. Ann was nice to me even though she was rude to other people. I think she was just shy, defensive, you know."

"Don't torture yourself. We all do things we don't understand. Getting involved with Michelle was easy. She is smart, beautiful, and seductive. She got to you by being sympathetic about Ann. She's obviously good at getting her way."

Teddy's tone was resentful. "I know you don't like Michelle. Just because she isn't femmy and talky like Ivette…"

"Do you believe Ann was Anna LaPlace?"

"What difference does it make what names she used?"

"Knowing who it was that died is a beginning for finding out who might have killed her, why she died. Maybe Ann was killed by mistake. Maybe somebody thought she was Anna LaPlace. BG faxed the Annie they knew at the dig. He thought she was there."

"Somebody—was it you?—gave a picture of me with Ann at the dig to the newspapers and Michelle and BG saw it. That's how they found out I'm a newspaper reporter."

"How did that picture get into the paper? I gave it to the police."

Lynn shrugged; then she asked, "Do you still have a picture of Ann?"

Teddy nodded and took her wallet out of a pocket. "That DEA guy tried to get all my photos, but I didn't tell him about this one." She pulled out a small photo of Ann in front of her tent, her face in the sunlight.

Lynn reached for the photo. "I need to send this off to my friend Del back home so I can confirm who Ann really was."

Teddy held it against her body possessively. "This is all I have left."

Lynn tried to reassure her. "If the police still have your pictures, I promise I'll get them back to you. There should be no problem, the case on Ann is about to be closed. The DEA guy has convinced the Belize police that it was suicide."

Teddy handed the photo over reluctantly. She stared at Lynn for a long moment. "Ann wouldn't do that. She was so positive about finally getting control of her life."

Lynn told Teddy about being left in the jungle. "Michelle was as mad as BG when she found out I'm a newspaper reporter."

"I don't believe Michelle would pull such a mean trick. Why would she care?"

"I think I heard her talking to BG about leaving me just before I heard the bus drive off. To her credit she argued with him, but that's all she did. Ivette says they've been dealing in mushrooms and other illegal substances for petty cash."

"You said you were drugged and you don't know who carried you into the jungle. I'll bet Michelle didn't have anything to do with it. She told me you had gone off by yourself, abandoned them so that's why they came back to Belize City. They didn't have enough money to travel without you."

"And Ivette?"

"Michelle didn't mention Ivette. I assumed Ivette was hanging out with BG."

"I haven't heard that Michelle called in to see if I was still alive."

"BG must have lied about you to Michelle."

"She and BG are on their way to Mexico now?"

"She has to get back to her job in Canada."

"Did you show her the picture of Ann?"

Teddy looked away sadly. "No, But she told me she had a crush on Ann too. How bad she felt that she was gone. How beautiful she had been. That's what Michelle and I have in common."

"You know when BG and Michelle saw Ann's picture in the paper, they said that Ann was not Anna LaPlace, the woman that they had traveled with. So Michelle never knew Ann."

There was a shocked, angry look in Teddy's eyes now. She whispered, "Maybe she was kidding you. She talked to me about Ann. I— You're telling me Michelle lied to me deliberately."

Lynn nodded. "Or to me. Or, to be charitable to Michelle, you thought you were talking about the same woman. I asked my policewoman friend, Del, back home, to check it out and she found out that Ann Wilson and Anna LaPlace really were two different people who happened to know each other back in the States. One of them was the Ann we knew and the other apparently traveled with Michelle.

The police claim it was Anna LaPlace who died. I can't figure out why the two would have switched identities. And where is the other one now?"

Teddy curled up on Sarah's bed with her face to the wall. Her little girl voice was squeaky. "Don't say any more right now... please."

Lynn stretched out on the other bed suddenly exhausted. She should send the photo to Del. Another dead end. Maybe Sarah was right. It was time to take a break. Sit on the beach. Her mind automatically brought up a picture of Ivette, golden tan and all. Oh well.

Teddy said, "You know what makes me the angriest?"

Lynn was too tired even to respond.

"It's the way everybody lied about Ann."

Lynn was suddenly wide awake. "What do you mean?"

"I told that DEA guy and the police that Ann wasn't taking drugs; she was off them. The needle marks were because of her insulin shots, for diabetes. But they wouldn't believe it. I don't get why they wouldn't pay attention to that."

Lynn sat up. Why hadn't DEA or the doctor mentioned that to anyone. She would have to get Del to check on that one too. Of course venom could easily be put into a container of insulin. "Maybe she was lying to you about the insulin to cover her drug habit."

Teddy shook her head. "It was why she was so irritable. Why she tried so hard. She didn't want anybody to know." She lay flat staring at the ceiling and whispered, "I should have gone out with you when you went after her. Sarah didn't know. Maybe that's why she died; the doctors didn't know either. I told the DEA guy but he said what you did just now—that Ann lied to me about it to cover her drug habit. I believed him for a while."

"The doctors would have picked that up I think. Dr. Alvarez didn't say anything about it to Sarah or me at the hospital." Lynn leaned nearer. "It isn't your fault she died, Teddy."

"But what if she was just in insulin shock and Sarah gave her the antivenin. And she hadn't been bitten by a snake, and—"

"If she was in insulin shock it was a deliberate choice. She was responsible for taking care of herself."

But someone could have tampered with insulin—put venom and heroin in an insulin container. Del hadn't mentioned that the rehab records said that either Anna LaPlace or Ann Wilson were diabetic.

But she hadn't asked Del to look for that. Lynn tried to remember if she had seen anything out at Ann's campsite or in her tent at the dig that might have looked like insulin. It came in small containers didn't it?—and there would have to have been disposable needles. They had been so worried about Ann that they hadn't looked that carefully around her camp. Of course the police would have collected any such evidence, unless... But why would the police or Grant have lied about that? They had said she was on drugs. Of course both could be true; she could have been taking drugs too.

Lynn left Teddy in her room and went to mail the photo to Del along with some more questions. She wanted to find out more about Bobby. She didn't trust Grant's information. Had Bobby been involved with the drug dealers that Anna had testified against? And what about the diabetes?

Then she went to find the doctor who had taken care of Ann.

# Chapter 20

Dr Alvarez was a very busy woman. She agreed to talk to Lynn between patients while she ate a perfunctory lunch in her office.

"Well of course insulin is a drug too. We did detect the diabetes right away. But there was no evidence that it was not controlled.

"That would not necessarily have made her more susceptible to the venom. But I am surprised that she hadn't told Dr. Donovan about it. Sometimes people are ashamed, see it as a weakness—don't like it to be known. They feel it is an embarrassing handicap. But in any case she was not in insulin shock when she came in. There were traces of venom in her blood and heroin of course."

The woman frowned. "But she was not stable when she left here. I felt at the time that with the proper precautions she should not have died. I told that military doctor..." She sighed. "I told them they should leave her here till she was more stable. They were so convinced that they should rush her off on that military plane. She was a US citizen. There wasn't much I could do with a relative present ..."

"Relative?"

"Her brother, a Colonel LaPlace."

"I thought her name was Wilson."

"Mr. Grant must have explained to you that the name Wilson was just an alias. She had a false passport, I understand, under that name."

"So there was heroin in her blood. Was that what killed her?"

The Doctor frowned. "Of course we checked for drugs right away. With someone so young and the needle marks... Then we realized about the diabetes. The venom could have been in an insulin shot as well, although there was heroin in her blood. The venom in itself would not have killed her."

"And not much venom."

"The antivenin would have taken care of that. Although a diabetic has special vulnerabilities... She shook her head. "...not much is known...it's not my field of expertise."

"So you understood why they would want to take her to a more comprehensive hospital."

"We have few specialists either in toxins or diabetes. With under two hundred-thousand people in the whole country—"

"They are calling it self-inflicted—suicide."

The doctor looked up from her folder. "I suppose that is possible. One would have to know a bit more about her personal history. It does seem unlikely. Why bother to make it look as if she was bitten by a snake?"

"That was my thought too. Did you expect her to die if she was moved?"

The doctor got up from her chair. "I have patients to see. We did our best for her. I'm not an expert in diabetes or snake bites. I didn't see her after she left this hospital. As I said she was alive when I last saw her."

Back at her hotel Lynn took out a pad of paper to make notes. What did she know so far? Not much. What she did know just left her with a bunch of questions. She wrote them down.

Who *was* the woman who died? Hopefully Del would clear that one up with Teddy's photo.

Was she murdered as the Belize police first thought, or was Grant right that it was a bizarre suicide?

What if Ann had thought the amount of venom and heroin would not be fatal? Instead, like many suicide attempts, it had been a call for help? Ann knew Sarah would look for her, rescue her. Sarah almost had. Bobby had claimed that Ann had attempted suicide before. Had she been trying to get his attention back? Then why had she avoided him the whole time she was at the dig?

But why make it look like she had accidentally run into a snake? Maybe a misguided attempt to get the sympathy of Sarah and the people at the dig? Even if she had found a way to buy a snake, would she have gone to all that effort—bought the snake, faked the bite and injected herself with the venom along with her heroin? Ann had been hostile and withdrawn, but Teddy who had been closest to her didn't think she was that depressed.

But assuming she really had wanted to kill herself, then the lethal dose of heroin and venom made sense, though it seemed to Lynn it would have been easier to put herself into insulin shock.

Or did someone kill her after all?

Who had a motive?

Had it been Bobby who gave her the lethal dose? Where was he when Ann went out in the kayak? And why had Sarah never mentioned him. No one at the dig had while she was there. Did he have connections to the convicted drug dealers that Anna LaPlace had testified against in spite of what Grant had said?

Grant had been interested in BG and the Canadians. Maybe they were involved with the convicted drug dealers. Why had Lynn being a reporter worried them? Had BG dumped her in the jungle just to scare her off or had he really meant her to die because he thought she knew too much? Not a bad method. If she had died from a combination of drugs and exposure, the police might well have concluded she was just a stupid tourist out of control.

After BG dumped Lynn did the Canadians find the Anna they knew in Belize City or San Ignacio? Was that why they had had money to buy the bus? Was Anna sharing the missing drug money the dealers that she had testified against had hidden?

Ivette hadn't been with BG and Michelle when the police stopped them. Sarah had said Ivette had been angry that Lynn had left her in San Ignacio and had left a phone number. And Teddy had not seen Ivette with Michelle. Maybe that really meant she was no longer traveling with BG and Michelle. She wanted to find Ivette; she might have some answers.

She called the number Sarah had given her. An older woman answered. Probably a local woman from the way she spoke. Lynn asks for Ivette and the woman put down the phone. Lynn heard her speak with a child, but she couldn't quite hear what they were saying. Then after a minute Ivette came on the phone. Her, voice was subdued. A whispered, *"Qu'est que vous voulez?"*

"It's Lynn. Sarah said you called."

"Lynn! Why the hell did you run away like that? I—"

Lynn couldn't hide the injury and anger in her own voice. "Your buddies tried to poison me. I got dumped in the jungle. I think some

Mayans finally picked me up and carried me to a bus stop."

"You think?"

"I was seriously out of my mind. I thought I was a rain goddess or something. Somebody put a chicken feather cape on me. Some sort if sadistic joke. Unless it was all a hallucination."

Silence of the other end of the line. Then swearing in French and then, "I'm so sorry. I should have known. He does get jealous."

"Jealous of who? You? I didn't know you were sleeping with him."

Ivette said angrily. "That doesn't deserve a response."

After a minute Lynn said, "Anyway, it's hardly an excuse. I could have died."

"I said I was sorry. Anyway I didn't dump you. Why did you go away from the highway? You would have gotten a ride with the Brits or even a bus...eventually."

"I think somebody else came and carried me into the jungle... I wasn't exactly in my right mind so I'm still not sure. BG put something in my soup."

"Must have been those magic mushrooms Michelle got in Mexico."

"I think it was more than that. I couldn't even move for a long time. So are BG and Michelle here in Belize City too?"

"Took off...with my bus. We had a permanent fight when I found out you were gone. They told me you took off on your own. I thought they had chased you away somehow. I should have figured they were lying—that they had done something stupid. They said you wanted to travel on your own. I should have known you would have told me. I told them I didn't want to be around them any more."

"They have your bus?"

"Borrowed, with my Canadian passport in it."

"Did you report them to the police?"

"Not my style. I'll get it back—if they make it home."

Lynn took a chance. She wanted to catch Ivette off guard, even if it upset her just a little. She wanted to find out what Ivette really might know. "The police haven't reported them crossing over a border...yet."

"You reported them to the police?"

Lynn certainly didn't intend to tell Ivette she'd talked to Phyllis and the bus was going to be stopped at the border, whichever one that might be. "Ivette, I could have died. They dumped me, not to mention drugging me. Of course I called the police. If you report your bus stolen you might even get it back."

Lynn waited for a long moment then said, "Ivette, are you still there? Tell me where you are. I'll come over so we can talk this through.

Ivette gave her the address. It was the same guest house where she had found the Canadians originally. That made sense—she had liked them, she would go back there.

Lynn hurried over to the house where Ivette was staying. The little girl let her in when she knocked. Ivette was standing in the doorway of her room, while the little girl and her grandmother sat at the dining room table unapologetically looking on. Ivette's eyes were swollen and she needed to comb her hair. She smiled at her landlady and gestured abruptly for Lynn to come inside her room. Then she stood by the window looking through the white lace curtains "You shouldn't have gone to the police."

"If it hadn't been for the Mayans—"

"You said you weren't sure what happened. It was just BG. I know Michelle wouldn't have tried to hurt you. She even left me some money to travel on in exchange for the bus."

"I thought none of you had any money. Where'd they get money to give you?

"I told you they did a deal—mushrooms or something. I did wonder —it seemed like a lot."

"Where were they going."

"They said they were going to Mexico. I think they were lying."

"Teddy said they were going to Mexico too. She met Michelle here in Belize City."

There was a dead silence at the other end of the room for a moment, then Ivette said, "You mean Ms. Sincerity Babydyke out at the dig?"

"Remember...you told me they had a date. I didn't think Michelle meant to keep it. She met Teddy in the van, without BG. Dumping people seems to be a habit with her too," Lynn said dryly.

There was a sigh. "He probably waited around some place for her."

"What will you do now? You should at least report your passport gone. Teddy was with her today. Maybe they are still in town."

"I have another one, a French passport. My father was French. I grew up in Canada, but I never gave up my French citizenship though I can't speak much French. My Spanish is better."

"And those two know you have a French passport?"

"Of course. Michelle wouldn't leave me stranded. She said she couldn't be bothered letting me search the bus for my Canadian passport right then. She was in a hurry suddenly."

"Teddy's pretty upset about Michelle."

"Michelle really gets into that romantic stuff. Poetry and all that. She's not a bad sort, really. She won't treat Teddy mean. Those young ones always move on anyway. They grow up. You know."

"So where were they really going after they left Belize City?"

"I think telling me they were going to Mexico was just to throw me off. Michelle talked a lot about Flores in Guatemala. She was originally going to go there with Annie. She seemed really happy. It pissed me off, she didn't really care that I was mad at her. I think she figured out where Annie is."

"Michelle and Anna were lovers?" Lynn asked.

"Sure. Why not?"

"Michelle didn't seem all that broken up when I told her Ann was dead. Maybe she already knew it wasn't Anna."

"Michelle wouldn't let you see how she felt. You were a stranger then. She's an expert at not showing her feelings. You have to know her for a while."

Lynn was convinced Ivette knew more, but wasn't telling. "So maybe they got the money they gave you from Anna."

"They *said* they did a deal, sold mushrooms and stuff. They *said* that's why they had to come back to Belize City—"

"How much money did they leave you?"

Ivette hesitated a moment, then she said, "Michelle gave me quite a bit actually—in dollars too. Enough to travel more on my own, get back to Canada."

"They must have sold a hell of a lot of mushrooms."

Ivette came over to her then and put an arm around her. "I'm sorry, Lynn. It's my fault. I should never have insisted on staying in San Ignacio. I'll make it up to you. Look, they're gone. Let's forget about them. We can have a good time; you've got a couple of days left. Let's take the plane to Tikal or go out to the islands, to Ambergris for the beach and snorkeling. To hell with BG and Michelle."

Lynn took a deep breath. Ivette was probably right. She shouldn't let BG ruin her vacation. And if the police and the DEA said the case was closed, why bother to pursue it?

# Chapter 21

Lynn and Ivette took a boat out to a quiet little island, and found a place to stay in a small hotel on the beach. It was evening by the time they sat down on the deserted beach near their room with drinks and contemplated the sunset. Ivette had bought a bag of limes and borrowed Lynn's pocket knife to cut herself a slice.

Lynn had to ask. "You miss Michelle?"

Ivette smile. "Lynn, I like Michelle but we were never lovers. She's not my type. Too angry. Somehow somebody has to be punished for the way the world treated her mother...and her. And nothing is ever enough. If she ate steak it had to be fillet mignon. She is always looking for the perfect lover. If anyone likes her that makes them imperfect."

"What is your type?"

Ivette squeezed lime juice into her seltzer and put a neat slice expertly on the rim of the glass. "We were poor too; my father drank too much, my mother yelled too much, but she always somehow made it all OK. Like this."

She cut another slice of lime and moved closer to Lynn, "You may only have a glass of water but with this you have a little elegance." She squeezed a little juice into the liquid and put the lime on Lynn's glass. "And it matters. She might have only a small piece of meat and a little wine but she could make a wonderful meal with it. Such a sauce." She kissed the tips of her fingers in a very French way and touched them softly to Lynn's lips. "Michelle doesn't understand this. I think you do."

Ivette took another slice of lime and reached inside Lynn's shirt touching the tip of each breast with the cool liquid. "And she taught me sometimes less is more." She touched Lynn's lips very very softly with her own and Lynn felt herself begin to melt. Yes, much much more.

When Lynn got back to her hotel there was a fax from Del. There had been no record at the rehab center of Ann Wilson or Anna LaPlace having diabetes. Neither Robert Donovan nor Ann Wilson had police records that Del could find. The woman in the photo was not Anna LaPlace. But so far she had not found an Ann Wilson that resembled the photo.

So if the Ann that died was not Anna LaPlace why had Grant claimed she was? Let the police deal with it. She sent Phyllis a copy of the fax and put the information in the file folder with her notes. Come hell or high water she was going to have a good time. She would finish the article for Gayle later.

Ivette was toying with her food. They were in the hotel dining room and bar.

A couple of drinks appeared at their table. The waiter pointed to a corner table where Ed Kelly was sitting alone. It was a local restaurant—not where she expected to find him. He was more the fancy resort-hotel type. Lynn wanted to refuse the drinks, but not Ivette. While they were arguing, he came over and sat down casually at their table without an invitation. He was leaner with a few days growth of beard. His designer silk shirt was grubby and he smelled of beer. He leaned toward them. "How was the trip to Tikal, ladies?"

Lynn said, "We never made it. ...San Ignacio was a bit too much for us."

Ivette smiled. "We're flying to Tikal tomorrow."

He smiled at Ivette and patted her hand. "Pretty amazing those ruins. But you know they say there are some here just as grand, still buried."

Lynn asked, "Where's your wife, Ed?"

He laughed and took a swig of his beer. "She went on home, back to Texas. Couldn't take the place, said it stunk." He took a handful of peanuts and chewed them slowly looking at Ivette. "Says she's divorcing me. Been a long time coming. Didn't fancy living permanent-like in this country."

"And you do? I thought you and your business partners were buying land for investment."

"I'm official now. Got my citizen papers. And a landowner."

142

Lynn tried to sound casual. "Jacob and Emma finally sell you their ranch?"

Ed laughed. "Hah. What do I need that puny piece of dirt for? Stubborn old man. Should have grabbed his chance. I got bigger things on my mind now." He sat up straighter. She could almost see him mentally sticking his chest out. He looked around for a moment then whispered, conspiratorially. "If it all works out my new corporation could own half of Belize."

There was an interested look in Ivette's eye that bothered Lynn.

"Sold the catamaran did you, now that you're...permanent here?" Lynn said dryly.

"No way. Now that the old lady is gone I can use it to...entertain." He gave Ivette a meaningful look. Then he laughed and glanced at Lynn. "...For entertaining business contacts of course."

"Marv still running it for you?"

"Sure. He's good with the motor. Got a sailing crew too and a cook." He glanced up. Someone caught his eye behind Lynn. "Got to go, girls, been nice talking to you. He put his hand on Ivette's arm. "Come for a sail, Sweetheart...when you get back. Both of you of course...I'll be back Wednesday. I'll take you out to islands nobody goes to."

Ivette turned to Lynn, excitement in her eyes. "I've never been on a catamaran."

Ed got up, his eyes still on Ivette his hand still on her arm. "I'll pick you up at one." He smiled meaningfully. Then he turned to Lynn. "At your hotel. Don't need to bring a thing."

How did he know where she were staying?

But Ivette nodded and he left before Lynn could open her mouth.

Ivette looked at her obviously surprised at her angry expression. "We'll be fine Lynn. Don't be such a party pooper..."

"He thinks you're interested. You led him on. You going to sleep with him?"

Ivette laughed. "I love you jealous. Don't worry; I can handle him. He is just an old teddy bear. Didn't you hear him? His old meany wife just dumped him. He deserves a little fun."

"Doesn't it bother you that he might be the one that killed Ann? How does he know where we are staying? He's been watching us."

Ivette stared at Lynn. "Annie's not dead. Michelle talked to her.

That other Ann, the one that died, I didn't know her. I thought you were through with all that. You said the woman killed herself. Why would Kelly kill anybody? He doesn't act like a murderer. If he did kill your Ann why is he still hanging around here?"

"Michelle talked to her? Why didn't you tell me?"

Ivette fiddled with her drink. "I don't want to get Michelle in trouble. She *is* a friend. And she had nothing to do with your Ann being killed. Anyway I didn't want you chasing off again after Michelle. I'm done with them."

Lynn grabbed her arm. "Where is Anna?"

"Why do you want to know?"

Lynn thought fast. "My boss wants an article. It's my job to follow up on new leads. Anna might know something about what happened here."

"I don't think I should tell you. You said you were going to give up on all that."

"Is that why Michelle took your passport? Because Anna is afraid to travel on the only passport she has—that of Anna LaPlace? Did she pay Michelle for your passport?"

Ivette pried Lynn's hand away. Her voice was tired. "I don't think so. Maybe she would give it to Anna. I don't know."

"Where is she?"

Ivette stared at her for a long moment and sighed. " She's working in a hotel. Michelle plans to meet her; I don't know when."

"Which hotel? What name is she going under?"

"How should I know. Somewhere in Guatemala. In Flores maybe. Leave it alone, Lynn. You're on vacation, remember. We're supposed to be having fun."

"I'm sorry but I think since we are going to Flores anyway we could just talk to her. Clear up a few things. She probably is somebody else altogether. But then I would know."

Ivette finally told her what hotel and the name she was using, Marie Wilcox.

The next day they flew to Flores and checked into that hotel. After a day of hiking around the ruins Lynn left Ivette resting in their room and went to talk to the desk clerk.

Fortunately, he spoke a little English. When she asked about

Marie Wilcox he said, "She works in the office. She is out at the moment. Would you like to leave a message?"

Shocked at her success she still had the presence of mind to say, "She's an old friend. It's a surprise. She doesn't know I'm here. Do you know where I can find her?"

At least he didn't sound suspicious. "She is probably taking a break in the back. She smokes there."

Lynn found her way down a dark walkway between two wooden buildings—workers residences for the hotel.

A slim woman with Ann's dark good looks, but a bit older and thinner stood in a doorway. Lynn was amazed at how much she looked like the Ann she had known. She said, "Marie?"

"Who the hell are you?"

Lynn held out her hand. "Lynn Evans."

Anna's stained fingers shook as she lifted the stub of an unfiltered cigarette to her lips. "What do you want? If it's a problem with your room you have to see the manager."

Lynn shook her head. "You were traveling with Michelle Arneau and Ivette Devereau—"

"How'd you know where to find me, anyway?"

"Ivette told me."

"You're lying. Ivette doesn't know where I am."

"Michelle hasn't been in touch with you? She told Ivette where you are."

The woman studied her carefully through squinted eyes "What's it to you anyway. What do you want with me?"

"You were a friend of a woman named Ann Wilson."

The woman shook her head, but she had a frightened look in her eyes. "Don't know her."

"My sources say you do. You were at a rehab center in the States. People there said how much you looked alike. They said that you looked so alike you could almost have been sisters."

"You a cop?"

It was Lynn's turn to shake her head. "You told Michelle and company that you would be at an archaeological dig on the Belize coast. They sent you a fax there. You never showed up."

"I don't know what you're talking about."

"A woman with Ann Wilson's passport died several days ago.

There was venom and heroin in her blood. The Belize police think she might have been murdered. I thought you might know why somebody would kill her."

Leaning over, not looking at Lynn, the woman took another puff. Her hand was steady now as if she was consciously controlling it but there was desperation in her voice. "You're lying—just trying to rile me. I know Ann's not dead. You can't pull that on me."

"You didn't see the photo in the paper?"

"I don't read the Belize papers."

"Didn't Michelle tell you about Ann's death when she called to arrange to meet up with you here?"

"What's it to you anyway? You must be a cop."

"No. I'm just somebody who doesn't like to have the people around them killed. The people who killed her thought she was you. Aren't you afraid they will find out that isn't so? After all it wasn't that hard for me to find you."

Anna's hand was shaking again. Her voice was harsh, angry. "So, assuming these guys are after me and know I'm not dead, what you going to do about it. You going to protect me?"

"Michelle is bringing you a new identity—right? So they won't find you?"

"I don't know any Michelle."

"Strange, I was traveling with her and she talked about you."

"She wouldn't."

"She thought you were dead. Then she saw a newspaper and knew it wasn't you that died. That's when she contacted you here."

The woman's face seemed to collapse inward. She bent her head and ground the cigarette butt into the dirt with the heel of her shoe as if she wished it was Lynn. "I've got to get back to work. I don't have time for this shit."

Lynn blocked her path. "Do you have a sister, Naomi. Or a brother, an officer in the US military?" Anna suddenly looked even more nervous, scared. She just shook her head.

"Naomi thought it was you that was in the hospital. She came to see you, but got there too late, she—"

Anna looked up and around suddenly, a hunted animal. "Why are you bothering me. I'm not the one that killed her. I liked her. We helped each other. I wouldn't hurt her."

"Then who would? Who might kill her?"

"I haven't the foggiest."

"Was it because she looked like you that Ann died? You have to admit it looks like a convenient way for you to disappear—everyone thinking you are dead."

"I didn't kill her. I never went anywhere near that dig."

"Then aren't you scared of whoever did kill her?"

Anna was silent. Lynn waited. She could see the glint of tears, reflections of a dim porch light as Anna lit another cigarette. "If I was running from somebody, how come I'm using my own name now?"

"Because you thought the guys you testified against would think Ann was you and be off your trail. So now it is safe and you can get the missing money and—"

Anna interrupted angrily. "If I had money do you think I would be working here in a fucking hotel under my own name? I don't know anything about any money. Stupid rumors those press guys started."

"But maybe somebody still thinks you do know. If they thought Ann was you—"

There were tears running down Anna's thin cheeks now. She dropped her cigarette and stamped on it. "He said he had a plan so they wouldn't find me, ever. I could live somewhere on a little island or something—somewhere safe and happy. You know—white sand beaches, palm trees, all the fresh fruit and all the booze you want. She laughed bitterly, "Like *Gilligan's Island.* I didn't know his plan meant Ann...maybe getting killed."

"Who?" Who had a plan?"

Anna wiped her face on her apron. "He shouldn't have done it."

So Anna knew who might have killed Ann. "Who shouldn't have?"

Anna looked up frowning now. "What you going to do with the information?"

Lynn decided to tell some of the truth. Anna might start regretting her decision before... Lynn needed her trust. "I'll give it to a Inspector Phyllis Thompson of the Belize police."

There was contempt in Anna's voice now. "She can't do anything; he's an American Citizen. If Ann is dead I want him locked up."

"People aren't usually allowed to kill each other. Even US citizens in a foreign country," Lynn said dryly.

"That's what you think."

"How about I tell the DEA—their agent Grant? Is the guy who killed Ann involved in the drug trade? Is that why was he was helping you hide out?"

Anna laughed. "I wouldn't put it past him. He was going to have me stay at that archeological camp too. Probably uses that step-sister of his for cover. Proud of himself for fooling her I bet. He said he just wanted to help. He sure fooled me."

"Bobby? Dr. Donovan's brother Bobby?"

"That's what *she* calls him. Nobody I know ever called him that."

"What do they call him?"

"Ann said his nickname was Skullhead, because he sometimes shaves his head."

Bobby was the one with the alias, B. Gerald Scully, Ann told Teddy about. "Skullhead likes to ride a Harley?"

Anna shrugged. "I don't know what kind of bike he rides. I got to get back to work. You got what you want. Skullhead's the one. Ann was scared shitless of him. That's why she left the States with me. Now you. You're trouble. You stay away from me." She turned to hurry off with Lynn right behind her.

"I don't get it. Bobby helped you. Why was Ann at his sisters site if she was so scared of him?" Lynn grabbed her arm before she went inside. "And the hidden drug money—is Bobby after it? Is that why you're hiding out here?"

Anna Marie looked around; there was nobody in the passageway between the buildings where they stood. She leaned against the wall. "You're set on getting yourself killed too I guess." Then she laughed. "I don't know about any money, but Bobby was pissed as hell when Ann dumped him. I don't know why she was stupid enough to hang out at that site. She wouldn't be the first to get back together with somebody like that. I sure as hell was going there."

"I though you were his girlfriend."

"Not my type. He helped us get out of the States. That's the only time I saw him. Then Ann took off with me."

"So you traveled with Ann?"

"Not for very long. It wasn't part of the plan. We were supposed to meet up again at that archeological site, but I never made it there."

"When are Michelle and BG coming to meet you? Have you seen them yet?"

Anna nervously stubbed her cigarette out on the stucco wall. "You know a hell of a lot for someone who just happened to have known Ann."

"Ivette is here with me. They took her van and she wants it back."

There was a scared little girl look in her eyes. "Who are you? I don't know shit about that. I wish the hell you'd all get off my back. I have enough troubles. Look, you got one woman dead. I'm sorry about that—I liked her—she wanted to help me. If you care about keeping people alive, just forget you saw me—understand?"

Lynn nodded. "I won't write anything, but—"

Anna pulled her arm away quickly and disappeared into the building turning the lock as she pulled the door shut.

Lynn's head was swimming. Poor Sarah with Bobby hanging around the dig to run his drug connection. Maybe he was one of those in the drug ring that didn't get caught. What a perfect cover Sarah made. But why kill Ann if Anna was the gang's target? Was it some sort of awful mistake?

Maybe it wasn't the gang after all. It was Bobby who killed Ann. But he didn't seem the jealous type, though one never knew. Lynn wanted to ask Anna more questions. She needed evidence before going back to Phyllis, not just hunches. What would link Bobby to the crime. Where was he when Ann died? Could he have been the one Ann was going to meet in the kayak, or did he send someone else to kill her?

She took a deep breath and headed back to their room. Evidence or not she should just go to Phyllis with all this and take Ivette to the beach.

But now Sarah was back at the dig with Bobby. Was he still running his drugs through the camp? She should ask some more questions maybe even go back to the dig. She should warn Sarah. Sarah would not believe her, but she had to try.

# Chapter 22

When she got back to Belize City, Lynn couldn't bring herself to call Sarah. She couldn't very well discuss Bobby being a drug dealer over the radio. She did put in a call to Phyllis Thompson but she still wasn't back. She thought about calling Grant but didn't trust him.

On the day they got back Ed Kelly showed up as scheduled to take them out on his catamaran. Lynn decided to try and ignore Kelly and enjoy the ride. Kelly was on his good behavior, shaved and in newly pressed designer silk shirt and jeans. When they climbed aboard Kelly took them for a tour of his boat. "I guess you've seen it before," he said to Lynn.

"Marv didn't give me the tour; he was too drunk to get up out of his chair."

Kelly smiled, the gracious host. "Now that's not quite fair to the man. He likes his beer but he's not an alcoholic."

They went into the main cabin. Ivette admired the Mayan art. She stood in front of a particularly impressive three-legged pot in the form of a Mayan god. "This must have cost you a fortune."

"A copy of one I got at home. My wife thought it would make the boat a bit more homey with some stuff. She never wanted to be on a boat in the first place, wanted to make it look like a house. We had to glue them down because of the motion of the boat. Wouldn't want to do that to the real thing. Besides the local authorities don't like it if you have the real thing. Might confiscate it for the museum they don't have yet."

"Speaking of that, how's your search for, what was it, the diamond skull going?" Lynn asked.

Ed shook his head, "You got that one wrong doll. What I saw was a crystal skull. Damn powerful too." He opened a drawer in the chest under the Mayan replica. In it were jade and stone artifacts. "Your buddy there is one of those skeptics," he said, addressing Ivette. "She thinks these are just cold stone. Doesn't understand how much power there is here. Those Mayan guys knew a lot of stuff, had powers the science types can't even imagine."

"Those copies too?" Lynn asked. Ed just smiled. Was Ed part of the illegal trade in Mayan artifacts? That might explain why he was so rich. "So how did you get rich Ed. Is this merchandise or just a hobby?"

He just looked at her and closed the drawer. "My daddy made lots of cash on Texas oil. I collect—for my own pleasure." He smiled at Ivette conspiratorially. "And what do you gals do for pleasure?"

Ivette had the good taste not to answer. She just blushed.

Satisfied with the effect of his comment Ed led them into another cabin. "This is for you gals for the day. Just help yourself to anything you need—towels, bathing suits, snorkeling equipment. If you want to dive we got all that too. Just let me know and I'll take you out to the deep stuff."

When they anchored the boat near a deserted and palm filled island with pristine, white sand beaches, Lynn noted another larger ocean going yacht anchored within swimming distance. Tourist on a day trip?

After a pleasant lunch served by one of the local crew members, they lounged on the deck drinking excellent coffee and talking about snorkeling to the beach.

Lynn was just thinking that Ed Kelly didn't seem to be a bad sort after all, the man who had served them lunch took off in the outboard toward the other yacht. Two men got in it and they came toward the catamaran.

Kelly said, apologetically. "I forgot to mention to you all that I got more guests this afternoon. You remember my business partners, Schmidt and Garcia? You met them in San Ignacio." He smiled at Lynn. "Carlos was the one that took a shine to you."

Ivette nodded. All Lynn could think was, shit, he planned this all along. But when they climbed aboard the two men seemed genuinely surprised to see them—and not pleased. Lynn and Ivette stayed in their lounge chairs while Ed went to greet them. Schmidt said something Lynn couldn't hear in answer to Ed's hearty Texas greeting that caused him to lead them off into the main cabin. After a while he came out and said, "I'm sorry ladies, I figured this might make a nice party, but my buddies here are in a bit of a hurry and want to talk business right off. You go ahead and do some snorkeling."

Something was wrong. Ed suddenly wasn't his confident boisterous self. He actually seemed nervous.

He disappeared into the cabin and Ivette and Lynn decided they would snorkel and swim to the beach.

There was nothing like floating along on the cradling waves watching swarms of yellow grunts pretending they were seaweed. A pair of French angels and a queen angel fish in royal blues, yellow and pink darted beneath her and they followed them—through a rocky chasm encrusted with fan coral and moss and soft coral. The corridor was just wide enough for them to swim without touching. Then they swam over white sand where a turtle grazed at a leisurely pace on sea grass and an octopus hid in the rocks staring at them with wide intelligent eyes.

They climbed out onto the hot white sand. Ivette's golden brown skin glowed under the shadow of dappled green of palm leaves moving in the warm tropical breeze. Lynn was aware only of soft lips and the rich red gold of flushed cheeks. They found a shady spot in the warm sand behind a screen of young palms, hidden from the boat's view and made love with the hot frenzy of new lovers caught in a moment out of time.

Ivette was peering through the palm leaves. "Ed's on deck with a pair of binoculars. We better signal that we didn't drown or he might leave us here."

"I'm not sure how much I would mind," Lynn said sleepily.

Ivette laughed. "You'd get hungry pretty quick. I don't fancy eating bugs or those pretty fish, if you could catch one." She pulled on her suit and went out on the beach to wave at him. Then she said, "We better go back."

Carlos and Renaldo were in lounge chairs on deck still drinking when they got out to the boat. They had clearly had more than enough. Ed said, a bit too cheerfully, "We were wondering if you drowned."

Lynn answered, "Sorry not a chance. We enjoyed the swim

though—thanks. It is a great…snorkeling spot."

Carlos got up, sacrificing his chair and smiled at Lynn. "We have brought our…negotiations to a happy conclusion…so now we can enjoy your charming company."

Renaldo took another gulp of his drink and rattled his ice cubes, staring rudely at Ivette's body. Ivette returned his stare as she marched off silently to their cabin to shower and get dressed.

Lynn wrapped her towel around her and accepted the lounge chair. Ed gave her a drink and she asked. "So what is it your corporation is setting out to do?"

The three men stared at her. Carlos finally said, rather apologetically, "We have bought up a large parcel of land in the mountains. An investment for the future."

"R-ight," Ed said slowly. "We're just working out the details right now."

Lynn took a sip of the strong gin and tonic. "So…you'll be doing some archaeological exploration up there."

"When I get my permit," Ed said, not looking at her. "Your Doc Donovan, she could be involved if she wanted. I wouldn't mind her help…if she cooperated with my plans."

"And those would be?"

"We'd have to talk about it."

"I'll tell her what you said," Lynn responded, evasively. She had a good idea just what Sarah would have to say. "Where exactly is this land you're buying?"

"Couple of ranches…near San Ignacio," Ed said.

Renaldo leaned forward, his eyes on her, making her feel exposed. She pulled the towel closer around herself. His smile was not particularly friendly. "I believe you've been there."

Lynn sat up, feeling chilled. Was that voice familiar? She reassured herself. After all, she had met him in the bar in San Ignacio and been bored by his conversation with Ed and Carlos in Spanish. "What do you mean?"

Ed offered her some chips. "He doesn't mean anything. He's had a bit too much to drink."

Renaldo laughed and took another gulp. Carlos was looking worried. He checked his watch. "Perhaps its time—"

Renaldo frowned. "Sit down Garcia, we just started to celebrate.

We got the rest of the day."

Lynn got up ready to get dressed and said dryly. "You really should try the snorkeling—it would clear your head."

In the cabin Ivette had gotten out of the shower and was wrapped in a pink terry cloth robe that must have belonged to Mrs. Ed.

Lynn said, "Schmidt said something odd. He said I had been on the land he Garcia and Ed bought near San Ignacio."

Ivette sat down on the pink bedspread toweling her hair. She didn't look at Lynn for a long time. Finally Lynn asked, "Is there something you know and are not telling me?"

The green eyes met hers. Ivette sighed and reached over for a swallow of Lynn's gin and tonic. "You know that money that Michelle gave me?" Lynn nodded as Ivette continued. "It's partly why I didn't believe them about you leaving San Ignacio on your own without telling me. I guess I sort of knew what BG meant when he said how much he appreciated you now you were gone, with that stupid smirk."

"What do you mean?"

"You know how I said BG was acting weird. He didn't get mad like he usually does when I say something critical. He thought it was funny that you were gone; said something about selling a dope not some dope, but a long, skinny drink of water. I thought he was just being stupid. Now I think he meant you. Somebody paid him to drug you and dump you.

"Besides, Michelle—she's usually so cool when we fight—she was really pissed at him. Told me to call Sarah Donovan if I wanted to find you. Now I think she wanted Sarah to know you might be in trouble. Michelle wouldn't have done it, but she took money from him to give to me. I'm sorry, Lynn."

"She could have told you the truth or called Sarah herself."

"She wouldn't want me to know she would let BG get away with anything so underhanded. Anyway, I think these two buddies of Ed's were involved somehow. Somebody paid BG. Maybe it was them."

The memory of those rough hands picking her up like a sack of flour came back. Men speaking Spanish. Maybe she hadn't imagined it. "I can see BG doing it, but who the hell would pay him and why? And how come you didn't tell me about this before?"

"It was over with and you were OK. I didn't want you mad at me about taking the money. I'm sorry Lynn, but I wanted us to have a good time. And we are. Forget those guys. They don't matter."

"I think you're underestimating them. I think they are trouble. I don't know what Ed had in mind, inviting us out here, but I don't like it."

"Oh come on Lynn, lighten up. They didn't try to kill you after all. If that was their intent there are a hell of a lot of easier ways to do it. It was just a stupid prank. You were rude to them. BG probably hatched it and talked them into paying him. It's the sort of thing he would do. They're harmless. A bunch of businessmen—we can handle them."

Lynn was really pissed. "You handle them."

She left Ivette sitting on the pink bedspread in her pink robe and found Ed in the kitchen.When she confronted him about her ordeal in the forest, he looked genuinely puzzled and almost sympathetic. He shook his head. "Your buddy BG did tell us you were a newspaper reporter and that you were still snooping around about that woman's death. The cops hassled me about that too, thanks to you and the shoes you borrowed from my boat, but I thought it was all settled that she did it herself."

"Somebody gave BG money to dump me in the wild, was it you?"

Ed chuckled. "You're not my favorite person, but that's not my style."

"What about your business partners? Your friend Schmidt implied that I'd been on the land you bought."

Ed shrugged. "Why don't you ask them?"

"Why would they do it? They don't even know me."

He smiled. "You said you were dressed up in chicken feathers. Maybe they wanted to scare the natives, make them think the white lady goddess wants them off the land. A few Injuns working at the hotel lends atmosphere. Trouble is we can't have too many of them living on the land. Probably just wanted to encourage the squatters to move on. It was clear, even to me, that guy, BG, wanted to get rid of you. And Renaldo and Garcia certainly wouldn't like the idea of any publicity on our deal—you know those environmental types getting into the picture. I could care less about that."

"What do you mean squatters?"

"Those Mayan farmers, they don't own the land but they move in, sometimes from Guatemala, and burn the forest, clear for their crops. It would be embarrassing to have to evict them—you know, once we start to develop the land. I don't really care. Those folks can help me with the digging and maybe even work in my hotel. Good for tourism. And as far as I'm concerned you can write what you want."

Lynn sighed. The man was hopeless. "I appreciate your support, Ed."

He smiled, missing her sarcasm, and went back to his drink mixing. "You must be ready for another drink. Want the same?"

"Thanks Ed. I think I'll just take another swim." She went out on deck, dove in and swam to the beach. Then she ran the length of it and back to think through what she had just heard.

When she swam back to the boat she was still not clear about what she felt toward Ivette...or what she would say. Just as she reached the ladder she looked up to see two figures struggling on deck. Then she heard a splash and looked up to see Ed Kelly's flushed face leaning over the railing and Ivette splashing in the water.

She called to Ivette, but Ivette said to both of them, annoyed, "I can get myself out." Lynn noted that she had her clothes on. By the time Lynn climbed up the ladder Kelly had disappeared.

She went to the cabin they were using to change. Ivette came in just as she was getting into the shower.

When Lynn came out wrapped in a towel drying her hair Ivette had left a pile of wet clothing on the rug and was curled up on the bed again in the pink robe.

Lynn asked, "What was that all about?"

Ivette reached over and snapped the lock on the door then stretched out on the bed and patted the spot next to her.

Still annoyed Lynn wrapped the big towel around her and sat down stiffly on a chair as far away as possible.

Ivette laughed nervously. Then she said soberly, "You were right, much as I hate to admit it, they are a sleazy bunch. We got a bit of a problem on our hands."

Ivette wasn't looking at her and the slight panicky sound in her voice frightened Lynn, but all she managed to say in a dry annoyed voice was, "So he threw you overboard because you wouldn't put out?"

Ivette's eyes were angry as she sat up and leaned toward Lynn. "We haven't got time for your stupid jealousy act. I...fell in. I was trying to talk to Ed. To warn him. He wouldn't believe me—that those two are a couple of real crooks. He thinks they are legit—business men investing in his projects."

"And how do you know there not?"

"They were talking in Spanish. They didn't know I was there."

Lynn could see that Ivette's fingers were trembling. Her own panic fluttered uselessly in her stomach.

"They were talking about...their work. They deal in coke mostly. They talked about how pleased their boss would be now that they could launder their profits through Ed's investments.

"And you talked to Ed about it?"

"Don't be silly. I just told him he shouldn't trust them."

"So, was he so annoyed that he pushed you overboard?"

"He thought I was using that as a way to come on to him I guess."

"So what's the problem? We just wait till we're back in Belize City and—"

"They think there's a woman DEA Agent working in Belize. At first they thought it was Ann. Now they aren't so sure; they think you have been snooping around working for the DEA. They talked about drowning you—taking back your body all weepy and tragic. Just another stupid tourist hits her head on a rock and drowns."

Lynn felt suddenly cold. Were they the ones that killed Ann? They had paid BG to help them dump her in the forest, maybe they had intended her to die but BG had botched the job...hadn't given her enough drugs to kill her. If she could just get to Phyllis or Grant with this new information. But she had no evidence—just what Ivette thought she heard in Spanish. "Would you tell the police what you heard?"

Ivette shook her head, her eyes a little wild. "You won't get me into court, not in this part of the world."

"Kelly could be involved in the drug trade too."

"No. He's not such a bad guy. He is in real estate, not drug running. I thought if I stayed close to him till we got off the boat I would be safe. I guess it worked, but Ed thought I was interested, you know. I fell in the water to get away from him..."

"What makes you so sure he isn't in with them?"

"I'm not so sure as all that, Lynn; what are we going to do?"

"Get off this boat as soon as we can."

"And how do you propose we do that?"

"We could stick together and hang around Kelly. We can't all die from snorkeling accidents," Lynn said hopefully.

Ivette just shook her head and began to cry quietly.

"Look, I know about boats, and boat radios. I could try to radio the police, maybe even get Grant."

"You can't get near the radio on this boat. It's in the main cabin. You would have to get past them.

Lynn took Ivette in her arms and tried to think. If they swam for it they would be stuck in swamp country even if they did get through the mangrove without clothes, a map, or a machete. The piece of coast near where they were moored was not near any village that she knew about. If Ivette was right maybe Kelly or his crew might help them. Ironic wasn't it, hoping to be rescued by Ed Kelly? Kelly liked Ivette.

And she wanted to get these guys, but she needed some evidence. If she went back to the city without doing some searching she would be no nearer to getting Ann's killers. She didn't want to waste this opportunity. Lynn gathered up her snorkeling gear; then she said to Ivette "Keep your door locked. I'll put out the word that you are passed out and need some time to sober up."

"They'll know I didn't drink that much. What are you going to do?"

"Check out their boat. There's nobody on it right now. The crews are out fishing in the outboard from this boat. In their condition those two drug dealers won't get far without their crew. I'll get their dingy. If we have to, we'll take their big boat. You just be ready. By the time those guys can come after us we'll be halfway back to the city."

"You know about boats?"

Lynn tried to sound confident. "I was in the Navy for four years."

Somehow Ivette did not look reassured.

Lynn swam along the reef toward the other boat, slowly in case they were watching her. The sun was behind her so its glare would make watching her more difficult, and she didn't see anyone on the

158

catamaran's deck. The crew were still out fishing, Schmidt and Garcia were still in the catamaran's main cabin drinking with Kelly. She would take a quick look at the other boat, try the radio. If she could just get some evidence of what they were up to. Maybe they had killed Ann.

As she swam nearer she realized that though the boat had the appearance of a shallow draft pleasure boat on the surface it was deep hulled, much more substantial than most of the boats she had seen here—big enough to cross open ocean easily.

Lynn climbed on board the yacht on the side that was not visible from the catamaran. She saw no one on deck so she left her flippers and mask near the ladder under some canvas. She listened for a moment and then checked the main cabin. Everything was ship shape—a well equipped, ocean-going vessel. As far as she could tell it had all the latest computer directed marine equipment.

Damn, the door to the main cabin with the radio was locked. Nothing obvious on deck to tell her what the boat had been used for except that all the obvious places to search were locked up.

She stood near the stair going below decks and listened for a few moments, but again heard nothing. There was still the possibility that there was another member of the crew left behind even though the boat was safely anchored. She went down below, past several locked cabin doors to a door marked Supplies Storage. This door was unlocked. She turned the knob slowly. It was dark inside. She slipped in.

There was just enough light from a high porthole to see dimly. Along one wall were shelves with ship stores of food. It looked like they might be planning for a long trip. Opposite were several large crates lined up beneath the porthole. At one end there were several locked metal boxes. She decided to start with the crates. She found a tool box and took a screwdriver to pry open one of the crates. She imagined them full of Mayan Treasures. The slats came away easily. Inside carefully wrapped plastic bubble packing were clay pots. But as far as Lynn could tell they were just cheap modern imitations of historical artifacts. The sort of stuff tourists bought in gift shops all over central America. She dug down and found nothing more.

Putting back the packing, she wondered where it was made. Most such packing was made of transparent plastic; this stuff you couldn't see through. Made locally no doubt. The stuff back home was more practical, not so heavy and dense. She remembered how much fun she and her dad used to have popping the stuff; used to drive her mom crazy. She couldn't resist popping a couple, but it didn't snap as satisfactorily and some powder came out making her sneeze. She started packing the box back together; no need to let anybody know she had been here. But everything took on an over-brightness and she felt slightly dizzy. Probably some plastic residual poison from the manufacturing process for the plastic filler, or was it? There was something wrong with her head. Suddenly she realized what the white powder was that had made her sneeze. She had found what she was looking for. They were smuggling cocaine inside the plastic packing for the fake art. She took some with her for proof and carefully closed the wooden slats and tapped them down.

She had secured the sample inside her bathing suit when she heard a click behind her. She turned to see a woman wrapped in a large towel standing in the doorway, a small gun in one hand. At first Lynn was too surprised to be afraid. The contours of the woman's face seemed to be distorted—the eyes narrow, the cheeks flushed. Lynn noted the traces of makeup with a clarity, as through a lens. There was something familiar about this woman.

Lynn said conversationally, "I'm sorry. I didn't know anyone was on board. I called out when I first came on but no one answered. I was looking for something to dry off with. The door was unlocked. I thought—"

The door slammed shut with the woman outside and she heard the lock click before she could move. Stupid. She had been so sure no one was on board. She should have checked more carefully when she first got on.

She checked the door to make sure it was really locked then called out to the woman to let her out, repeating that she had only been looking for someone to get her a towel. No answer.

Her heart pounding in her throat, Lynn climbed up on the crates to look out the porthole. It might be just wide enough for her to climb through if she could get it open. She could see the catamaran. Was that Ivette on deck? If only she could signal, warn her. Surely if Ivette realized Lynn was in trouble, she would go to the police or find Grant when she got back to Belize City?

She had to get out—she struggled with the porthole but she couldn't get the latch to budge. She would have to break the glass. She watched the crew return from their fishing trip and Schmidt and Garcia hurriedly climb down into Ed's outboard. The woman must have radioed them. Lynn climbed down and had just settled on a heavy screw driver as the best weapon to pry off the porthole when the door opened. It was the woman again, now dressed in shorts and silk shirt still unbuttoned at the top, her makeup restored. This time there was no gun visible. She smiled and apologized for having been so rude and asked Lynn to please come into the main cabin.

The slight suggestion of the Southern US accent in her voice soothed Lynn momentarily. She had imagined the woman French or German or from some exotic Latin American community with her dark eyes and damp blond hair neatly and done up in a French twist. Lynn did as she was asked. Perhaps there was no problem after all; the woman had just been frightened by Lynn's intrusion.

Once in the main cabin Lynn turned. The woman was no longer smiling; she stared at Lynn with a Marlene Dietrich, eyelid-lowered disinterest or perhaps disdain. Then she sat down on a couch, took her gun from a pocket in her shorts and placed it next to a plate of crackers and cheese She sighed and broke a cracker in half, her eyes still on Lynn.

Lynn imagined in another time she would have taken a puff on a cigarette. Instead she took a tiny nibble, neatly biting at the edge of a cracker with a brisk snap that broke the stifling silence in the room.

There was an almost audible sigh. "What *are* we to do with you?" Lynn did know this woman from somewhere.

She thought about trying to run for it or lunge for the gun, but as if she had read Lynn's mind the woman finished her bite and picked up the gun.

Instead Lynn said, "I can just swim back to the catamaran It's not very far. I'm sorry I startled you. I was just looking for a towel. I didn't know anybody was on board. I stayed in the water and got too tired. I'd better be getting back. My friend will be worried about me.

The woman, smiled a slow upturning of her lips. "Your friend knows you are here. We told her you were going with us."

"Thank you, but that's not necessary—"

The woman looked past Lynn, a slight frown marring her brow.

"Come Renny and bring Carlos."

Lynn turned. Schmidt and Garcia came in looking sweaty and rumpled from their drinking...and clearly annoyed at being disturbed. Carlos dropped Lynn's backpack inside the door. Garcia dropped down on a couch and Schmidt stood leaning against the wall near the door. Both men stared at Lynn and she felt particularly vulnerable still in her damp bathing suit and t-shirt.

The woman put down the gun again and took another cracker this time with a bit of cheese. "I'm sorry." She gestured toward the plate with the cracker, "Help yourself."

Lynn shook her head. Still trying to be hopeful, she said, "I can still swim back to the boat. I have no reason to stay here. In fact, my friend is going to be rather upset when I don't show up right away."

The woman looked up. "That won't be a problem. Mr. Kelly so kindly offered to explain to anyone concerned that you found a free ride back to the States. It was good of you to have packed up your things so Carlos just had to fetch it from your cabin."

Back to the States! The situation was getting worse and worse. Lynn felt like she was drowning— going down for the last time. And to compound her disquiet the engines started.

Clearly amused by whatever Lynn's face was showing, the woman said, in an exaggerated hostess voice. "Darling, we just happen to have a cabin free for you. Just relax and enjoy your trip home. I'm sure the airlines will be happy to refund your unused ticket."

Now she remembered where she had seen this woman before. Ann's sister, Naomi—at the hospital—or someone pretending to be her sister. Lynn decided it would be better not to let on she recognized Naomi. Maybe Naomi had also been the mysterious woman who bought a live snake from the Mayans—and even been the one that had met Ann out in the bush. Had this woman been part of the original drug ring? Or was it Garcia or Schmidt who had carried out the drug ring's vendetta? She tried to remain calm as she said conversationally, "That's very kind of you, but I need to be back at work in the States on Monday."

It was Schmidt's turn to laugh. Lynn thought about getting past him through the door. She could still swim back. The catamaran. was still visible through the porthole. She was desperate now.

"It's too bad for you...sweetheart...that you're such an inconve-

162

nience," Schmidt said. "You see, we know what you are."

Lynn could not hide the desperation in her voice. "I am a newspaper reporter if that's what you mean."

The woman's eyes bored into her, wide, accusatory. "A newspaper reporter who also happens to work for the DEA."

Lynn shook her head hopelessly.

"Of course it doesn't really matter; the press, in its way, is as dangerous as the police. Too much information spread around isn't good for us. But we still have the problem of what to do with you."

This time when the woman spoke Schmidt and Garcia suddenly came to attention, their eyes on her. "We could drop her off a few miles out to sea, Margo," Schmidt said.

Margo put her cracker down with some distaste and said something incomprehensible in Spanish. Then gave a dismissive wave of her head and the two men left the room. It was clear they were working for her.

Margo went to a refrigerator and took out some juice, cheese and cold cuts and put them on the table on another glass plate. "Help yourself," she repeated, "you must be hungry after all that swimming." She sat down and resumed nibbling on the same cracker, her eyes on Lynn. Lynn felt like a mouse under a cats paw. What was the game? —Let's watch Lynn squirm.

Lynn decided not to play. She took some juice, made herself crackers with cheese and sat down on the sofa opposite Margo. "I'm sorry that I came on board without your permission, I apologize. Really, I have no particular interest in you or your boat. I don't work for the DEA or any other government organization and I have no idea—"

Margo nodded slowly, saying,. "Of course, I must have been mistaken. Don't worry, we will...drop you off...in due time. Like I said, it's too bad...sorry that you have been so inconvenienced."

The tone was authentic, only a shadow of irony in her voice. For a second Lynn could almost believe she was actually sorry. "I don't see how I could be a threat to you—"

Margo leaned over and put the gun softly against Lynn's neck, then she said. "If you aren't interested in us, why the hell take such chances, snooping around our boat, newspaper reporter or not?" Margo shook her head, a bare flick of incredulity showing with the slight raising of the eyelids.

Lynn said half-heartedly, "I don't know what you mean. I was just getting out of the water for a minute. I was tired from swimming...."

The woman leaned back, and smiled lightly. "Of course. And you were at the archaeological dig because you love to grub around in the dirt. And you snooped around Mr. Kelly's boat, not to mention ours, just for the fun of it. And who was it you happened to hunt down in Guatemala?"

Lynn was horrified. Had Anna been right that Lynn's questioning was dangerous for her. "Did you do something to Anna?"

Margo shook her head. Lynn could tell she was pleased to have gotten a reaction. "Unfortunately by the time we realized who she was, little Anna was long gone—thanks to your snooping. Some of our friends, the ones looking for her, were truly disappointed. She would never have taken off like that if you hadn't found her."

"I was trying to find out who killed Ann Wilson. Sarah, Dr. Donovan, is a friend of mine. The police suspected her. I was just trying to help. It was all so confusing. The papers reported that the woman who died was Anna La Place—" Lynn realized she was talking too much.

Margo smiled, a shadow of triumph in the faint glitter in her eyes. "Your DEA friends must think we are truly stupid."

Lynn was beginning to panic. "They're not my friends. I came down here on vacation. I—"

"Have a nasty habit of showing up where you are not wanted. With her eyes still on Lynn, Margo stood up and reached for the radio's headset.

Lynn thought about trying to overpower her. The gun was almost in reach. But even if Lynn succeeded she would not be able to get past Carlos and Renaldo waiting outside.

Margo called the catamaran, the gun resting against the headset. Margo's voice sounded sweet, even naive, as she said, "Ed dear, will you let me speak to the young woman, the one who is still on your boat. Yes, Ivette, what a charming name."

She handed Lynn the headset and whispered, "Tell your little friend you have decided to come with us. She can have your things you left back in Belize City as a momento of your..." Margo smiled. "...time together. You can thank her for that." She waived the gun.

"Nothing more. Don't mention me. Otherwise she might have to join you here."

Lynn took the headset reluctantly and heard Ivette's voice on the other end. "Lynn, are you all right?"

Margo didn't even bother to point the gun at her, and, of course she was right. Lynn had no choice but to cooperate. "Hi, Ivette—Look, these folks are on their way to the States. They've offered me a free ride back to Miami."

Ivette's voice was hurt and angry. "Merd, what the hell you want to go to Miami for? I'll pay for your fucking ticket home."

It was hard but Lynn followed the drill, Margo's eyes still piercing her. "Thanks, Ivette for the good ol' time. You can keep my stuff back at the hotel as a momento if you want." What could she say that would clue Ivette in? "I decided to take your advice and live life...with out a twist of lime."

Margo took the headphone out of her hand and switched it off. Lynn hoped that the anger in Ivette's voice had been feigned, for Ed's hearing. Ivette was smart; surely she would figure it out—eventually.

Lynn was worried about Ed's involvement with this crew. Hopefully Ivette was smart enough to play dumb around him. But Ivette hated the police. Would she go to them or even the DEA?

Margo wanted Ivette to think they were on their way to Miami. That had to be a lie. So where were they intending to deliver their cargo? Hopefully, they thought Ivette was intimidatable, or just dumb. At least she would be OK. After all they hadn't talked about drowning her.

As if reading her mind Margo said. "Don't worry about your little friend. Ed has agreed to...entertain her for a few days. Console her for your desertion." Margo smiled, obviously enjoying her power over Lynn.

Lynn took a deep breath. Better not lose her cool now. "Look this is stupid I am not a DEA agent."

Margo moved away from the radio and stood over her. "It's true—if you were a US agent you've been incredibly sloppy, but your snooping would be understandable—just not very smart. If you're not..." She laughed. A faintly unpleasant sound." But you wouldn't be the first stupid agent—the last one snooping around ran into a viper."

Was she saying that Ann had been a DEA agent? So that explained why Grant showed up with the Belize police.

"So it was you who arranged to have Ann Wilson run into a snake?"

Margo smiled gently, totally in control now. "Why bother? Agents are too easy to avoid. One doesn't need to kill them. Only dumb, desperate or crazy people ever resort to violence of that kind."

Lynn certainly wanted to believe that this woman never resorted to violence. But if it wasn't these three who had killed Ann, then who had and why? Maybe Carlos and Renaldo without Margo knowing?

She tried another tack. "It was rather clever to bring in the snake. It almost worked. We were convinced that the viper venom killed her. If it hadn't been for the doctor being suspicious…"

Margo looked slightly annoyed. "It did work. She was known to be a drug addict. Nobody was charged." Then her brow smoothed. "Whoever did it was clever, but of course, I was not involved."

Lynn nodded. "Look I believe you. And I really don't know who any of you are or what you might be doing that you find me such a threat. And I don't care."

Margo sighed, lay the gun on the table and cut herself a paper thin piece of cheese, delicately placing it on her tongue. "I know you're a newspaper reporter. I did check that out. It doesn't really matter what you are…by the time you have anything to say we will be long gone. As I said, I've no need to have you on my conscience. After all, I'm not a criminal; I'm a business woman. Your sweet Ivette is safe too, especially if you cooperate with us."

Lynn was feeling desperate. "Why should I believe you?"

Margo looked at her pursing her lips and frowning in a faux look of concern. "Don't worry, she won't come to any harm. Not any she has not brought on herself. But I am jealous. Your face tells me you care about that bit of fluff. Am I not just as…attractive." Margo softened her face into a seductive pout.

Lynn was furious at the cruelty of the teasing. But she would not be baited. All she said was. "What do you mean brought on herself?'

"She has been flirting with Mr Kelly. No?"

Lynn didn't say anything. One of the infuriating things about Ivette was her unapologetic flirting.

Margo ran a teasing finger gently down Lynn's face into the

space between her breasts and left her hand resting there. Lynn felt her breath quicken, her heart beat faster. She wanted Margo to mean what she said about Ivette. It was the only hope she had. Margo said, "Don't worry, Mr Kelly, that harmless lecher for women and land and treasure is as gullible as he is greedy. He thinks we have whisked you away so that he can have your little Ivette to himself." Margo laughed again. "Your face is getting an attractive pink—is it sex or anger I wonder? Either turns me on. She kissed Lynn a long slow kiss. Lynn wanted to cry with humiliation and rage. She pulled away feeling herself start to shake. She had to think. This need to play with her prisoner like a cat with its prey, was a weakness, a vulnerability. Something to take advantage of. Margo was watching, waiting to pounce.

"So you like to torture your victims, play with them before you eat them?"

Margo smiled slowly. "Ed Kelly won't hurt her. He believed us that you decided to go home with us. And we *will* return you safely to the States. Sweet Ivette will be free to go where she wants once we are far enough away. Of course to be truly safe, neither of you should mention the rumors you have heard about us. We will protect ourselves...if necessary. Even if you do talk to your friends at the DEA, they will never find us. Like I said, it's an inconvenience for us, but we will move on. Our business opportunities are endless."

Margo sat down on the couch, her smile, her posture, inviting. The smile softened her features, made her seem almost vulnerable. Her hand with the gun relaxed on the arm of the couch. "Don't look so worried, Lynn. Just enjoy the trip. You get a free luxury cruise home. Carlos is an excellent cook. Nobody will get hurt. And you have an exciting tale for your memoirs." She leaned forward and put a caressing hand on Lynn's arm. "I certainly am looking forward to the company."

Lynn shook off the beginnings of complacency that Margo was clearly cultivating. "Treating me this way does make me think you have something to hide, like drug dealing. If that's true why should I believe that you didn't kill Ann or plan to kill Ivette for that matter?"

Margo laughed. "I don't recall telling you that we were ever drug merchants. Where could you possibly have gotten that idea? I would think working for a newspaper you would have better investigative skills. However, even if I did decide to buy and sell an illegal commodity, I would certainly do it within the context of my own, purely rational, moral code. Not that it is one that most ordinary, law-abiding citizens would understand."

In response to Lynn's puzzled look Margo continued. "After all, it is just an accident of history that cocaine and the opium poppy were outlawed and tobacco and alcohol were not. I see no difference, ethically and morally in buying and selling either. Their use is a matter of personal choice in the pursuit of pleasure. Doesn't your own constitution say you have the right to pursuit of happiness? Certainly your own government looks the other way when it's convenient for them. They financed their war on Nicaragua with drug money, not to mention the decades that their buddies the Chinese Nationalists survived on their proceeds from opium in the Golden Triangle of Asia."

"Can I quote you?" Lynn asked facetiously.

Margo looked at her for a long moment. "It might be refreshing for your readers to hear another point of view."

Lynn imagined now that maybe, just maybe she might survive this trip. She would go along with whatever weird game this woman played. She had nothing to lose but her dignity...and maybe her life to gain. She tried to smile. "I'll write your story if you like...when I get home. I assume you would want to be anonymous?"

Margo's eyes looked haunted for just a moment, her eyelids dropped in a quick series of blinks and stayed lowered, controlled—her voice had a slight angry note. "Now you are teasing me. I know what your public thinks of people like me. I know what you think."

Lynn turned away for a moment. The woman might not be as tough as she had seemed at first. Maybe she did care what people thought. Being a crook must be terribly isolating, particularly for a woman.

Lynn took a deep breath, turned and smiled at Margo. "Do you? I don't think so. I am interested in your point of view. But I could listen better without the constant threat of being shot. What is your point of view about the use of guns?"

Margo looked down at the gun and stroked it gently the way she had Lynn's cheek. "This is a tool like any other. It can be used well or badly. I am skilled with it. I can wound you so that you are harmless but not dead. As I said only stupid people need to kill. She looked up at Lynn again her self-confident, slightly amused manner restored, her tone teasing again. "But being shot wouldn't make your trip home very fun." She shook her head. "And I would be bored and annoyed. I'd have to leave you in the care of Carlos and Renaldo."

Lynn said, "I guess I will have to cooperate then. No use being a difficult prisoner. I meant it when I said I would like to hear your story. I am interested...even if I might not be able to print it."

Margo put the gun in her pocket. When she looked up at Lynn, her eyes were wide and a little out of focus...and suddenly innocent—shinny and damp. It was a frighteningly profound change that caught Lynn off-guard. It was as if there were suddenly a different woman in the room. The tones were soft and intimate and confessional, "We will write it under the name Margo—Margo Blavatsky. Yes, that would be appropriate. You see she was a great-great aunt of mine. I have always admired her, wanted to be like her. She had her own moral code too. Was never as crazy as people thought, and so very clever."

A chill ran up Lynn's back and she looked down to mask her reaction. Was this some sort of act to disorient her. She decided to continue to play along. "I'll need a notebook, or a tape recorder...Margo."

Margo opened a cabinet behind her and produced a fresh note-book. Crisp paper with lines, light blue cover, and a matching blue pen. The old Margo was back as she handed the notebook to Lynn. "I'm so sorry. You're still damp." She shook her head. "I can be so inconsiderate." She pulled open a drawer underneath the cabinet and handed Lynn a terry cloth robe. "Take off your wet things and put this on. There are some of my clothes in your cabin you can put on later." The calculating eyes caressed her hips. "I know they will just fit you."

When Lynn hesitated Margo said, impatiently. "They won't be back—I told them to stay outside."

Lynn thought about the sample of cocaine hidden in her bathing suit. If Margo saw that it would confirm her suspicions of Lynn. Lynn quickly took off her damp suit and t-shirt her back to Margo, slipping the sample into the pocket of the robe as she put it on. Then she spread the notebook out on her lap feeling like Scheherazade. As long as she could keep the story-telling going she might still be OK. She looked up expectantly.

Margo had cut herself another slice of cheese, this time more generous. She took a bite and contemplated Lynn with wide liquid eyes. "My business is providing people with what they want like any other free enterprise organization. If the government wants me out of the trade, the best way would be to make my commodities legal and reduce the profit margins. The government could even be in the business like they are with alcohol in some places or put on a tax. Selling antiques would be more profitable then drugs then." Margo chewed, her lips slightly parted. The southern accent was gone; her speech was pure midwest.

"Do you want this written as a personal statement of your point of view or shall I do a profile?" Lynn asked.

Margo pouted seductively. "You're making fun of me."

All Lynn could do was shake her head. Something of her fear must have shown in her eyes because Margo said, leaning closer and patting her cheek, "Don't worry hon. I really don't kill people however inconvenient they might be. I couldn't hurt a fly. I'm a vegetarian. You can write that down."

Lynn did so dutifully.

Margo continued. "As I said, killing people isn't practical. It causes too much trouble. That's why I wouldn't have killed Ann. Look at what happened when she died. The police and the DEA start snooping around. That archaeological site was a perfect contact point for us—tourists coming and going all the time. Nobody noticed a few extra boats now and again. That woman's death blew our cover; we'll have to start again someplace else. A drag for sure."

"You mean Ann Wilson."

"Whatever her name was." Margo looked at her hard. "Agents come in many packages, so do traitors." Margo smiled and patted Lynn's cheek. "But of course you are neither so you don't need to be afraid."

Renaldo peeked in at the door and said something in Spanish about their course.

Margo's face changed. She responded in clipped Spanish, then stood up. Now her eyes were cold, her face drawn as she said harshly in English, "Carlos will take you to your cabin." And then she abruptly left.

Carlos was waiting outside for her, frowning at her suspiciously.

He had a gun in one hand with which he waved her along the passage and through an open door. Then he pushed it closed behind her and locked it.

It was a simple, tiny cabin, hardly room to stand up next to the bunk, probably meant originally as a crew cabin. There was a bowl of fruit, a bottle of wine and some sandwiches on the tiny table. The only other door led to a cubbyhole of a bathroom. She thought about flushing the sample of packing from the crate down the toilet, but was prevented by the image of it floating forever on the surface of the ocean. Instead she hid it it a crack in the wooden backing behind the toilet.

She found some clothes in the small closet and put on a pair of shorts and a silk shirt that fit her perfectly.

There was one porthole, too small to crawl through. Outside all she could see was water. She entertained herself trying to pick the lock on the door without success. Then she paced the tiny room worrying about Ivette. Ivette was just as much a threat to these people as Lynn, but of course they couldn't know that. Did Margo really leave Ivette with Ed Kelly or had she been lying? She had no way of really knowing that Ed wasn't dealing drugs too.

Still Lynn had to admit Ivette could handle herself pretty well—could talk herself out of most situations. Lynn fervently hoped Ed was just a cover for money laundering in Belize. Ivette had thought that. Maybe Ivette was OK, maybe even on her way back to Belize City. But would she go to Grant or the police if she had the chance?

Finally she ate the sandwich. If she was going to die , being poisoned was better than being shot or drowned. Of course all they had to do was throw her overboard once they were out to sea so why bother poisoning her.

Finally she went to sleep. She was awakened when someone crawled into bed with her. She struggled to get away when her assailant whispered. "Don't be afraid. It's just Margo."

Lynn felt a soft hand caress her face. Then soft lips reached for hers. Her body stiffened involuntarily as Margo stroked her gently.

She could just see the contours of Margo's face and body in the moonlight streaming through the porthole. Margo was either very confident of her power over Lynn or she was showing her vulnerability. Lynn wasn't sure yet how she would make use of that, but it seemed like her one chance to survive this ordeal. And if she was going to get tossed into the briny tomorrow— So much for her scruples about not having sex with strangers. She ran her fingers over the silky shoulder remembering how it had looked framed in the doorway above the damp towel. Interesting, first Ivette in a damp towel, now Margo...

# Chapter 23

Lynn was about to fall asleep enjoying the comfort of the soft body curled against her, the smell of sex and sweat lulling her. But she fought sleep and started to ease her body away from the sleeping form. If the door was unlocked, maybe... She lifted her arm and slid away. The women next to her stiffened. Lynn quickly slipped out of bed and moved toward the door, but her bed mate moved across the tiny cabin and out the door even faster.

Lynn just had time to slip the cover of her notebook into the crack in the closing door when the lock turned—but not quite all the way. She waited until she heard another door close down the passage. Then she put on some clothes, took a deep breath and waited five...ten minutes. Listening for any sound, she gently pulled at the door and the notebook at the same time. Miraculously the door came open.

She slipped down the dark narrow passage. Not a sound. All the doors closed, no light under any of them. Light came down the narrow stairs from the deck. She crept up the stairs onto the deck keeping her head down. Carlos was nodding at the wheel, on watch. She looked through the railing on both sides of the boat. They must be in open ocean; there were no shore lights. What had she thought she would do when she got out of the cabin, try to swim for shore? She leaned against the hard cold metal of the main cabin wall. What were the possibilities? If she could overcome Carlos maybe she could figure out where they were and radio...who? She had handled a boat radio before in the Navy—not a part of her life that she liked to remember. But, as a high school graduate, it had been a way of getting away from an indifferent home life. There was no chance to lower the outboard dingy into the water without overpowering

Carlos. Even if she could get it in the water alone. There was an emergency inflatable life raft with no motor. But she preferred her chances with Margo to dying of dehydration mid-ocean.

Just then a door slammed down below. She prayed that Margo hadn't gone back to check on her. What if she came up on deck— where could she hide? She found a canvas awning that had been taken down and piled on deck and crawled under it.

She heard footsteps, then a conversation in Spanish between Carlos and someone down below, then more footsteps on the stairs. Someone passed her hiding place. More time passed. She was desperate to look but didn't dare move. There was enough light from the cabin that any movement of her canvas hiding place might be seen.

She lay still for longer than she imagined possible. Then the boat slowed. After a few long moments she heard a splash. Were they anchoring the boat? That would mean they were near shore, maybe even near a town. She couldn't believe her good luck; she might even be able to slip overboard and swim for shore. If she could just get to her flippers; if they hadn't already been found and moved.

Soon it was silent again. She ventured out of her hiding place. Now it was dark, just small warning light at the bow and stern. If there was a shore out there there was no evidence of it; she could see no comforting house lights—nothing there but blackness and silence. But they had to be near shore; they were in shallow enough water to anchor the boat.

Not even stars visible above. It must be completely clouded over. Was there still someone in the cabin on guard? She had to take the chance. She hoped they snored at least to let her know they were there. She made her way slowly toward the main cabin where she had spotted the radio when she first came on board.

Fortunately there was enough visibility from the warning lights to see the outlines of the boat and she found the door. It was open. She slipped inside. There were small lights on some of the instruments. There was no one on guard, her luck was holding. She took a deep breath and looked around.

A chart was spread out on the table. From what she could see in the dim light from the instrument panel, it looked like someone had traced their movement on the chart with a pencil. They were following the Yucatan coast north. All she had to do was let somebody know. Then she would consider trying to take the dingy.

Right now the question was who she could reach by radio. What instrumentation there was was rather basic and old-fashioned. Lynn switched on the radio and tried to remember what she knew. She sent out a general SOS with the location from the chart, repeating it several times. She included a request to contact Grant at the DEA with her name and the location. If she did end up floating out there or on a deserted beach somewhere she might actually get picked up. She imagined a British Navy ship coming to the rescue.

Then she imagined Margo greeting them with her enigmatic smile. "Sorry boys it must have been some sort of silly prank. We're just fine." Even if the US Navy stopped them would they know to search? Would they find the cocaine? Maybe she should just go back to her cabin and trust Margo to let her go when they had safely delivered their cargo rather than trust her luck on some dark deserted coast... Yeh, right. Trust Margo. She shook her head; she was losing it. It was time to get off this boat before Carlos and Renaldo did dump her overboard mid-ocean.

She repeated her message several more times, listening for any responses. Nothing. Everybody in listening distance was asleep. Well, maybe there was a ship out there with its equipment on automatic record. She imagined a sleepy operator finding her messages in the morning. She tried again putting as much information as she could in the message and hoped some of Margo's friends didn't pick it up.

She was trying another channel when she heard a sound. She quickly turned off the radio and dropped down between the table and the bench built into the side of the cabin. Damn, she shouldn't have waited so long to go overboard. Somebody was out on deck; she could hear them checking the anchor line. She crawled to the door. Nobody was near. Was it better to try to slip into the water while they were at the back of the boat or wait on the chance that she could get to the dingy? Whoever it was would would certainly hear her drop into the water. She slipped out the door and crawled back under the tarp. Somebody went into the cabin and switched on a light. She peeked out. It was Renaldo. He settled down on the bench and pulled a comic book out of his pocket. Clearly he was there on watch.

Unfortunately the ladder on the side that would let her get into the water without being heard was in Renaldo's direct view. If only she had seen some sign of where the shore was. She didn't relish finding herself on a deserted beach, but better that than open ocean if she should swim the wrong direction. She could wait till he dozed off, then try to swim for shore. Surely he would doze off before dawn. Even if he didn't, at dawn she would have a better chance to see where to go. She tried to make herself comfortable in her hiding place.

She was awakened by the sound of a motor. It was still dark. Renaldo was standing on the deck not far from her. She could see a light out on the water—another smaller boat. They pulled up along side and he threw them a rope. Then she saw Margo and Carlos pass the crack in the canvas. Two men started hauling some crates aboard with the help of Carlos and a crewman. Of course, they had stopped here to make a pickup. In all, a dozen large crates were pulled on board. Lynn wondered if those too contained fake art packed in plastic packing material. She could try to slip overboard while they were busy with the cargo. Maybe she could hang onto the side of their boat in the dark and get pulled to shore.

She could see Margo talking to someone from the boat but couldn't hear what they were saying. Then Margo called Renaldo to her and he hurried down the stairs. He came back a few minutes later and shouted, "She's gone."

Of course, the people in the other boat must have picked up her message. Stupid, she should have gone overboard right away. Now she would have to chance it with them all on deck.

She was at the rail about to slip over when Renaldo spotted her. She started to climb under—to slip into the water, but it was too late. He had her by the silk collar of Margo's shirt. She tried to take it off but Carlos was there helping him to pull her back on deck.

They stood her in front of Margo, arms in a hammer lock behind her back. The man from the other boat stood next to Margo.

Margo said to him not looking at Lynn, "A minor problem." Her eyes bored into Lynn. "An ungrateful...relative." Then she said to Renaldo. "Put her back to bed."

As Lynn was dragged down the stairs, she heard Margo say, complacently, "Would you believe it; I rescued her from a mental hospital. I thought the tropics might do her good. She keeps trying to do herself in. I might just let her one of these days."

For two days and nights Lynn was locked in the cabin. She felt like a prisoner on death row. She saw no one except Carlos who silently brought her a tray, always with Renaldo behind him. Each dish was well prepared and aesthetically presented. She wondered if Carlos was making a statement of sympathy, or it was Margo's sadistic joke to make her wonder if each meal was to be her last. She told Carlos how good his cooking was. Though he never spoke, doubtless under Margo's strict orders, Lynn felt sympathy in his sad eyes.

Finally on the second day, when Renaldo turned to look out to sea, she tried to whisper to Carlos asking for his help. He still didn't speak, just looked at her.

Still, she tried to keep herself sane, told herself that the fact that they hadn't already thrown her overboard, or whatever, should make her hopeful. She let herself believe that somehow she would survive.

But clearly her radio messages hadn't gotten through—the boat was not being stopped or followed. She saw a few boats off on the horizon. She hadn't a clue now where they were going. The shore, when it was visible at all, was just a faint line on the horizon. Even if she were a long distance swimmer she wouldn't make it. And she kept having images of Diana Nyad in a cage, swimming through shark-infested waters.

Ivette was just a faint memory of happiness long past, her own life in the States, distant history. Several times she woke up at night imagining Margo moving outside her door—then she would lie awake waiting. But there was nothing but silence and the sound of the waves on the side of the boat and the creaking of the structure as the boat rocked.

Finally someone did open the door. It was late, after midnight— this time she heard the key turn in the door. For a moment she feared it was Renaldo. Maybe it was time to throw her overboard. She got out of bed ready for a struggle. But then she saw a woman's profile against the faint light of the doorway. Margo took off her silk shirt and dropped it over the lampshade, turned on the light, and whispered, "I'm sorry, I meant to come sooner. They're so uptight. You shouldn't have tried to run away. We don't like it when people disappoint us."

Lynn sat down on the bed, the sheet wrapped around her shoulders. She suddenly felt cold. "Are we almost there then?"

Margo looked puzzled for a moment, caught off guard. "Almost where?"

"Wherever it is we're going. Wherever you're dumping me."

"Not quite yet. We still have a little time."

"If we are so close why do I have to be in solitary?"

"Don't blame me. It isn't *my* fault you have to be watched all the time. We thought you would be sensible. After all we mean you no harm."

Margo pulled at a corner of Lynn's sheet and played with it between her fingers. "Lets be friends. We could have such a nice time. I know you like me." Two wide eyes reflected the lamplight almost innocent.

Lynn felt totally indifferent to this strange woman in front of her. No not indifferent. She was angry. The anxiety of the last days turned to hopeless anger now. "A friend would get me off this boat, back to shore, to my life. A friend—"

Margo jerked her body away and stood with fists on her hips. Lynn could imagine her throwing a tantrum, lying on the floor screaming if she didn't get her way. "I told you we will. Why don't you believe me. If we wanted to kill you we would have done it a long time ago." There were tears that reflected the lamplight. "I just wanted to say good-bye...in a nicer way. I won't see you again, you know."

Lynn felt she was in the middle of some bizarre piece of theater. Maybe she was still asleep. Was she going crazy? She was this woman's prisoner. She knew it was best to go along with the program. She did want to see Ivette again and Sarah, and Del, and— She felt tears coming into her own eyes. She was incredibly exhausted. She just couldn't play the game anymore. "Goodbye then." She crawled back into the bunk and covered her face. Margo had won. She was giving up. She didn't even care if they threw her in the ocean. They said that drowning was a good way to go.

Margo tucked the covers around her and kissed her cheek. Lynn did not even look. She heard the door click shut and the lock turn. Then she fell asleep, the best sleep she had in three days.

Sometime later as it was just getting light, Renaldo dragged her out of bed and waited while she dressed. Up on deck Carlos was there looking sad, but didn't say anything. Renaldo carried the gun and had a grim determined look on his face. Lynn could not see land anywhere on the horizon. The swells were high and there was a good breeze blowing. They must be farther north in the Atlantic—the water had a green tint, not turquoise like in the Caribbean.

Renaldo said something in Spanish to Carlos and Carlos shook his head.

Lynn said, "Thanks Carlos for all the good food. You are a great cook." Carlos didn't say anything; he couldn't even look at her. He just turned away.

Renaldo unlatched the cord and lowered some stairs over the side of the boat. Then he said, "It's your choice Amiga. You can swim for it or we dump your body with enough lead to sink it. That way the sharks get you sooner." Lynn heard Carlos choke, then he leaned over the railing and threw up.

Lynn looked down at the churning water and watched Carlos' breakfast float away. Maybe the sharks would go for that instead.

Carlos said in a Spanish that Lynn managed to understand, that Margo would not like this. Renaldo said, clearly choosing to speak English to make sure that Lynn could understand, "It's no concern to her if this one talks. Margo will just disappear again and leave us to take the consequences."

Lynn thought about yelling. Maybe Margo would hear her and interfere, but the ocean was making so much noise that they were already shouting to be heard. She said to Renaldo, "No chance you'll let me go back for my passport? I'll have to go through immigration in Miami and they're tough."

He didn't even crack a smile. He just tilted his head toward the water. Lynn stared at him. Even now she weighed whether she could get past him before he pulled the trigger. What would Carlos do?

Carlos was standing near a life preserver, his head leaning against it, clearly resigned. It didn't look like he intended to throw it. Then he looked at her and winked. She did not move. How many days could she stay alive in the water even if she had that piece of styrofoam? What was the chance that somebody could spot her in the water even if they were looking for her—which they surely weren't? Renaldo gave her a shove with his foot. She hung onto it as long as she could but he hit her knuckles and then the side of her head with the butt of his gun.

She hit the water dropping down through green glass for a long time, admiring the colorfulness of sunlight—thinking only of water words—dappled, crystal clear, green and blue and gold. Then after an eternity of gasping choking reality, her head emerged and she took in a gulp of pure air…and something hit her on the head again. This time it was the life preserver. Carlos' last gesture for somebody who appreciated his cooking.

The boat disappeared behind a swell then appeared again. She could see Carlos leaning on the railing watching her. Renaldo was pulling up the ladder. Then she could hear him swearing at Carlos. On the next swell she could see him lean against the cabin wall to steady his hand. She heard the bullet hit the water a bit too close. She decided she preferred to drown at her own leisure rather than bleed for the sharks. She stayed under the water holding onto the rope of the preserver until Renaldo got tired of using the preserver for target practice. Fortunately it was Styrofoam and continued to float.

Soon enough they were out of range and she could relax, resting her head on the preserver and staring at the clear blue of the sky. Waiting for what?

After a while she explored what her world was now—the island of the preserver. This was not what she had ever imagined being marooned on a desert island would be like, although this one was deserted enough. So what did she have? The long t-shirt she had been sleeping in and a piece of floating styrofoam on a length of rope…tied to nothing?

But then, miraculously, she found something attached to the rope near the foam preserver—a battery operated noise-maker—the kind that rescue workers could pick up even from a distance and a strobe light. Standard equipment on most boats. Crew members tended to wear them around their necks in bad weather in case somebody fell overboard. Carlos had been attaching it while Renaldo was occupied with making her walk the ladder, so to speak. In any case she was incredibly grateful.

Of course, she would have to wait until they were far away enough not to pick up her signal themselves and come back for her. She lay her head inside the preserver watching the sun turn the horizon pink purple and gold. When the sun was well up she turned on the signal and waited. If she was in US territorial waters there just might be a chance.

She waited through the bright day, resisted the temptation to drink the salt water as the sun beat down on her and she got more and more dehydrated. She was grateful for the respite of a quick evening shower though there was nothing to catch the water in. She lay with her mouth open and the drops cooled her tongue. Then she got a little more water by wringing her t-shirt into her mouth.

She didn't really start to give up until it got dark and she began to shake with cold. She turned on the strobe light knowing how short its life would be and tied herself upright so that even if she became unconscious her head would stay above water. She woke up at daybreak, but passed out when it got hot again.

# Chapter 24

Someone was beating on her chest. Lynn opened her eyes and saw a face, a familiar face, above her. It was Sarah's brother Bobby. Was she drowning? It felt like there was fire in her lungs—she must be in hell. Her mother had been right after all. And how appropriate—the devil torturing her had Bobby's face.

The devil made another lunge at her anatomy and she felt as if she were being turned inside out. After the spasm of coughing her intestines out, she heard the Bobby-devil say, "Hey. Bill, I guess she'll live after all."

It was DEA Grant that leaned over her. Another devil look-alike?

Then it was a Sarah-devil who looked down at her. Wait a minute—maybe she was actually in heaven...

But not with Bobby there.

The Sarah look-alike helped her sit up for the next spasm of coughing and throwing up and then handed her a towel. After the spasms had quieted, Lynn reappeared from the towel's comforting folds and looked around. Maybe she wasn't dead after all. It couldn't be heaven or hell with both Sarah and Bobby there. She must still be alive.

The crystal green water and bright sun reassured her that she was indeed still alive. She was on what looked like a coast guard boat. Of the three people watching her, only one was wet and that was Bobby.

She thought about thanking him but couldn't quite manage it. She would try again later. It would be an exercise in self-discipline.

"Let me guess," she said to DEA, "Your initials are BG, right?" It had to be. This was hell after all.

DEA looked at her puzzled. "William Grant actually. but everybody calls me Bill."

Sarah handed her a glass. "This should help," she said in a mothering voice.

After swallowing a slug of brandy, Lynn rasped out to Grant, "If by chance I am really alive how the hell did you find me."

"Your friend, Ivette, came to see Phyllis Thompson and she contacted me. Apparently she finally convinced Mr. Kelly that his friends were drug runners and she was afraid that you were being held by them. He didn't believe her at first, but he did some of the checking he should have done in the first place and realized they weren't who they said they were. He brought her back to Belize City and came with her to see me after Inspector Thompson contacted me. He may be an unscrupulous businessman but he doesn't like the idea of drug dealers as business partners. He gave us a description of the boat, but by that time it was long gone."

"So how long did he keep her on his boat?"

Grant shook his head. "They didn't talk about that. They came to me a day or so before we got your message from the Navy. They were a bit puzzled by it. When they didn't find a boat at the location you gave them in the SOS, they thought it was some crazy crank fisherman or yachter's prank—somebody out too long on the open seas and bored. But then some Navy guy thought it might be drug-runner code and had the good sense to check it out with us soon enough so we could use your coordinates for a beginning of our search. It helped that Kelly gave us an accurate description."

"When you did find it and why the hell did you wait until after they tried to drown me to get them?"

They all looked at her in silence for a moment. Then Sarah said, "They were waiting for the boat to get into US territorial waters."

"You wanted to get to their contacts here in the States, right?"

"Unfortunately you were no longer aboard by the time they were arrested. But we sent out a search and heard your beeper."

Lynn shook her head.

Sarah said, "If they had tried to come aboard on the open sea you might have been shot."

Grant nodded. "They were arrested as they began unloading. We got the guy on shore as well as the two men who held you. The crew were hired on with the boat. They thought they were carrying trinkets for the tourist market in Miami and that you were a guest. They were allowed to take the boat back to Belize waters. As far as we can tell the company that owns the boat is clean."

"What about the woman?"

She was greeted with blank stares. "There was no woman on board," Grant said. "Just the two men, a Carlos Garcia, and a Renaldo Schmidt and the three crew members."

"Three crew members?"

"Two Belize citizens and a young boy from El Salvador, Miguel Alvarez. He has his temporary papers in Belize. All three were employees of the boat company."

In spite of herself Lynn was amused. "There was no boy on board. That was Margo or Naomi or whatever she calls herself. She's the chief honcho. The other two just work for her. She said you would never catch her."

Grant turned abruptly, no doubt going to radio to try and stop the boat. Lynn said after him, "I doubt she will still be on board."

Bobby, not at all chagrined for not being thanked, went off cheerfully to put on dry clothes. "I should have thanked him." Lynn, said absently. She looked at Sarah apologetically. "I though it might be Bobby that killed Ann."

"Lynn, Bobby is as obsessively good as I am. He can't help it. It's in his genes. My father—"

"As long as he keeps it there." Lynn said remembering Bobby's seductive hand shake and their earlier conversation.

Sarah didn't laugh. "Lynn! Bobby is devoted to Ann. He just likes to flirt. Most women like it."

"Is?"

"Yes, they deceived me too. I haven't forgiven them yet for all those days thinking I was responsible for Ann's death."

"You weren't responsible, but what do you mean is? Who was it that was killed. I met Anna LaPlace or someone who called herself that. Were there three women?"

Sarah shook her head and laughed. "You see the network of drug runners locally had found out somehow that there was an Agent there."

Lynn nodded. "I know. Margo thought I was an Agent. So Ann was an Agent?"

Sarah smiled. "Is an Agent. She had just managed to get in touch with the drug network and had set up a meeting, ostensibly to buy drugs from them."

"A new voice, a woman's from down below said, "It was my job. But yes, that they tried to kill me showed that they suspected who I really was. Better for me to disappear." She came up from stairs next to the bridge. It was Ann!

Lynn blinked twice. Yes, she, Lynn, was dead. Here was Ann, who she had seen rushed into the hospital comatose, smiling at her cheerfully.

Ann sat down on the bench next to Lynn, who hardly recognized the neat almost collegiate woman next to her with a stylish hair-cut and a crisp white shorts and sleavless t-shirt that showed of her smooth tan.

Ann leaned closer to Lynn, smiling. "I was at the dig because someone there was suspected of using the location for drug deals. When you got there I was already getting close, but I was also getting nervous. Being aloof and rude helped me keep my cover. I didn't want to take the chance that somebody might be able to catch incon-sistencies in my cover story."

Sarah said, "They were going to meet Ann out in the bush. That's why she went out in the kayak. A very risky move."

Lynn was overwhelmed. She took the brandy bottle from Sarah and took another swig. Then she asked her fellow ghost, "So the BG Scully story you told Teddy…and Anna was part of your cover? And you led Anna to think that Bobby was one of the bad guys?"

"Anna came up with her own version of my story. I just didn't dis-abuse her of it. Yeah. BG. Scully… He was just some guy I knew was arrested for domestic violence. Teddy was very persistent. I told her that he was my ex and was chasing me to shut her up. I had no idea that he would show up in Belize."

"He didn't. I thought the Canadian guy, BG, was Scully for a while. You were the one that got Marv to get Sarah away that day. What did you give him?

Ann shook her head. "It didn't take much.I told him I just want-ed to take a look around in the kayak and that Sarah didn't want me doing survey alone. Just took a few beers. He thought it was funny he could get her to pay him when it was me who wanted her out of the way."

"But why meet the drug dealers alone?"

Ann smiled indulgently. "They wouldn't have agreed if I had com-pany. I needed them to start trusting me. I thought if I could get the trust of the local guys I could get to somebody bigger."

Bobby, back now in fetching white sailing clothes that brought out his own magnificent tan, said to Ann, "You were just supposed to keep your eye on the archaeological dig. Find out if anybody there was in the drug network."

Ann just looked at him and shook her head.

"So you were at the drug rehab place as an undercover agent?" Lynn asked.

Ann nodded. "We thought Anna LaPlace was going to be an important link. I was there to keep an eye on her. It turned out she didn't really know much. Just a minor player, but I liked her and she needed help. So I invited her down to Belize. But she never got to the dig. She did give your Canadian buddies Sarah's address and they wrote Anna there. I got the fax from them and was going to tell them that she had never shown up. Unfortunately—"

"Why didn't you tell Sarah about your diabetes? We could have told the Doctor about that after we found you—you could have died."

"Bobby knew. Once the military picked me up they dealt with it. Anyway, I thought I had it under control and my needle marks helped convince the dealers that I was a potential customer.

Lynn nodded. "So when you were in the hospital somebody, Grant maybe, decided to move you out to the States and then put out the word that it was Anna LaPlace that was dead so the people she testified against would stop looking for her."

A familiar hunted looked came over Ann's face. "And whoever tried to kill me would think I was dead. All the loose ends tied up."

Lynn wrapped the towel tighter around herself. "So who was it that met you out there in the bush and tried to kill you?" Lynn asked Ann.

"Your buddies Garcia and Schmidt were the ones I made contact with in the trade, but I never met them." Ann looked out over the blue water thoughtfully. "I took the survey stuff so nobody at the dig would be suspicious. I knew I would get in trouble with Sarah, but I figured Bobby could take care of that. Once I was at the rendezvous point I waited and waited. Then I must have dozed off. I don't remember the snake. Somebody grabbed me from behind and stuck a needle in my arm. They held on till I passed out. The next thing I knew I woke up on the plane going back to the States."

"So you're not sure that it was Carlos and Renaldo who tried to kill you?"

Ann shook her head. "It was likely them. I'm pretty sure they were the ones I was supposed to meet, but I never actually saw them.

Lynn couldn't stop shivering in spite of the hot sun, and the brandy was making her dizzy. "Margo as much as said it was. I'm glad you got them, although I will put a good word in for Carlos. He's a damn good cook."

Sarah took the brandy away from her and handed her a cup of hot tea. Lynn turned to Grant. "So you sent my picture with Ann to the papers?"

Grant sighed. "An article was necessary. After all we did want the information that Anna was dead to get back to the drug dealers. They looked enough alike. We didn't supply the picture. Some local reporter got that, probably from the police." He smiled. "They are an independent agency in an independent country after all."

"Does Phyllis Thompson know all this?"

"We finally had to let her in on some of it. Most of the time we can depend on the locals moving pretty slow. She's an exception; she got a bit too close on her own, with your help of course."

"Somebody should have clued me in. I hope I didn't blow Anna's cover in Guatemala."

Ann shook her head. "Sorry about that."

Lynn asked quickly, "I liked her. I was afraid Carlos and Renaldo might have found her."

Ann nodded, "She's OK, in a safer place now. Finally agreed to go into the witness protection program. We got very close at the rehab center. She was having a hard time keeping off drugs. She changed her mind about coming to meet me when we found out there were people connected to the crew she helped put away looking for her in Belize too—wanting revenge for the part she played in convicting their buddies. With Schmidt and Garcia put away she will be a little bit safer."

Lynn shook her head. "She should have had a false passport."

"We tried to get her to take on another name but she refused. Said she wasn't going to hide out all her life. She had changed her name once when she got married and that had been a big mistake. Fortunately she has changed her mind about that now."

Lynn leaned back in the deck chair and sipped her hot tea. Ann sat across from her smiling—safe, alive. Sarah looked out to sea, no doubt already worrying about her research. A wonderful sense of well-being settled over Lynn as she fell into a well earned sleep.

# Epilogue

After making her statement and leaving DEA office in Brownsville, she and Sarah sat out on a veranda overlooking the Gulf having lunch.

Over coffee Sarah said, "You don't have to go back to work yet, you know. I called your boss, Gayle, and told her you disappeared and we wanted to make sure you hadn't just gone home. She was pretty upset. Your friend Del threatened to come down. I told her you were probably on a boat in US territorial waters. I guess she has a thing about water. When I called them back after we found you, I told them you were OK, but just need a little recovery time. They were just happy to know you were alive."

Lynn suddenly had a vision of Ivette's silky nut-brown body slipping through turquoise blue water. She smiled, "Thanks Sarah."

# MORE BOOKS FROM NEW VICTORIA PUBLISHERS
## PO BOX 27 NORWICH VERMONT 05055
## OR CALL 1-800 326 5297    EMAIL  newvic@aol.com
Home page    http://www.opendoor.com/NewVic/

# SIX MYSTERIES BY SARAH DREHER

*"The touchstone of Dreher's writing is her wit and her compassion for her characters. I don't think I have ever read better or funnier dialogue anywhere."*–Visibilities

### STONER McTAVISH    $9.95
The first in the series introduces us to travel agent Stoner McTavish. On a trip to the Tetons, Stoner rescues dream lover, Gwen from danger and almost certain death.

### SOMETHING SHADY    $8.95
Stoner finds herself an inmate, trapped in the clutches of the evil psychiatrist Dr. Milicent Tunes. Can Gwen and Aunt Hermione charge to the rescue before it's too late?

### GRAY MAGIC    $9.95
Stoner finds herself an unwitting combatant in a struggle between the Hopi spirits of Good and Evil.

### A CAPTIVE IN TIME    $10.95
Stoner mysteriously finds herself in Colorado Territory, time 1871.

### OTHERWORLD    $10.95
On vacation at Disney World. In a case of mistaken identity, Marylou is kidnapped and held hostage in an underground tunnel.

## MYSTERIES BY KATE ALLEN

TAKES ONE TO KNOW ONE – an Alison Kaine Mystery    $10.95
This third Alison Kaine mystery finds the Denver cop and her delightfully eccentric circle of friends travelling to a women's spirituality retreat in New Mexico.

GIVE MY SECRETS BACK – an Alison Kaine Mystery    $10.95
A well-known author of steamy lesbian romances has just moved back to Denver when she is found dead in her bathtub. Suspecting foul play, cop Alison Kaine begins an off-duty investigation.

TELL ME WHAT YOU LIKE – an Alison Kaine Mystery    $9.95
In this fast- paced, yet slyly humorous novel, Allen confronts the sensitive issues of S & M, queer-bashers and women-identified sex workers.

I KNEW YOU WOULD CALL– a Marta Goicochea Mystery    $10.95
Phone psychic Marta investigates the murder of a client with the help of her outrageous butch cousin Mary Clare. Marta, helped by her psychic insights, struggles to get to the deeper truths surrounding the killing.

**INDIVIDUALS order from NEW VICTORIA PUBLISHERS**
**PO BOX 27 NORWICH VT 05055**
**CALL 1-800 326 5297        EMAIL NEWVIC@AOL.COM**